# EXPOSURE

A Novel

By

Alexandra Y. Caluen

# EXPOSURE

*The Playlist:*

Vogue - Madonna

Smooth Operator – Sade

I Move On – Catherine Zeta-Jones & Renée
Zellweger

Love Voodoo - Duran Duran

Killer Queen - Queen

Don't Talk Just Kiss - Right Said Fred

If I Were You - k.d. lang

Looking Glass Sea - Erasure

The Book of Love - Peter Gabriel

*Author's note:*
*the torch song "Maybe You'll Be There" was written*
*by*
*Rube Bloom and Sammy Gallop*

# EXPOSURE

Chapter 1

November 2012

Andy looked for Brando, as he always did, on his way home from morning class. It wasn't that they had a bond, or even a civil relationship; it was more that the old alley cat was almost always good for a photo. At first it looked as if Brando was asleep, curled up in the sun on top of the nest box the Brewery's unofficial carpenter had built. Then Andy got closer and realized that he wasn't asleep.

He sat down on the concrete step by the box and laid his hand on the cat. Brando's rough orange coat was warm, but only from the sun. It was the first time Andy'd ever touched him. He stroked the cat's body, oddly moved.

"Well," he said out loud, "not a bad way to go, I guess." He stood up, thinking, *we should have a ritual. Everybody knew this old bastard.* Out of habit, he took a few pictures with the camera he always carried. Then he went upstairs and composed a quick email to his friends around the complex.

They got together that night, a whole gang of them; nearly forty people, including guests of residents, showed up for the send-off. Someone had decorated a box to lay the cat's body in, others had organized a potluck, many brought beverages, and three people brought contraband guitars. They ate and drank, compared scars, told stories and sang for a couple of hours, then said a few words and consigned the deceased to the incinerator.

Victor turned away from that not-very-solemn ceremony, smiling at something the tattoo artist was saying. Then he glanced across the pavement for a moment and saw somebody, and stopped moving. Tall, dark-haired, standing under the building's harsh floodlight and looking as though he were at center stage. "He's here?" he said out loud.

Lola turned her head and followed his gaze. "Who, Andy? He lives here. You know him?"

Victor met her mildly-interested eyes. "Not really. I did a play this year. He did the photography, the lobby cards. He was good to work with."

"Too bad you've got fresh ink, you could get him to do an update for you. He does lots of portfolios."

Lola might have meant that to sound like a suggestion; Victor certainly took it that way. "No time like the present," he said. "Who knows when I might get out here again. And my head shot is three years old." That was true. He hadn't updated it since he landed the part on 'L.A. Vice.'

"Better catch him before it gets too late. Nice working with you today." She offered her hand; Victor shook it; they parted ways. He walked away thinking about 'too late.' It wasn't that late. If he was about to do what he thought he was about to do, it wasn't late at all. *What am I doing.*

Five months since that photo shoot. Five months since walking into that scruffy concrete rehearsal room, greeting the director and the other actors in the play, and being introduced to the photographer. Tanith said, Hi Victor, thanks for being on time, this is Andy Martin. Victor said something polite and shook hands, grateful he was an actor. *Why now. Why this one. What is happening.* He was thirty-five. The world thought he was straight. Keeping up his cover had meant some lonely years, but he was used to it. He thought he was resigned to it. His reason for playing straight had a time limit, after all, and five months ago it had seemed all the more important to maintain. But oh, it was tough to do. Tough to get in character as the bad guy, and follow Andy's direction or Tanith's, and not look past the lights and *wish*.

Victor's reason still existed. She was even more important now that time was running out. He should not be doing this, should not be walking over to Andy. No matter how gorgeous he looked, laughing at something. Victor should not be letting the loneliness and the hunger get the best of him.

He kept moving.


As the group dispersed, Andy felt a touch on his shoulder. He turned and recognized a recent photo subject. "Well, Mr. Garcia," he said with a smile, because who wouldn't smile at this guy. "What are you doing here?"

"Getting some new ink from Lola," said Victor, also smiling, pushing up the sleeve of his loose denim shirt to show the fresh dressing on his forearm. "Do you live here?"

"Yeah. Moved here four years ago."

"Friend of the deceased?"

"We had a gentlemen's agreement. I wouldn't try to touch him, and he wouldn't put any more claws in my leg." Andy indicated the parallel scars across his shin.

"He did that?" Victor leaned against a wall, apparently in no hurry to go. "Shame to mess up one of those legs."

Andy blinked. He habitually wore dance shorts around the complex, but no-one ever remarked on it. He wasn't even close to being the most eccentric resident. Since he wasn't certain Victor's comment meant what he thought it meant, he went with a reference to a project they had both worked on. "I hear the play was quite a success, in spite of everything. Congratulations." He was tempted to say more, maybe something about the photo shoot. About that electric moment when their eyes met. But Victor had gone straight into character then. Andy followed his lead, because the room was full of people and they were there to do a job, and maybe it was all Andy's imagination anyway. A moment of wishing, because someone that beautiful didn't walk into the room every day.

"It went well, thanks," Victor was saying. "Definitely the weirdest theater experience I've had, but it was a good little part for me. Even if I was the bad guy." His tone said he didn't mind playing bad guys.

"You were a good bad guy," Andy said. "I went to the fourth performance. It ran really smooth."

"Everything shook out by then." Victor gave him a look up and down. Subtle, but unmistakable. Andy kept his face still with an effort. This was *not* his imagination. Victor was studying him in a way that had nothing to do with his next words. "I liked the photos you did for the production. Do you have a minute to talk about updating my portfolio?"

"Yeah, I guess." Andy thought fast, because evidently he was not, after all, tripping. Was his studio space a mess? Was the kitchen clean? And why did he care? *Maybe,* he admitted to himself, *because this is the hottest guy who's spoken to me in years, he's practically inviting himself up to see my etchings, and I'd like him to get a good look.* Some guys weren't turned off by domestic disorder; some – like Andy himself - were.

"You're sure it's a good time?" Victor smiled a little, and shifted his body in a way that made Andy flash back to his performance in the play. When he'd played a seducer. The implication was dual: 'it'll be a good time all right' and 'this could take a while.'

*Fuck, I hope so.* Andy straightened up, making the most of his height for a change, and tried on a smile. "Sure. Let's go up." If anyone was listening, they would hear a totally innocuous exchange about an actor's portfolio. They'd have to be really paying attention to catch that subtle body language. If Andy weren't well aware that Victor wasn't out, he would have thought the guy picked people up all the time. He wasn't entirely sure why the guy was picking *him* up right now, but he had no intention of questioning it.

Victor followed Andy to a door, up some stairs, up a rampway. Watching those legs move and asking himself, all the way, *what am I doing.* But the people outside didn't care who he was. Nobody had paid the slightest attention to him. It was the safest place he'd been in for a long time, more than a year since his last time, and here was the man who'd been on his mind for months. Victor might be risking everything. Andy knew who he was. But he'd played that little scene perfectly. He had to know what it meant to not be out. So if this was a chance to be himself for a little while … Victor was going to take it.

When he opened the door, Andy was relieved to see that he'd left his studio-slash-apartment in an acceptable state. He closed the door behind Victor, threw the deadbolt, and watched while the other man surveyed the space.

The room was open on the main level, with a desk surface and bookshelf across the entire wall facing the door. Two big monitors stood on the desk in front of two task chairs. Andy kicked off his shoes, walked past Victor, and set his high-end DSLR camera on the desk. His guest (for lack of a better word) was still examining the room. *What is he learning about me*, Andy thought, interested. It made him look at the space with fresh eyes. Bathroom, kitchen, and laundry areas were tucked under a sleeping loft. To the right was a huge multi-paned window, with all but the top row of glass panes whitewashed. The sole soft furnishing on the main level was a slipcovered couch under the window. It was large enough for four people to sit and watch a movie, or for two men to lie down together. The entire space was painted hard white; all the color on the main level was in the books, and in the oversized Underground Cabaret posters hung above the shelf.

"Wow," said Victor slowly. "Those are your work?" He removed his shoes too, then walked across the room to get a better look at the posters. Talking to Andy downstairs had been an impulse; he hadn't even thought about what the other man's living space might be like. This was serious. A working space.

"A friend of mine starting doing video of their shows and hooked me up. It's easy when you have subjects like that." Andy heard the habitual self-deprecation and reminded himself not to do that. He was seven years into this new career; it was time to accept that he was making it work.

"I've never seen them. Are they good?" Victor was studying the row of books on the shelf now. Art, design, and photography. Thinking about that last comment. He heard things like that a lot. Nobody in show business ever really believed they knew what they were doing.

"I think they're really good. If I were still dancing I might even try to get in on a show." *Why did I say that?* Andy never told people about his history. Talking about it still hurt. But whatever was happening here, he wasn't the one at risk. He wondered again why Victor was here. Not here at the Brewery – obviously that was for the new tattoo – but here in Andy's home. If he didn't want people to know he was gay, why come up with someone everybody *did* know was gay? Andy watched the other man study his space, reminded himself about the whole 'update the portfolio' exchange, and waited.

"You were a dancer?" Victor turned around to look at him again. "That accounts for the legs." The legs were amazing. That might account for the it's-just-luck tone a minute ago, too. A second career. *How old is he?* He didn't look much older than Victor, even in this white space with its almost clinical lighting. It didn't really matter. He was old enough for what Victor wanted. He was everything Victor wanted.

Andy watched Victor think, fairly sure he could read the other man's mind. That hot stare was not really open to more than one interpretation. "Well, I do still dance." Again it was as if something else had control of his speech. "I take class with Mandy, she's a ballet teacher, every morning here at the complex. She has this class for residents. I just don't audition anymore." *Shut UP Jesus Christ he doesn't care.*

Except maybe he did. "Why is that?" Victor came closer. His expression was warm, intense,

7

interested. His voice had a husky quality that was doing bad things for Andy's composure.

*Did I notice that before? Was it there before?* "Um, too old? Not cute anymore? Broken heart?" Andy stopped talking, appalled. But Victor didn't seem to be considering a quick exit.

"Who said you're not cute anymore? Would that be the asshole who broke your heart?" Victor was standing very close now. He was maybe two inches shorter than Andy's six feet and he looked like heaven. His skin was a couple of shades darker than Andy's. The thin mustache he wore for his role on 'L.A. Vice' was, Andy noted with an attempt to focus, his own and not an appliance.

Andy wanted desperately to kiss that mustache and everything near it. "Um," he managed, "would you like a drink?"

"Maybe later." Victor kissed him. Andy stood still for a moment, but when Victor put a hand on his side, sliding it around to the small of his back, running his fingers up the indent of Andy's spine, he took the other man's head between his hands and dove in. Victor made a muffled sound and pressed his body close.

"Ow! Shit," Victor said breathlessly.

Andy let go of him. "Crap, sorry. I forgot you saw Lola today."

"I did too." Victor sat up, shaking out his arm. They'd sprawled across the slipcovered couch under the window, touching and kissing, all over each other like teenagers. Andy'd shed his flannel shirt within seconds and the rest of his clothes soon after. Victor was down to an undershirt. The dressing on his new

8

tattoo was awry. He straightened it, patted down the adhesive, then peeled off the shirt.

Andy propped himself up on his elbows, took a good look, and blew out a breath at the sheer beauty of the man. "God Almighty," he said. "What is happening?"

"I think we're about to fuck," said Victor, amused. "Is that okay?"

"What do you think?" Then he had a moment of rationality. "Wait. Condoms?" He had some, of course, but they weren't conveniently located. He hadn't gone down to Brando's funeral thinking he would come back with a new lover.

"Hold on a second." Victor leaned over to find his pants, which had landed under the couch. This maneuver brought his mouth close to a very interesting bit of Andy. He retrieved what they needed, got them both ready, then spent several minutes doing things with his mouth before he straightened up, flushed and smiling. Andy's head had fallen back and he was gasping. Victor stretched out on top of him.

*This isn't what I came here for*, thought Victor. *What am I doing?* But the slim body beneath his was too much for him. He lowered his mouth to Andy's throat and let desire take over.

Andy made it easy. It was clear almost from the start that Victor's experience hadn't included a few of Andy's favorite things. When Andy said, No, this way, he was surprised. But he was amenable to taking direction. He was careful, thoughtful, observant. And God, he was beautiful. To see each other's faces while Victor was inside, to be kissed, to watch him come through the haze of his own orgasm: it was the best fuck Andy'd had for years. Almost perfect. The only thing that could have made it better was a thing he knew he wouldn't get. *Once might be all I get. It'll have to be enough.*

Later, they had a snack scavenged from Andy's kitchen, and a couple of beers. They talked about nothing in particular, mostly about work. Victor showed no sign of wanting to leave. Andy certainly didn't want him to. When they landed on the couch again they did another thing that seemed new to Victor. Whether it was sixty-nine itself that was new, or doing it naked, or doing it with the lights on (though not that obnoxious overhead light; he'd switched that off before kneeling between Andy's legs), Andy couldn't tell. He didn't ask. He didn't care. They tidied up again. He thought Victor would go then. Surely twice was the limit, and it was well after midnight. But he didn't. He moved, almost hesitantly, into Andy's arms. They stretched out together and went to sleep for a while.

Deep in the night, Andy talked Victor into posing for a series of photos, including a few artful nudes. More than a few. He let Andy take the sort of photos that anyone might shy away from. If they'd been laughing through this whole encounter, it would have been funny how that turned them both on again. *Personal best*, Andy thought, and now he thought he might share that with Victor someday. It might be possible; this might not be the one-time thing he'd expected. Especially after he put Victor up against the wall, felt his initial resistance, then felt his surrender. Heard the sound he made when he climaxed, something between a curse and a prayer, and the softer sound he made when Andy finished. They stood together, both shaking, with Andy's arm wrapped around from behind and his cheek against Victor's hair. Andy wanted to say something, but he didn't dare. Instead he brushed his lips over Victor's cheek one more time, disengaged, and took him into the bathroom for a shower. They washed each other (with Victor's freshly-inked arm held up out of the water), dried each other, kissed.

They slept again, off and on, tangled together on the couch under a flannel quilt. Every time they woke up, they started kissing again. Neither of them could seem to stop, even though they were both completely spent. When the big window was pale with dawn light, they got dressed and had coffee. Andy scrolled through the digital images, deleting the few that Victor didn't like and tagging those he wanted for his portfolio.

"Use them or don't use them," he said. "I'll email them to you. No charge for this update." Victor didn't reply. Andy's heart sank. *Oh hell.* "Everything okay?"

"I didn't mean to do this. I didn't even know you lived here." Victor was looking at Andy's hands, graceful as the rest of him. He wore a wide silver ring on his right index finger and a brown leather cuff on his right wrist. It wasn't the usual studded, belt-like affair; it was braided cord, flexible, a bit slippery. It felt like the serpent of temptation against Victor's skin. He'd examined it during a break in the action, sometime after midnight. After the camera came out but before he'd been up against the wall with Andy pressed to his back, ringed hand on Victor's throat and bare hand on his cock.

Andy heard the change in Victor's voice. "I didn't know you had any idea who I even was. I was only the photographer."

"No, you weren't." *You're so much more. You're everything.* He couldn't do this. It was too perfect, it

11

was everything he'd never even realized he wanted, and if he stayed – or if he came back - he might as well take out an ad on the front page of the Hollywood Reporter. He had to get out of here. He couldn't come back. This man did not deserve to be hidden. He deserved someone who would kiss him for the world to see. That couldn't be Victor. Not now, maybe not ever. He didn't know what else to do, so he draped an arm over Andy's shoulders and hugged him. "You're great. Super great." His voice didn't sound like his own.

"But." Andy knew what was coming. That long pause said it all. It was what he'd expected all along. He'd thought, maybe, something about the night might have changed the outcome. It really shouldn't have mattered what Victor said next.

"I'm … kind of in a relationship right now. I shouldn't have done this. I'm sorry." He wanted to say more. He wanted to tell the truth. As always, he was afraid to. Except that he was sorry, because he never meant to hurt Andy and it was all too plain that he had. *Selfish, careless cabrón.* He had just been so hungry. So lonely. So he'd taken, and taken again, through that glorious night, and now he had to ruin it.

"Okay," Andy said quietly. "That's okay. I wouldn't have missed it." He tried to smile, which was a mistake. *Get a grip you idiot, it's only a fling, stop it don't cry STOP IT.*

Victor wanted to kiss him again, didn't quite dare. Instead he squeezed Andy's shoulders and stood up. Then he reached over to the desk, where a pad of blank release forms lay under the computer mouse. He wrote out and signed a release giving Andy permission to use the photos.

"You shouldn't do that."

12

"I trust you. You know who I am." Andy heard it, but didn't think about it. Not then. He was still trying to maintain. "I'll call you sometime," Victor said, sounding uncertain.

"No," Andy said calmly, looking up. The eye contact was painful. "It's probably best that you don't."

After a moment, Victor nodded. He made a move, as if to put his hand on Andy's shoulder again, then stepped away. He looked back for a second when he got to the door. Andy was staring resolutely at the monitor. Victor's head was telling him to get out, but his heart was screaming *stay*. If Andy had turned his head Victor would have let go of the door handle and gone back to him. That didn't happen.

Once the door closed, Andy dropped his head into his hands for a minute. *I never learn*, he thought. It probably served him right. Payback for one of those times he'd been the one to pick someone up, make love to them like they mattered, and then walk away. *In a relationship*. He didn't want to believe it. Didn't want to believe it was possible for someone to surrender like that and for it to be a lie.

Out in his car, Victor didn't start the engine right away. Instead he leaned back and closed his eyes. He was exhausted, satiated, sore, and perilously close to tears.


December 2012

Andy was conscious of Not Moving On, and he didn't like it. He had things to do – plenty, thank you – and was getting them done, but there was a persistent sense of unfinished business. It wasn't the first time someone had told him No. Not by a long shot. It was simply that a No had never landed after a night like that. Possibly because there had never *been* a night like that. He forced himself to acknowledge and dismiss it, treating it like a posture correction: oh yes, there's that knife in my back again.

Before ... that ... happened, in and around all the usual work – head shots, portfolios, glamour shots, weddings, souvenirs - he'd been working on his usual post-exhibit project. His fall show was a series on empty theaters. From the beginning he'd thought maybe this wasn't the best choice, but it had proven commercially successful. Nearly all the exhibit prints were sold, some others had been ordered, and at least one of the unexhibited images from each theater's shoot was now in his portfolio of stock photos. But he couldn't stand to look at them anymore, certainly didn't want to put in the time to make his usual personal-record book, and therefore simply abandoned it. Maybe someday he'd go back to that folder and think, okay, now I can.

Instead he decided to concentrate on the next show. He'd been playing with the concept for a while and already had several models lined up. He needed half a dozen more, so he put the word out to his contacts. The title for the show came to him in the middle of the night about a month after that devastating No. He'd been looking through the photos of Victor Garcia, trying to decide if he should delete them, and conceding that he couldn't. He had sent the photos Victor liked, as promised, but without comment and from an alias address. He didn't want so much as a 'thanks,' and couldn't stand the thought that the man might offer to pay for the photos. Maybe someday he could contemplate them without pain. For now they were an effective reminder, as if he'd needed one, that he was better off alone.

That probably wasn't the best thought to go to sleep on. When he woke up at something like three in the morning with the words 'Cut Open' in front of his eyes, he thought it was about Victor. There were those scars, after all. But then he realized it was right for the new show. He wouldn't use Victor's photos. For one thing, he was planning to shoot this series in black and white. For another, it wouldn't be fair. And maybe it didn't make sense to care about that, but he did.

He didn't tell anybody about the project title except the actual models. He was avoiding his particular friends, the ones who were apt to ask about his love life (or at least his sex life). The only people he told about that night in November were his mother and a not-too-close friend. Someone who didn't have a personal stake in Andy's well-being, and therefore someone he could tell about that night in a way that re-framed it. It was almost a joke: the one who got away. Almost everybody had one, after all. If only he'd been able to laugh about it.

Victor didn't know if he had ever felt so alone, and he didn't know what to do. Didn't know if there was anything he *could* do. His agent sent a few possibilities for fill-in work during the mid-season break, but Victor didn't think he could give anything the concentration it required, and decided he might as well go to Puerto Vallarta. Spend as much time as possible with his mother. They both knew they weren't going to get a lot more.

Once there, though, with nothing they could do except talk, it was almost worse. Because what Victor wanted to talk about, he couldn't. Couldn't say, Mama, I met the man of my dreams. We had the night of my dreams. I left him, I lied to him, what can I do.

15

Couldn't say, Mama, I think I'm in love, I'm afraid. Of all the things to be afraid of, when she was dying. But he was, so afraid, afraid the chance was gone. He couldn't decide if he would rather he'd never had that night at all.

His Tía Susana helped. She was there every day after work, bringing stories about her job – in the same hotel where Mama used to work – or about Victor's cousins and their families. They all had families, even the twenty-two-year-old youngest. All married and with at least one child, though for the youngest that child was still 'expected.' Mama said she hoped she would be around for the christening. She didn't ask Victor, this time, if he was seeing anyone special. He was grateful he didn't have to add to that long string of lies.

When he went back to Los Angeles it was with a combination of relief and resentment. Plus, of course, guilt about both things. He shouldn't be relieved at escaping that little apartment with all the medical equipment, all the drugs, the smell of sickness. And the landlord hovering, always wanting Victor to confirm the rent would be paid. As if he hadn't been doing that for years, so Mama could use her own money for things she enjoyed. Victor made sure the landlord knew Tía Susana was keeping an eye on things. That his mother wasn't to be harassed or troubled for any reason, and that Victor would know if she were. The landlord would get his new tenant soon enough.

Then there was the resentment that he had to go back to work, which made doubly no sense, because he was so grateful to have the work to distract him. He told the show runners it wouldn't be long now, and was grateful all over again that the back half of the season gave his character something to be angry about. Because he was so very angry. Angry at his mother for being sick, which was horrible. Angry that he had to lie to every single person in his life. Angry that because of all those lies he had no one to share this grief. He was getting noticed on the series this season, and even that made him angry.

When Tía Susana called, Victor went straight to the show runners. The way the series was shot made it possible (if not easy) to reschedule a few things so that he could go back to Mexico. His colleagues were kind. He'd had his bag packed for a week, since his aunt said 'soon.' He was on the next available flight.


Andy told himself it was stupid to watch 'L.A. Vice' now when he never had before. He told himself it was, if not actively self-destructive, at least a species of sabotage. He was hoping that Victor wouldn't be good. Except he wanted him to be good: wanted the performance to reinforce his sense that the man had been worth the pain. Fortunately, he was good. He was so angry, though. Andy couldn't help wondering why. There was more going on there than the script could account for. It might have been the basic anger of someone who couldn't live his life in the open, allowed to develop because of the storyline. There'd been no sense of anger in November. Nothing negative at all, in fact, until the morning. Whatever had caused Victor to walk away, it was something he was able to box up entirely during their lengthy encounter.

Or maybe he was simply a much better actor than that stupid show really needed him to be. "Oh well, whatever, never mind," Andy sang to himself, then shut his mouth so he could finish shaving off the

17

damned beard. If certain people saw him like this, he'd never hear the end of it, and it was time to show his face again. What was he trying to do, anyway, be a different guy than the one who fucked Victor Garcia? He should've had a beard in November. Then his normal self would look nothing like that guy. "Get over it," he said to his dripping face in the mirror. "Move on."

Chapter 2

March 2013

On the flight to Puerto Vallarta, all Victor could think about was his mother. On the flight back to Los Angeles, all he could think about was Andy. He wasn't angry anymore. He was empty, hollow, exhausted.

The whole ordeal was over, finally over, the more-than-a-year of pain and fear and dread. Now Mama was with God and Victor was more alone than ever. He didn't know how it was possible to hurt this much and still live. Tía Susana said, let it be. Let yourself go. Don't hold it in. But holding it in was all he'd ever done. He didn't know how to do anything else.

His father wasn't there, of course. Or perhaps that wasn't fair. They were in touch; John had asked, should I come. It was Victor who said no. The cousins, all Mama's friends, they knew John was only in her life at all because of Victor. It had been years – seventeen years – since he'd been to see her. The last time had been a year after Victor went to live with him in Escondido, when they were doing the paperwork for Victor to become a U.S. citizen. Mama was stoic about that, as about so many things. She knew he would have more opportunities in California. He had a good education; he had talent; he spoke perfect English. He had the body and the face to get noticed, to get hired for local TV gigs and as a model, even that first year when he wasn't at his best.

And John had money. He said, I'll stake Victor for a year in L.A. If it doesn't work out, he can come back and work with me at the car dealership. But it had worked out. Mama was so proud. Victor sent her discs whenever he could. If he played a bad guy she would say, oh you should have been the hero, you would have been so much better. If he played a good guy she would say, nobody could have been better. When she saw the recording of the most recent play, she said, ay m'hijo you are such a star. He'd laughed with her on the phone, promising her one day he'd be the one on the movie poster. He'd been promising her that for years. That last time, both of them knew she wouldn't live to see it happen.

He'd be going back to work on the TV series right away. They would have a week of catch-up to do. He was lucky they'd let him go at all. So even if he'd wanted to let go, to cry and scream and grieve, he couldn't. He had to maintain. He had no idea why that thought led to Andy. Or why, having arrived at the subject of Andy, his mind wouldn't leave it.

For months he asked himself why he did that. Why put himself through that, why do it to Andy. The answer was always the same: because he's beautiful, because he was there, because I wanted him from the start. Then the question changed, and he asked himself why he didn't tell the truth. He'd signed that release. Andy knew who he was, knew he was on a TV show. Victor had put his whole life in the other man's hands the moment he walked up and said that stupid thing about his legs. But still, no one knew. Victor's closet door was still securely shut. Andy didn't sell him out.

When Victor sent a cell-phone picture of the healed tattoo to Lola, she texted back saying *did you get your new head shot?* To Victor, that said: Andy hasn't mentioned you. Because of course, sometime during that long night, they'd talked about Lola. Andy knew her. He knew everybody. And he respected Victor's privacy. He didn't go to his ballet class and say, this TV actor fucked me over. He didn't go to Lola and say, that guy you inked is an asshole. *I could have told him.* Could have said, my mother doesn't know, so nobody knows. Will you keep my secret. *We could have been together all this time.*

That was only a dream, because it still would have been a lie. Sneaking, hiding, denying. He wanted, so very much, to make it true. He couldn't get that time back. Couldn't cancel out that devastating lie. Didn't know if it was possible to be forgiven, to make amends.

He had to try. Now that Mama couldn't be hurt, he had to try.


The studio was set for Andy's new show and he thought it looked good. "What do you think?" he asked, without turning his head.

"It's good," said his friend Rory. "It's great, actually. But what's wrong with *you*?"

"What do you mean?"

"You're, like, askew." He'd been friendly and funny as usual, but Rory had known him for a long time. "You've been avoiding us for months, we've only seen you for the Cabaret shoots. What happened?"

Andy looked down at her, tempted to make an excuse about the press of business. That kitten face said 'no bullshit please.' "You really want to know?"

"Yes, I really do." She tugged him over to the couch and they sat down. "Tell Mama."

Andy snorted. She was ten years younger than he was. "The short version is, I had a fling way back in

November, going nowhere as usual, the guy is high profile and not really out, plus he had a relationship, plus oh what does it matter," he wound down.

"Jesus, this is like Sam and Mateo all over again," she muttered. "What is it with you guys?"

"What are you talking about?"

"Your star subject there," she said, indicating one of the photos of her friend Sam, who featured heavily in the 'Cut Open' show. "He had that I'm-not-worthy thing going with Mateo. He was like, I'm too old, he's too beautiful, not for me."

Andy made a stagey but sincere gesture of rejection. "Hey, honestly. It's not that I thought I'm not worthy. The guy made a pass at *me*. It's that after an epic night he said oops sorry, shouldn'ta done that, never again, gotta go."

"But none of that is anything to do with you."

"Which, EXACTLY."

Rory winced. She always forgot how he could project. "Oh."

"I was kind of shattered at the time, but basically I've been mad as fuck ever since, and I can't seem to get over it. I mean, it's not like what he did was *wrong*."

"Well, actually, yes it is. It was wrong. He was cheating on somebody."

"Okay, yeah. But who? That endless procession of beards I see him with? Oops." Andy heard himself a moment too late. He must have really wanted to talk about this.

"Uh, hey now." Rory snorted. "Are you stalking this guy?"

"NO. I can't help noticing when he gets a press mention. Okay, I might have a Google alert set. That's not stalking."

"Eh, no, I guess," she said with half a laugh. "It's not exactly 'moving on with your life' either."

"At least I'm still dating." *Sort of*, he thought. Drinks with a friend might count.

"So," she said, thinking. "It sounds like what you're most mad about is the fact you can't tell who he is - or was - really with. So you don't know if that was the truth or if he lied so he could bail."

"Yeah. 'Kind of in a relationship' were his words. And since I've seen no evidence of that, I'm forced to conclude it actually meant 'kind of not really interested.' And that makes me mad because then WHAT THE FUCK were the previous eight hours all about."

"Eight *hours*?" Her eyebrows went up. "Damn, Andy, I'm impressed."

He snorted. He'd been kind of impressed himself. "Not, you know, uninterrupted."

"I'm, like, deeply invested now. Are you willing to tell me who this guy is?"

"You have to promise … *promise* … not to tell anybody. Not even Dana. I mean it, he is high profile and he isn't out and I don't want to be That Bitter Queen who ruins someone's life out of vengefulness."

"It'll be in the vault." He knew if she said it, she meant it. Rory kept secrets well. So he got up, went to the computer, dug through several layers of security, and opened the file. "Holy *shit*," she said, eyes wide. She studied the index screen. There were a lot of photos, ranging from head shots (that guy looked amazingly good with what had to be two-in-the-morning shadow) to, "Wow." She couldn't believe the guy let Andy take those pictures. No wonder he was

23

bent about the whole bailing-out thing. "He gave you a release for these?"

"Yes he did." They stared at each other for a second. Andy knew he didn't have to say more. Being a Latino actor was tough enough. Being a gay Latino actor, and being out? Even at his angriest he hadn't considered blowing Victor's cover. Even now, he couldn't imagine why Victor had put this much trust in him, and then walked away. The relationship thing still didn't feel true.

Rory looked again. She didn't want to bang the guy but she could certainly appreciate what she was seeing. She touched the screen, scrolling the index so she could see everything. "We don't watch that show. Maybe we should. Goddamn, he is beautiful."

"Yeah." At least he'd gotten these pictures. Rory probably suspected he was using them for improper purposes. *Only once or twice*, he thought, feeling not at all guilty about it.

She might have read his mind. "Nice ink, too." One of the tattoos was on his right pec, a stag's head beautifully rendered in bright rainbow colors. The shot was framed from the ribs up. The subject's hair was disheveled, eyes sleepy, mouth not quite smiling and distinctly reddened. He looked freshly fucked, or about to be. *That is not going in his portfolio*, Rory thought, almost cracking up. Another image showed a tattoo on the front of his hip. She tapped the image to put it on full-screen. Naturalistic – almost photorealistic – except for those same brilliant colors.

*Thanks for nothing, girlfriend.* Just looking at that was enough to turn him on. Andy averted his eyes from the gecko with its tail curling up toward Victor's hipbone and its tongue curling toward his half-hard cock. In retrospect, he couldn't quite believe Victor let

24

him take – or keep - that picture. Or the one of the similarly-rendered rattlesnake wrapped around the top of the opposite thigh. "That's why he was even here. Getting a new one from Lola." He waved a hand toward one of the many images where the fresh dressing was visible.

"Sorry," Rory said, looking at him with sympathy. There had been times when she could give him crap about his love life. This wasn't one of those times. She exited the full-screen view, wondering who the other tattoo artist was. Someone as good as hers, that was for sure.

Andy shrugged. He felt better for sharing it, and he told her so. "But I've got to finish setting up, and you have to get back home because, if I recall correctly, you have a show of your own to do very soon. What's the number?"

"'Trust in Me,' from 'The Jungle Book.' The Sterling Holloway version."

The mental image that supplied was delightful. Andy giggled. "I won't miss it."

"You'd better not."


Rory got home and immediately told her girlfriend Dana why Andy'd been absent from their lives. "No details because I swore not to," she said. "He met somebody, it was epic, and then it was over. He's hurt, he's mad, and he's not getting over it the way he usually does."

Dana was happy to be interrupted – she was reading a very lousy spec script – but not to hear about Andy's trouble. "If he's hurt it's because he cared. He's had his share of flings."

"I keep hoping he'll find his one and only, you know? His Dana." She bumped her shoulder against

25

Dana's. "On the plus side, the show is stupendous. His photos of Sam are killer and some of the other stuff will break your heart."

"Is he coming to Chrome?"

"He promised."

"Good. Save me from this stupid script. What a piece of garbage." Dana threw the spec script across the room and pulled Rory down onto her lap. "Tell me a story."

"Your agent never learns. Okay. Once upon a time there was a sexy blonde who lived in a little cottage in WeHo."

"I like this story already," Dana said, smiling.


There weren't many people for Victor to talk to. He didn't have the first idea how one went about coming out. There didn't seem to be much point in doing it unless Andy was willing to give him another chance. So when he got in touch with his friend Janis, he made it about dinner, and the photographs. They met up at Sisley in Sherman Oaks, a location that was mutually inconvenient. Los Angeles being what it was, that was often the most considerate solution. Otherwise one person ended up doing all the driving.

She was already there when he arrived, sitting at the bar with a glass of wine. "Victor," she said, and came straight to him for a hug. "You look like shit."

He couldn't help laughing a little. "Thanks?"

"I'm so, so sorry about your mom. Are you actually okay?"

"Eh." He shrugged. "This too shall pass." She made a sympathetic sound. "What's new with you?"

"I'm going to try to make an album. Let's get a table and get you some wine and I'll tell you all about it." So they did that, and it was a great distraction. Janis was a pianist and singer. She was one of the musicians working on that play last year, hired by the arranger, who was now also a friend. They talked music for a while. Janis reminded Victor that he needed to do more with singing. Then she said, "I went to see that exhibit you told me about, out at the Brewery. I don't know quite how to describe it. It was great, a little disturbing, but also kind of uplifting."

"What kind of pictures were they? All I really knew was the title." It was Andy's show, of course, which Victor knew about because he was practically stalking the guy. The title was 'Cut Open,' and he'd had a moment of fearing this was when Andy retaliated. Because he'd seen Victor's scars. He'd taken pictures. And Victor had signed the release.

"They were black and white, white-box background, super sharp. Unforgiving. One of his subjects was this guy, mixed-race I guess, dark skin, incredibly handsome except his nose had been broken and there was this scar across his face." Janis lifted her hand and drew a line with her finger, from the outside of her eye to the corner of her mouth. "It was like someone took a box cutter to the Mona Lisa. But he looked so, not resigned, but resolute. Everything about him was like, we shall overcome. Lived through that. Your petty attack has no power over me. Every one of the subjects was that way, and some of them had much worse damage. I asked the guy, the photographer, how he gets people to trust him like that. He said, I ask questions, and then I listen."

*Yes he does*, Victor thought. Janis knew, she had to know, why Victor asked her to go to the exhibit. He'd said 'this person is important to me, and doesn't know it.' She knew Victor wasn't out. And only an idiot – which Janis most definitely was not – could fail to grasp that Andy was gay. "Thanks for going to see that."

"Thanks for sending me over there," she said, draining her glass. "I told Valerie to go. Actually I told everybody to go. I'm not usually the person for the visual arts, you know, I can barely dress myself. But that guy has something. So." She regarded him for a moment. "You're back at work, I assume."

He nodded. "I was lucky they let me have a week. Some other people are having to put in extra time so we can catch up with my stuff."

"I'm sure they don't mind. What're you going to do?"

They stared at each other for a moment. They weren't super-close friends; Victor didn't really have any of those, because he'd been lying to everybody his whole life. But she was the person he'd thought of when he wanted some connection, however tenuous, to Andy. Even if that connection told him 'this man hates you.' That clearly wasn't the answer. If Victor was on the wall at that exhibit, Janis would have said so first thing. "I lied to him," he said after a moment. "I'm going to see if he'll forgive me."

"Do you want a relationship?" She said it softly, keeping it between them. They both knew what the consequences could be. Maybe Victor's show runners, or the production company, or the network, or the series stars wouldn't care if he came out. But maybe they would.

"I don't know," Victor said honestly. "I've never had one."

"Jesus, Victor."

He smiled, shaking his head. "Yeah. But something has to change, and I think it's me."

28

She set her hand on his arm. "Don't change too much. Because you're pretty close to perfect. I hope it works out." He picked up her hand and kissed it.

On the third weekend in March, Andy showed up at the Hollywood nightclub Chrome to see the Underground Cabaret. His poster for the new show - called 'On Safari' - was by the back entrance. The four principals were all in animal costumes of the scanty variety, meaning mostly body paint. He glanced at it with approval, then said, "Hi Julio. How's it hanging?"

"Long and low, gangsta." The doorman, who knew Andy wasn't asked to pay admission, waved him in.

Rory's number came toward the end of the first act. As expected, her striptease to Kaa's song brought down the house. Andy took a lap during intermission, meeting and greeting. After more than a year working with the Cabaret, the nightclub felt like a second home. He picked up a drink at the bar, chatting with the bartender for a few minutes till the house lights dimmed.

When he turned around to go back to his table, he almost crashed into Victor. A little too much experience with dousing the flames of burning bridges kept him from saying the first thing that came to mind, which was 'fuck off.' Instead he said, "Well, this is unexpected."

"Hi Andy," said Victor uncertainly. "I hope you don't mind."

That really was unexpected, but his voice stayed cold. "Why should I mind? It's a public place." Victor flinched. "If *you* don't mind, I'd like to see the show." Andy brushed past and went to his table, heart pounding. *That was not nice*, he thought. *That was hella rude. Good for me.* Half of his cocktail was gone before the lights went down.

He tried to concentrate on the show, but he was aware that Victor stayed by the bar throughout the second act. At the end, Andy stayed at his table. Pretending to check his phone for messages, pretending he didn't know Victor was approaching. He heard his name, and looked up. "What do you want, Victor?"

"I want to talk to you. Preferably in private."

Andy studied him. Victor didn't look like he was on top of the world. In fact, he looked tired and sad. Andy melted a little. "If you can hang out, we could go in the green room in a bit."

"Good. That's good. Thanks."

"So." He couldn't sit there not talking indefinitely; there were too many people who might notice. "How's the TV show going?"

"It's going well. One of few things in my life that is right now. I saw you were doing a thing at your place. Wanted to see it, but I … wasn't sure you'd want to see me there, so I sent a friend. She said it's really good work."

"I've sold a lot of the prints, so I'm calling it a success." Andy thought, *be a grown-up now.* "I have my working copy for the book in the car if you'd like to see it."

"Yeah! Yeah, I'd like to." Victor was swamped with relief. Coming here tonight had been an act of desperation, a Hail Mary before actually turning up at the Brewery again.

"Hang on, I'll go get it." Andy produced a quarter of a smile as he stood, then went up the stairs in record time. He shot past Julio and out to his car, got the binder, and then walked normally (to catch his breath) on the way back. He slid back onto his stool. "Here we go."

"That was fast." Victor was still standing by the table.

*Why do you have to look like that*, Andy thought. The other man was wearing a white denim jacket over an indigo tee shirt and jeans. Aside from the fatigue, he looked like he'd come from a photo shoot. "Yeah, well," he said. "My athletic friends tell me it's good to get my heart rate up occasionally. Take a seat."

Victor pulled a seat close and said, "Show me?" Andy opened the binder and paged through it, giving some of the background for his subjects. Victor glanced at him. "When I heard the title, I thought you might have put me in it."

"This one had a particular theme," said Andy. "You might have fit, yeah. But I didn't know enough about you to know if what I'd seen had a story. Or a story you'd want to share."

The knife scars definitely had a story, but not one Victor was ready to share. He'd put his phone numbers on that photo release. He wondered if Andy had ever considered using them. "You could have called me."

*I wonder if he has any idea how many times I almost did.* "No, I couldn't. It was none of my business. This kind of image … people talk about them. They ask questions. It's super intrusive. You have to be braced for it. This guy Sam," he tapped a photo. "He was at the opening and he got mobbed. He told me if we hadn't talked all the way through the shoot it would have really freaked him out." He gave that a second. "Whatever your story is, I figured it was exactly what you *wouldn't* want people to know about you."

"Well." Victor looked away. "I appreciate your discretion." More than he could say.

"Is that why you came?" Andy didn't really think so. Victor didn't answer right away. Andy looked around and noted that all of the Cabaret people had cleared out except for Rory and Dana, who were at the bar. "Wait here a minute." He went over to his friends. "Is the green room empty?"

Rory looked past him to the table. She kept her face neutral, with only the usual interest of someone in L.A. spotting a TV actor. "Yeah, everybody's out."

"That's my friend Victor Garcia," said Andy, mostly to Dana. "He asked to talk privately. I think he's having some personal issues."

Victor was watching their conversation. He recognized the pretty blonde, an actress. They'd never worked together. He'd never met her girlfriend, the cute Pacific Islander.

"Go on back," Dana said, aware of Victor's gaze. She'd recognized him immediately. She didn't ask why Andy and Victor couldn't talk privately somewhere else. She'd find out later. Andy wouldn't be able to keep it secret now. "You want us to stand guard?"

"Do you mind?"

"Nope," said Rory and Dana together. Rory added, "But we'd love to hear all about it later if you can talk about it." She couldn't read Andy's expression right now. It wasn't one she'd seen before.

He nodded. "Maybe. I'll be in touch. Thanks girls." He kissed each of them and returned to Victor. "We can go backstage now if you want."

"Yeah, thanks." Victor followed Andy, hoping he could say the right things this time.

In the green room, Andy set the binder on a chair, then dug a couple of bottles of water out of the case kept under the makeup counter, handed one to Victor, and flopped down on the couch. "So. You look a little rough. I mean, you still look like you look, which is great, but … what's up?"

"Thanks for that." Victor smiled a little. "My mother died last week. Back in Jalisco."

"I'm sorry to hear that," Andy said sincerely. "My condolences. Was she sick?"

"She had cancer. She'd been sick for over a year. She didn't know," he said slowly, "that I'm gay."

"Oh." Andy knew that sudden comprehension was all over his face, which was generally the lousiest poker face in the history of faces. That was the simplest and most obvious explanation for why Victor wasn't out, and it was one he hadn't even thought of. "Say no more."

"But I want to explain."

"Really, Victor. I understand. You couldn't be with an out guy, even if you wanted to, and seriously there was no reason for me to think you wanted to. We had a great night, you were cool with me, and it's fine." It wasn't fine, not really. Andy wanted to scream at him, *why didn't you just TELL me?* Why give him that release, hand him all that power, and not simply tell the truth? Andy could take it. He'd have preferred to hear 'this was awesome but I can't do it again for this actual and comprehensible reason' versus 'shouldn't have done it because of this transparent and unnecessary lie.' He was so close to angry again that he almost missed what Victor said next.

"There *was* a reason for you to think that I wanted to. I *did* want to." Victor knew his voice sounded strained. He was trying to manage it, but he could feel that anger, and it felt like one blow too many even though he knew he deserved it.

"Oh." Andy recalibrated, casting about frantically for something to add to that useless word. This actually changed everything, because if Victor knew he couldn't have a relationship but suddenly wanted one, no wonder he panicked and said the wrong thing. Andy was about to put that in words when he looked at Victor, really looked, and saw someone teetering on a knife edge of grief. He set down the water bottle and stood up. "Come here." He put his arms around Victor, and held him while he cried.

After a while Victor got himself together. Andy brushed his hair back, and kissed him on the forehead. Then he went to get a clean cloth from the makeup counter, wet it with water from the bottle, and soothed Victor's hot, tear-stained face. "Thank you," said Victor. His voice was a little scratchy. Everything else felt so much better. To get that permission, to be held, to feel that casual caress and the kiss. Even if this was the last thing, it was so much better than how they'd left it before. "I haven't been able to do that till now."

"Were you with her?"

"Yeah, they gave me some time off. So at least I was there."

"Have you slept?"

"Not much."

*No wonder*. "Do you have a call tomorrow?"

"Two o'clock."

"Then you should try to sleep now, it's past midnight already. Did you drive yourself here?"

34

"No. I took a taxi. My concentration hasn't been good enough for driving." It wasn't really good enough to deduce why Andy was asking these questions, either.

Again Andy thought *no wonder*. If he'd lost his own mother he'd be catatonic. "Let me take you back to your place."

It took a second to sink in. Victor said, "Okay." He wanted to say more, but was afraid he'd start crying again if he did.

Andy figured that anyone left in the club wasn't likely to be hounding Victor, but he took a few minutes to give the other man a little camouflage with supplies from the makeup counter. Victor sat passively, apparently too tired to have an opinion, until he finished. "Come on." Andy picked up his binder and they left the green room. Dana and Rory were still waiting; he mimed a *call you later thank you love you,* then walked Victor up the stairs and out of the club.

Chapter 3

They didn't speak in the car, aside from giving and confirming directions. Andy pulled up at Victor's apartment building twenty minutes later. "You have your keys, right?"

"Yeah. But could you come up?" The question escaped him. He was so tired, and still – again, always - so lonely. "Could you stay?"

"Are you sure you're in the right state of mind for that?"

Victor shook his head. He didn't mean sex. "I don't want … I don't want to be alone." *I want to be with you.*

Andy was fairly sure this was a bad idea, but he wasn't the guy who could walk away from that much pain. The front of the building was deserted, the doorman the sole sign of life. "Where should I park?"

"Through there. Guest parking."

They didn't see a soul on the way up. "Is this building full of old people, or something?"

Victor cracked a smile. "Exactly." He let them into his apartment. Andy didn't pay much attention to it. He was mostly concerned with getting Victor into bed before he collapsed. He got his jacket off, and sent him into the bathroom. A few minutes later, Victor came out in his tee shirt and briefs. Andy couldn't help noticing the tattoo that had been new in November; it was a monochrome portrait of what had to be Victor's mother, but the woman was depicted as an Aztec king. He liked it. He didn't mention it, though. Instead, he pulled down the covers and tucked

Victor in. *Oh fuck being tough, he's a mess*. He stroked his hand through Victor's hair, let it rest for a moment on the side of his head.

Victor turned his face into that hand, eyes closing. "Thanks, Andy," he said drowsily. Andy stroked his thumb across Victor's cheekbone, thought *get out*, and left the room.

The primary mission was accomplished. He should leave. Andy kept telling himself that while he rooted around in the bathroom, borrowed the high-end toiletries to refresh himself a bit, then returned quietly to the bedroom, carrying Victor's discarded jeans. He dumped them on a chair in the corner and looked around. There was a framed photo on the dresser, a snapshot of Victor with two women. One was the model for that tattoo, and the other was so much like her that Andy automatically thought 'Auntie.' Victor was sound asleep. Andy stood there, undecided, noticing the shadowed eyes again, and the lines of strain that hadn't eased even in sleep. *I want to GO, but that would be shitty, so heckity hecking fuck anyway*. He switched off the light, stretched out next to Victor, and lay awake for a long time.

Victor opened his eyes in the still-dark room and thought *what's different*. After a moment he realized there was an arm across his chest, and a long, lean, fully-clothed body on top of the covers but pressed against his. He turned his head cautiously and saw Andy asleep beside him, head on the second pillow over his other arm. Victor's arm was bent, also under the pillow, his hand touching Andy's. He wouldn't have moved it for anything. *I don't deserve this*. He looked up at the ceiling, blinking away tears and grateful to his bones not to be alone. He listened to the other man breathe and, after a while, went back to sleep.

Andy woke up when he heard the shower go on. It took him a second to remember the events of the previous night. Now his late-night thoughts rushed into his head. *This is not going to be easy*, he thought with regret.

He got up and took a quick roam around the modest apartment. It was almost as impersonal as his studio space. Only a stack of plays and scripts by a chair in the living room told him an actor lived here. He couldn't find anything to leave a note with, and his own notepad was in his car. He jingled his keys, strongly tempted to make a break for it, but knew he couldn't. He sat down to wait.

Victor left the bathroom after about ten minutes, wearing a robe. He went into the bedroom, toweling his hair. When he didn't find Andy, he came back out to the living room. "Hey. Thanks for staying."

"You were out cold. Feeling better?"

"Much. You want to … ?"

"Thanks. Be right out." Andy went into the bathroom to take care of business. Relieved, he opened the door to find Victor halfway into dressing. Meaning, halfway naked. *Give me a break, universe*, he thought, but allowed the universe to give him another look at the stag's head on Victor's pec, its pink antlers spreading to the bottom of his clavicle and its violet mane to the ribs below that shapely muscle. There were bright green accents in the fringe of that mane. He averted his eyes. "Listen, I'm going to have to go. Do you have a car coming for you?"

Victor froze for a second. *Don't go.* "Yes."

"Okay, cool."

"Andy. Can I call you?" Victor turned away from the mirror to look at him.

Andy met his eyes; there was nothing but guarded hope there. He couldn't quite hang on to his cynicism. "Okay. We need to talk. I'm free on Sunday. Otherwise … we'll set something up." He pulled out his wallet, extracted a business card, and handed it over. Shoved the wallet back in his pocket, hoping he wasn't opening himself up to another disappointment.

Victor held the card without looking at it. He was still gazing at Andy. "Thank you," he said, face relaxing. "Thank you for that, and thank you for staying. I'm free on Sunday too. Can I take you to breakfast?"

"I'm not usually a morning person. And we might want this conversation to be a little more private."

"You're right. Yeah. Um … how about I pick up some stuff and bring it over, like around noon?"

"Fine. I'll see you then. Keep sleeping." Andy sketched a wave with that ringed hand, a thoughtlessly theatrical gesture that would have made Victor smile at any other time. He backed toward the door, and was out before Victor could move toward him.

*Damn it*, he thought. *I'm fucking this up all over again.* He didn't know how this was supposed to work, and had no clue who he could even ask. He sighed, put it away, and finished getting ready for the day's shoot.


"Hi Mom," Andy said on the phone early the next day. "What are you up to today? Oh really. And I suppose Pop is out on the boat. Did you tell him to bring back some actual edible fish this time?" He laughed, listened, made encouraging noises. "Oh, the usual. Except there was a thing. I told you about that disaster in November. Well, I saw the guy again. Eh, not exactly. Turns out his mother was dying, and she didn't know, so that whole in a relationship thing was true but the relationship was, yeah." Listening again, grateful he could talk like this with his parent, grateful she was still in his life, feeling a stab of vicarious pain that Victor went through that alone. *Wasn't your problem and may never be*, he reminded himself. "Well, sort of. We're going to talk this weekend. I have no idea. You might imagine that I have some trust issues after getting slapped back like that. He's really confused. He needed parents like you and Pop." His mother said the usual things. Andy made a dismissive noise. "Mom, you know to the extent I have ever achieved anything, it's because of you. I love you. Yes, I'll let you know if anything interesting happens. Tell Pop to stop smoking. Talk to you soon." He put down the phone and went to see how many emails had come in. There was always a burst after a show, but the response to this last one had been like whacking open a piñata.

Victor wasn't conscious of approaching his work differently, but apparently he was. The head writer dropped by the set toward the end of the week and asked if he was okay. Victor stared at him for a second, thinking *my mother just died, so no*, and said, "Is something not okay? The director didn't say anything."

"We had a meeting yesterday. Nailing down the arcs for the last six episodes. Somebody said, what's up with Garcia, the LAPD consultant said something."

There was a roster of media liaison officers who helped answer procedural or legal questions. Victor hadn't even noticed that week's person. "Well, what did he say?" He was getting concerned. This was really not the time to get fired.

"I asked the same thing," said the head writer. "Apparently the lieutenant said, quote, whatever switch Garcia flipped, you might want to find it for the other guys. That shit was legit, end quote."

Victor was speechless for a second. Then he said, "Did he mean the arrest?" They'd taped a long, complex scene involving execution of a warrant. Because this was fiction, it played out with maximum drama, including broken doors, gunfire, and yelling. (They'd all heard *ad nauseum* that most arrests were quiet, nonviolent affairs.)

"Upon investigation, yes. So we ordered some food and analyzed the dailies and sent a memo to the director, who as you know is also directing the next episode. There's going to be a cast meeting early next week. Anyway, thought you might want to know. Good work." Message delivered, the writer gave a brisk nod and went away.

"Thanks," Victor said to his back. Of all the ways that could have gone, this was the most unexpected. After he got home, he sat with a shot of sipping tequila and thought back through the scene. Tried to think what he'd done differently, what had made him seem like a real cop. When he finally thought he had it, he said "Huh" out loud. It had nothing to do with the lines, or the well-rehearsed action. He'd bet anything it was because when he'd kicked in that door, he wasn't playing fear or aggression or that sort of cynical disgust about yet another scumbag. He wasn't thinking of a desperate criminal on the other side. He was thinking of a way through to what he wanted.

*Here's to getting the job done*, he thought, *whatever it takes*.


By the following Sunday, Andy had settled himself down, and Victor had worked himself up. A few good nights' sleep restored his energy level. With it came a level of general pissiness that he knew had nothing to do with Andy. It was all over him when Andy opened the door, though. The tawny skin was fresh and smooth, but the eyes were hard.

"Mr. Garcia," said Andy, stepping back to let him in. Victor was hoping for the shorts again, but Andy was in jeans today, as he had been at Chrome. Instead of the African-print shirt he'd worn at the club he wore a white button-down, sleeves rolled up. "You look like someone cancelled your show and charged you for your costumes."

Victor lifted his gaze from Andy's hand, saw amusement in the other man's face, and felt himself blush. *He knows what I was thinking.* "That's kind of how I feel. I got a whole lot of mad and I don't know where it's coming from."

Andy closed the door. "The wisdom of my age says, you just realized you get to be yourself now, and you don't know how to do it."

"How in the *hell* - " Victor stopped and stared at him, astonished. "How old *are* you, anyway?" Andy laughed, full out. After a moment, Victor smiled, shaking his head like 'I didn't mean that the way it sounded.'

Andy wasn't offended. "I'm forty-six," he said, "but I've been out all my life. I've met a lot of guys along the way who had to figure it out later. It's never easy."

"I'm thirty-six," said Victor. "And I haven't had an honest relationship, with anyone in my life, for thirty years."

"Now's the time to start."

"You may already know me better than anyone else. Including myself."

"That is ... well." 'Awful' was the word, but Andy didn't say it.

"I don't even pick out my own clothes, I have a personal shopper." Victor glanced down at his outfit, jeans and a madras shirt with huaraches.

"She does fine. Do you like it?" Victor shrugged. Andy shook his head, smiling. "What did you bring?"

"A little of everything." Victor toed off his shoes, carried the deli bags into the kitchen, and started unpacking. Andy set up another pot of coffee and sniffed the half-and-half in his fridge. Between them, they assembled a smorgasbord, starting to eat standing up while they waited for the coffee. Andy generally felt people were in the way, but he and Victor seemed to move easily around each other, sharing the small space without awkwardness. Victor noticed too. He wondered if it was because Andy was a dancer. "Tell me about yourself," he said.

"A to Zed?"

"Sure."

"Born in Miami, mother Puerto Rican, dad white, thus my Anglo name is legit Anglo and not a stage name, although I considered changing it when I moved to New York because Andy Martin was so non-memorable."

43

Victor almost said 'the name, maybe,' but caught himself. "When did you move to New York?"

"When I was eighteen." He'd already blown his cover, so he went ahead with the history. He could ask Victor to keep it quiet. "Chorus boy for twenty years, mostly on tours the last eight years, and then I came out to L.A. because some friends had settled here and I knew I couldn't keep dancing forever. I've only done one dance thing here, it's photography now. I've been, you know, making a living." He almost added 'I don't want to talk about it.'

"You probably don't want to talk about it," Victor said. "People would be all over you for stories all the time instead of paying attention to what you do now." *He didn't expect me to say that.* "That's a long time to work on stage. Good for you."

All of a sudden, perversely, Andy did want to talk about it. "I was lucky. Tall enough but not too tall, naturally skinny, and if I stay out of the sun I can pass for white."

Victor picked up the cue. "I can't, I get a tan if I walk by a window. What was your favorite show?"

"Probably 'Cats.' I loved the choreography. And however rough I looked, it didn't matter, because of the costume and makeup."

"You still look good to me." That probably went without saying after the way he'd behaved in November. "I thought you were my age."

Andy gave him a sideways smile. He was tempted to make a joke about vodka being a great preservative. Instead he took the compliment at face value. "Yeah, well, I don't have to dance eight shows a week anymore. And it's been a long time since I got beat up."

"How many times has that happened?"

"Three ... no, four. Twice in high school, once in New York, and once on the road."

"I never got beat up. I got stabbed."

*Thought so.* Andy had seen plenty of scars during the 'Cut Open' photo sessions. A knife scar was distinctive. Victor had more than one. "Yeah. About that."

"I was at a club in Mazatlán with ... a friend. We got jumped outside it."

"What happened to your friend?" asked Andy, afraid he knew.

"He died."

"Shit, I'm sorry."

"After I got out of the hospital, that's when I moved to the U.S. for good. I was seventeen."

Andy resisted imagining what that whole ordeal must have been like. "So tell me about your family."

Victor sighed. "My mama worked in hotels in Puerto Vallarta all her life. She met a white man, an American, and had me. He was cool, a stand-up guy. He gave me a place to stay, got me a job, and did all the paperwork so I could get citizenship."

"Where does he live?"

"In Escondido. Owns a car dealership."

"You're not out to him, either?"

"Well, I think he knows. He's got a couple of gay friends and he's pretty mellow. He wouldn't mind, but he won't bring it up unless I do."

"So you've got a decent relationship there."

"Yeah. I don't see him much though because he's married, and had other kids. Grandkids now, too."

"So." Andy looked down and realized they'd eaten almost everything. "Let's take some coffee over there." He poured, let Victor add cream or sugar as he liked - turned out he used both - and they went over to the couch. Neither of them referred to what they'd done on it before.

"I want to come out," Victor said suddenly. "I'm afraid, though. Of the press and, like, how to even *be* out."

"Well, you could start living life and deal with it as it comes." Andy knew his tone was skeptical.

"Is that what you'd do?"

"Not really. That'd mean dealing with it over and over and over and *over* again. And personally, I like to deal with things once and move on."

"Yeah. I got that idea." Victor was suddenly even more grateful that Andy had been willing to talk, at the club and today. "So what do you recommend?"

"You could have a press conference," Andy suggested. "Then follow it up with a good interview, like with The Advocate or something. It would be awkward as fuck and there's bound to be some blow-back, but you could, you know, get it over with. What do you think would happen with your job?"

"No idea. My character's never had a relationship. I can't remember that we've ever defined his sexuality. Most of us on the show, it's that way. Only the three leads have any personal life in that world. I've never played it one way or the other, because all of my scenes are about the job."

Andy nodded. "You have good chemistry with the guy who plays your partner, but yeah, very neutral." *And yeah, I watch the show*. "But you've been on 'Vice' for a while now. Got a good rep?"

46

"Yeah, I think so."

"Any reason to think the company is homophobic?"

"No, not really."

"Worth taking a chance? Could you afford to get fired?" Andy knew that was a possibility. "Bear in mind they can't fire you for being gay, they'd have to come up with some story to write you off, and that would take some time." Not a lot of time. It was really easy to kill off a TV cop. It would take longer for the production company and network to come up with a plausible explanation for canning a well-regarded cast member that wasn't 'well he's queer.'

"I could afford it. I live cheap." Victor checked in with himself. "I don't know if I could afford it in terms of, would I ever get hired again. I can't think of many out actors making a living, especially not actors of color."

"Okay, moving on. Personal life. Clearly you know your way around a cock." Victor laughed, blushing. "And while you may not have been *looking* for action last November, you were certainly *ready* for action."

"I try to be prepared," said Victor. "I don't get many chances. And I had my eye on you during the photo sessions for 'What Went Down,' so when I saw you again, and you had those shorts on … well."

Andy waved that off. "Why me, for God's sake?" He thought he could be forgiven for wanting to hear it.

"I like your face. I like your body. I like *you*." He wanted to say, or do, more. He could have run down the list: I like those big brown eyes, I like your nose, I like the way your hair wants to break out of that part, I like your laugh, I like the way you move. *I like your mouth.* He looked away, because he was getting turned on, and now was not the time.

Andy veered off the conversational track, because what he wanted to say was 'I like you too' and that wasn't going to accomplish anything at the moment. It would make the next thing he needed to say that much more difficult. So he said, "Why the tattoos? And why those tattoos?" The portrait of his mother: obvious. The gecko and the stag and the rattlesnake curling around Victor's thigh – even more suggestive than the gecko – all made a less-obvious statement.

"I know," Victor said, reading his mind. "The casting notices always say no visible tattoos. I didn't get the deer till I was doing parts where I got to keep my shirt on." Andy snorted. "This one of Mama, it's borderline. You can't see it unless I have my sleeves rolled up to my elbow. But I wanted her where I could see her." He shrugged. "The others, all three of them, that was like … they remind me of who I am. I'm Mexican. And I'm gay. The art, it was a way I could say that until I could actually say it."

Andy nodded, drank some of his cooling coffee, and wondered if he really wanted to say what he needed to say. *Of course you don't want to say it, bitch, but say it anyway.* He sighed and got on with it. "Victor, to be perfectly honest you are one hundred and ten percent of my catnip, but there's a big huge problem that's going to take some time to solve."

"What's the problem?"

"You ever see 'Notting Hill'?"

"Yeah."

"Well, I'm the bookstore guy and you're Julia Roberts. You could fucking *flay* me. We're talking way beyond heartbreak here. I can't afford you until you've been out for a while and know this is really what you want."

They stared at each other for a long minute. Then Victor smiled. It was a calculating, seductive smile, with a slight narrowing of his long-lashed eyes, and Andy thought *holy guacamole*. "How long will it take to prove it?"

"A year," Andy said without thinking. "Give it a year."

Victor didn't argue, or try to persuade. "I'm going to be back here," he said softly, "in a year and a day, and I'm gonna make you scream." The hairs rose up on Andy's neck, and his scrotum contracted. He huffed out a breath. "But I have some conditions," Victor went on. "Fair enough?" Andy made a 'well, let's hear them' gesture. "I get to see you. Socially. Like a friend. I won't try to kiss you, I'll keep my hands off of you, but I'm not, like, banned from the presence."

Andy was relieved. He hadn't meant 'don't come near me for a year.' "And?"

"I'll be safe, I'll stay clean. You do the same." He knew Andy would. A person didn't get to forty-six looking that good without taking care of his health. What he meant was 'I won't put you at risk the next time we fuck.' *Or the next time we kiss*.

Andy gave it a second. "That's it?" Victor nodded. "Okay, fair enough."

They stared at each other for another minute. "So. Who broke your heart?"

"Oh, that." Andy waved his hand dismissively. It was another theatrical gesture, one that would read all the way to the back row; this time Victor couldn't help smiling. "It wasn't a who so much as a what. One too many failed auditions. I decided I was done getting rejected that way."

"I get it." There was another pause while they studied each other from opposite ends of the couch. Victor didn't want to go. He wanted to get closer. He had an idea. "Is dancing allowed?"

Andy had no idea where he was going with this. "That depends."

"On what?"

"Dancing in a club with a head full of vodka is probably a no, bad idea, nope. But dancing like my kind of dancing, probably okay." Also probably not something Victor would consider. Andy hadn't seen anything in his internet stalking to indicate Victor had any dance background. He couldn't imagine him at morning class.

The younger man surprised Andy again, by swerving. "During the show last year, Felipe got me turned on to milongas. Ever been to one?"

"No."

"Then can I ask you to do this for me? Would you learn some tango?"

Andy said, "Yes," again without thinking, or at least without thinking more than 'ask me anything I can say yes to.' "I haven't done any since 'Chicago' but I wouldn't mind brushing it up."

Somehow Victor knew he didn't mean the city. "Where were you in that?"

"Local production, all male, seven years ago."

"What part?" He could almost guess.

"Velma Kelly."

Victor bit his lip. He would have guessed right. "I wish I'd seen that." *Those legs in fishnets ... Jesus.*

50

Andy looked across at Victor's hot eyes and thought *get him out of here NOW.* "Never again. That number, 'I Can't Do It Alone'? It's a fucking killer. I'll show you the tape," he said. "In a year and a day. But now you'd better go."

Victor nodded reluctantly. He stood up and moved toward the door. Andy went with him, stopping when he did, a step behind. "A year and a day," Victor said softly, facing the door, one hand flat against it as if to hold it closed. "That's a long time. Can I have one kiss?"

If he'd turned around, if his posture had conveyed anything but the expectation of denial, Andy might have resisted. The line of Victor's neck and head - turned a few degrees as if he wanted to look back but was afraid to - was submissive, not confident. Andy took that one step closer, because even though he knew Victor was an actor, at that precise moment he didn't care. There was simply no good reason for Victor to ask for a kiss unless he really wanted it. There was no reason for him to even be here unless something about this was real. But Andy had to keep it as light as possible, because if he didn't Victor wasn't going to be on the safe side of that door for a long time. So he said, "If you're trying to set my pants on fire you're doing a spectacular job," turned Victor's face a few more degrees, and kissed him. He meant to make it fast, he truly did, but Victor's mouth opened under his, and he made a sound that went straight to Andy's groin. When he stepped back again, more than a few minutes later, they were both breathless. "That was a bad idea, catnip."

Victor leaned his head on the door, eyes closed. After a moment he straightened up, inhaled, and opened the door. "Worth it," he said without turning around again. And then he was gone.

51

Andy leaned on the closed door, in a state of such profound arousal that all he could think was *why didn't you at least fuck him again first, you idiot* until finally he started laughing at himself. "A year and a day?!" he said out loud. "Asshole!"

Chapter 4

He was still inclined to giggle about it when a text came in from Rory: *So we've been very patient, what do you have to tell us? Bottle of wine with your name on it if you'll give us the scoop*

He picked up the phone and sent back *I have doomed myself to sexual frustration for 366 days. There is not enough wine in the world*

*WTF have you done? Two bottles and lasagna await, if you're gonna be sexually frustrated you might as well eat*

*True. When?*

*Duh, now*

*LOL okay, on my way.* He knew Rory knew it would take him a good forty minutes to get to West Hollywood. And he knew that the first bottle of wine would be dispatched before the food ever got to the table, because even if Victor didn't go through with it, even if he didn't come out, even if Andy never saw him again ... he had to tell somebody. Rory and Dana had been his friends for a long time. They'd be there for him no matter what. He cleaned up the kitchen, looked at the chaste couch regretfully, and hit the road.


"So tell us about this vow of chastity," Rory said when she opened the door. "Or whatever the fuck it is."

"I have not made any such vow," Andy said, handing over a box from Michel Richard.

"Oooohh," said Dana, hovering behind Rory. "Is that what I think it is?"

"I'm going to drink all your wine, so bringing the lemon meringue tart seemed like the least I could do." He kissed them both and closed the door. "Remember that guy at the club?"

Dana snorted. "Uh yeah, that guy. Frankly, we were hoping to hear about that guy a week ago."

"There were reasons. Reason number one, his mother just died and he wasn't out to her. And since he wasn't out to her, he wasn't out to anyone else. Now he says he wants to come out."

By now he and Dana were sitting in the dining den at the back of Rory and Dana's cottage. Rory was pouring the wine, but glanced at him. "And it took a week to arrive at that decision?"

"Maybe not, but I had shit to do this week so whatever conversation we were going to have, it had to wait till today. Dana, I told Rory about this before 'Cut Open' and I apologize for not sharing with you then," he said, accepting a glass. "The gentleman's situation was at the time not fully known to me. We had a … thing. An encounter. A one-night stand." He took a sip of wine, then a larger mouthful. "Jesus, Rory, what is this? Did you open the good stuff?" She turned the bottle around so he could see the label, then sat down. "I love you with all my heart. Anyway, he was at the Brewery last November and invited himself up and we spent all night doing what you'd imagine and then he said yeah, no, gotta go." He tipped his head at Rory.

"That's basically all he told me," she said to Dana, "except he showed me some pictures so I knew who it was."

"Pictures? What kind of pictures?"

"That kind of pictures." Rory shook out her hand like 'wow so hot.'

54

Dana laughed. "So what happened today?"

"A very necessary conversation. It was about him being ten years younger than me and never being in a relationship and not knowing what the fuck he's doing and therefore me not trusting that he will not break my heart into one thousand tiny sharp pieces. He says he wants a relationship. He says he wants me. But it is Notting Fucking Hill."

"And thus a year and a day?" Rory said skeptically.

"I swear to Christ I said a year and immediately thought YOU ASSHOLE." People a block away probably heard that. Dana laughed again. Rory had to set her wineglass down, she was giggling so hard. Andy took a long drink from his. The absurdity of it still amused him, even though he was terrified. "I could have said six months, three months, a month, whatever. But no, I had to say a year. And he agreed, and now I have to wait a year to see if he's going to come back."

Dana said, "You don't think he might try to push the schedule?"

"Honey, he made it to thirty-six in an airtight closet, you don't think he knows how to manage?" Andy sat back and drank some more wine. "This shit is good. Anyway, I'm pretty sure I could call him up and say, you know what, never mind, let's just do it till we can't stand up. But I actually want him to see other people, get out there, learn what it's like to be himself. If he doesn't have that experience, how is he going to know I'm really what he wants?"

Dana rolled her eyes. "So you're being *noble*. That is so like you. And you're going to wait for him like a princess in a tower?"

"No, I'm going to keep doing what I always do, which is hang out with all my friends and occasionally go on a date." Andy didn't think he was being noble. A complete idiot, maybe.

"And no sex?" Rory had her eyebrows up. "Is that for real? Because the last I heard, you like sex."

He stared at her over the wineglass as he emptied it. Handed it to her and waited for a refill. Took the full glass back and stared into it. "I've had plenty of sex in the past thirty-two years. He didn't ask me not to. I didn't tell him I wouldn't. It's conceivable that at some point over the next year I will. It's also conceivable that I *won't*, because I can't imagine being with someone else and not wishing it was him." He looked up and they were both staring at him. "Yes, I know what I just said."

"Andy, you're one of my best friends in the world, you're the brother I never had and always wanted, and I am here for you no matter what," Dana said. "I really, really hope that this works out. Because you are the best thing that could ever happen to that guy."

"All of that, because you know my brother is a doofus. And also if that guy fucks this up he will never work in this town again," Rory promised. Andy cracked up.


Victor left the Brewery that day painfully hard, frustrated in every possible way, and yet full of hope. He didn't believe for a minute that Andy didn't want this to work. He'd accepted Victor's apology, he'd given him that night of comfort, he had not said no. Eating together, talking like friends. Giving Victor advice. There were dozens of places where he could have said nope, not worth the trouble, good luck to you, moving on. Clearly he was a guy who moved on: there was not a single thing in that live-work space that said 'sentimental attachment.' Maybe there was something up in the sleeping loft. Maybe Victor would find out someday. *A year and a day*, he thought. *That ain't nothing.* He was going to kick open that closet door, and take whatever came through it. But first, he was going to the gym. He needed to be physically tired when he got home. Right now he felt like he could fuck a brick wall. *Santa sangre, that kiss*. He could have come right there. If Andy had turned him around, if he'd put his other hand on Victor – anywhere – he would have. It took two cold showers to get through his workout.

When he did get home, he ordered some food. Finally took himself in hand while he waited for it to arrive, because he couldn't stand it anymore. Then he was calm enough to eat his dinner, reading his pages for the next week's taping and then reading something else for a while. Reading kept the memory of that kiss at bay, a little bit at least. Then he set the book aside, thinking. Had he actually apologized? Did he ever say 'I'm sorry I did that to you?'

"Fuck," he said out loud, realizing he hadn't. He lunged for his phone and composed a text: *Andy thank you for today. I realized I never said I'm sorry. I think you forgave me anyway but I want to do this right. I am sorry I did that to you. It was stupid and cruel. I could have told you the truth. I wanted to, and I should have. I am sorry.* He sent it without reading over it, positive there was more he should say but unsure what it was, or how to say it. He realized that for the first time since that kiss, he wasn't turned on to the point of indiscretion.

It was very late when a reply came in. Victor was already in bed, still not turned on because he'd been worrying ever since he sent that text. Worrying that Andy hadn't seen it, or had seen it and didn't think it merited a response, or had seen it and was thinking of some way to say 'fuck off' after everything they'd said. Waiting a year to try again had seemed no problem at all – aside from the playback of their one night, which had been running ever since that kiss – when he felt sure Andy wanted to try. Waiting out a year of 'maybe' when it might actually turn into a forever of 'no' seemed intolerable.

Then the phone buzzed. Victor grabbed it off the nightstand so fast that it almost flew out of his hand. "Shit." He closed his eyes, took a deep breath. This was so unlike him. Whatever it was, he'd have to handle it.

The text read: *Hi Victor been out with some friends, sorry for delay. Yeah you know I thought you DID say you were sorry. Whatever you said, it must have come across. Thanks for finding the words. I do forgive you*

That was all, but it felt like more absolution than Victor had ever received from a priest.

Over at the Brewery, Andy waited to see if he'd get some kind of answer back from Victor. It came almost immediately; the guy should have been asleep by now. *Thank you* was all it said. "You're welcome," Andy said out loud, so as not to send a return text. He was determined to keep his distance. Not to push Victor away, not to play games, but also not to lie down and say 'walk all over me.' He hadn't been lying to Dana and Rory. He honestly thought the only way this could work was if Victor sorted himself out, and came back to Andy with a full awareness of who he was and how he wanted to be in the world. Because Andy wasn't the secret-lover kind of guy. He was out and proud and he had no time to waste. If he ended up choosing celibacy for the year, and it didn't work out after all – if Victor called sometime and said you know what, I met somebody else, thanks for not tying me down – even though that thought was sickening, Andy would at least not have spent the intervening weeks or months letting that face, that body, that mouth ruin him for whoever else was left out there.

*You keep telling yourself that, bitch.* He put the phone on its charger and went to get ready for bed.


For the next few weeks, Victor concentrated on his work, and set the wheels in motion to change his life. He had his agent Parker arrange a press conference, confirmed the time and the venue, and went to face the music. There weren't that many people there; somebody from each of the local broadcast stations, stringers from a couple of cable news programs, and people from three online entertainment sites. "Thanks for coming today," he said. "I'm Victor Garcia, I play Detective Alvarado on 'L.A. Vice,' and I'm thirty-six years old. A few weeks ago my mother died." There was a murmur of sympathetic confusion. "Out of respect for her, I have been living a lie for thirty years. It's never been an issue with my work, because I've never had a relationship to play. Probably a good thing, because I don't know anything about real relationships. I want to learn, and there's only one way to do that. I'm here to tell you that I'm gay." Now there was a flurry of questions. Victor waited to hear one he could answer.

"Your mother didn't know?"

"She didn't know. I went to Catholic school, I wasn't supposed to have a sex life." Scattered laughter. "We never talked about it after I came to the United States. I've been focused on my career."

"What's going to happen with that?"

"God knows," he said, and a few of the reporters laughed. "I'm hoping nothing bad. Like I said, I've never had a relationship to play. The parts I've done, nobody needed to know or care about the character's sexuality. We never spelled it out for Alvarado. It was irrelevant. We've never even seen where he lives. I'd be happy to keep playing my character the same way as long as they want to keep me on the show."

"Have you got anything else coming up?"

Victor wasn't sure whether that was meant to be innuendo, or whether he was still thinking about that last kiss. "I'm working with my agent to find a hiatus project. I'd love to get a part where I get to play a relationship. Gay or straight doesn't matter. I think love is love. Sure hope I'm right about that." More laughter.

"So what about your personal life?"

"I haven't had one." That got another laugh. "I'd like to have one." A bigger laugh. "I'd like to have the same kind of personal life everybody else wants. Going on dates. Meeting each other's friends. Being able to talk about anything and everything, and never having to lie."

"What about sex?"

"Yeah, I'd like to have that too." Huge laugh. Victor thought this was going well. Then a question he hadn't expected, that he wasn't sure how to answer.

"Do you have a particular person in mind?"

He hesitated. No doubt everyone could tell that meant 'yes.' If he said no, he'd be lying, and he didn't want to do that anymore. "Yes I do," he said eventually. "I'm not going to tell you who it is, because my case of arrested development is not his fault and shouldn't be his problem. Let's say I'm inspired by this person. But a thirty-year habit of pretending to be something I'm not is not going to get corrected overnight. I need to figure out who I really am." He glanced at his watch. "And we're out of time. Thanks again."

The whole thing was surprisingly painless. There was no immediate reaction from his employers and only a little from the press, mostly neutral. Social media had some things to say, but for once he was glad that he wasn't a big star, with the kind of fans who got really invested. And he was really glad that he'd never had a public 'romance' that could come back and bite him now.

He'd never had a close friend either, one he could talk to about anything. The wish for that kind of relationship had always been tempered by the fear of saying too much. Now that everything was out in the open, Victor found people all around who he could talk to. It was like stepping out of a hot car at the beach, feeling the wind and seeing all the way to the horizon. He had dinner with Janis again, heard all about the arrangements she was building for her album, and told her all about the Andy situation.

"That's quite a situation," she said, setting down her fork and picking up her wine glass. "But I did see him at the exhibit so I kind of understand." Victor nodded, raising his eyebrows. She studied him. "You look so much better though."

"I've been working out a lot," he said. "And I've been sleeping better than I have for about a year."

"My brother died when I was seventeen." Janis was holding her glass in both hands, staring into it. "Suddenly. It was about eighteen months before I was back to normal. Still in touch with anyone in Mexico?"

He let her change the subject. Her brother was none of his business. "My Tía Susana. My cousins on that side, none of us are really close after all this time. I have no idea what they're thinking about me now. My aunt is fine," he added. "She always knew."

Janis smiled. "She never told your mother?"

"No." Victor sipped his wine. "I wonder if I should have."

"I'm guessing if you thought not for all that time, you were probably right. If she was open to it, she might have brought it up to you. Like, hey, kiddo, are you ever going to bring home a nice girl, or is there something you want to tell me."

Victor laughed. She had a point. "Anyway, the door's open now. All I can do is wait and see what comes through it."


He checked in with Andy a few times, by phone or email or text. He didn't ask if Andy saw the press conference, or – if he had – what he thought about it. A month after, when people had mostly stopped asking about it, he wrote *Andy, I'm glad I did this. Thanks for helping me get there. Don't forget why I wanted to*

Andy didn't write back till late in the day. By then Victor was wondering if he'd write back at all. But the message read *Hi catnip, been on a stage memorializing a very boring-looking play. They needed you to spice things up a little. Glad to hear the whole putting the top down thing is working out. Glad I could help. Hear anything from your auntie?*

Victor was surprised. *How'd you know about her?*

*Picture at your place*

*Oh yeah ☺ Guess what, she already knew. Never told Mama though*

*Glad you have someone at home who has your back*

*Me too.* Victor wanted to write more, to keep it going, but he still wasn't sure how to pitch this. Too flirty and Andy might put on the brakes, too casual and he might think Victor was losing interest.

Before he could think of the next thing, Andy wrote back. *Gotta go, doing a shoot for the Cabaret tomorrow. Thanks for keeping in touch*

*Thanks for everything. Especially that kiss.* He held his breath.

*Still worth it?*

*I think about it every night*

*So do I, but don't forget why we're doing this*

*I won't. Good night Andy*

*Good night.* Andy set down the phone and walked away from it so he wouldn't be tempted to write again. Or so he'd be at least *less* tempted.

Victor muted his phone and looked around his apartment. There was not much about it that said 'Victor Garcia.' One of these days he'd figure out who that was. At least now he didn't feel so alone. *Worth it*, he thought. Determined to do the work – it was almost like creating a new character – he started going through his things the next morning. A couple of hours later, he looked at the results and sighed.

A stack of scripts, bound plays, and books about theater and acting. A comfortable chair to read in, with a good lamp. A small metal-framed mirror from Mexico, and a Oaxacan folk-art monster that lived on his kitchen counter. And the vintage Armani suit he'd worn in that play last fall, that he'd bought from the wardrobe mistress afterward because it made him feel so sly, so slinky, so villainous.

He woke up his phone and took a picture of the suit, sending it with a text to his personal shopper: *I want to change my look. Let's talk.*

She texted back a reply that made him laugh out loud: *Ooooh yeah!!*


May 2013

They didn't arrange to meet for the Underground Cabaret's 'Lost in Space,' but somehow Andy wasn't surprised to see Victor at Chrome. He was sitting at the bar when Andy went to get a drink during intermission. "Well hello there," Andy said with a smile. "You're looking good." Victor was in dark gray jeans and a pale gray silk shirt. The top two buttons were undone to show a silver rope chain and a mouthwatering triangle of tawny skin. 'Good' was an understatement.

"Thanks." Victor studied him for a moment, checking out the constellation-print shirt, the long jeans-clad legs, and those hands. "You too."

*Stop it*, Andy thought delightedly. "How's things with the show? Any backwash from the press conference?" It was the first time he'd mentioned it. He wanted to ask if he was the person inspiring Victor. It seemed like he must be, but maybe that was wishful thinking, and he really didn't want to know if he wasn't the guy.

"Contract renewed." Victor smiled now. "Nobody even said anything, except a couple of high-fives from some queer folks in the crew."

"That's great! Must have been a relief. So who's your inspiration." *Oh fuck me, did not mean to say that, shit shit shit.* "You don't have to answer that."

Victor could tell the question had slipped the leash. Could see that Andy regretted asking. *He's afraid I'll say it's someone other than him.* "There's this photographer," he said, very softly, so nobody else could possibly hear. "Used to be a Broadway dancer. Gorgeous, sexy, smart. Knows what's what. Great role model. He's Latino, too, so he gets that part of it." They were staring at each other. Victor could tell Andy wasn't breathing right. A little short, a little shallow. *Me too, God I wish you would kiss me right now, Jesus this is torture.* He broke eye contact, realized he was leaning ever so slightly toward Andy, settled back and took a much-needed deep breath. "I did an interview with 'Out' magazine. They're going to be contacting you about photos. I told them I only wanted to use the ones you'd taken."

Andy was busy trying to box up the flood of *want*, and was grateful for the change of subject. Then he was surprised. "Well, thanks. Do I get to read the interview?"

"They said they would send you the semifinal version. You should get it pretty soon." He studied Andy for a second. "I don't need to see what you give them." *I trust you.*

Andy heard the subtext. It was all he could do not to grab the guy. "Cool." Then the house lights went down again. Instead of going back to his table, Andy stayed at the bar, standing beside Victor. They didn't touch, but the near-contact was both comforting and thrilling. After the show, Andy gave him a sidelong glance. "So I'm taking lessons. Per request."

Victor smiled again. One of the performers, reaching past him to pick up a drink at the bar, stood back and said "Whoa." He turned his attention to the lovely blonde. "Excuse me," she said. "That's quite a smile you have there."

"Thanks. You were great tonight."

It was her turn to smile. "Thanks! I'm Michelle Matsumoto. This is my husband Kenji." The handsome Japanese man behind her bowed.

Victor slid down from his stool so he could return the greeting properly. "Victor Garcia. I've seen you perform twice now. A real pleasure."

"Are you a friend of Andy's?"

Victor looked at Andy, who produced a complicated expression saying 'somehow, I don't know how, that seems to be true.' "Yeah, I am. He's my friend."

"Do you watch 'L.A. Vice'?" Andy asked. When Michelle shook her head, he went on, "That's Victor's regular gig. I met him when I did promo photos for that play last year, the one at the Million Dollar."

"I didn't get to go, Dmitri and I were prepping our show dance debut. Ballroom," she added, for Victor's benefit. "So are you a dancer, too? Salsa, maybe?"

"Claro que sí. I've done some other stuff here and there. My current favorite is Argentine tango."

"A couple of our regulars are really into it. I love to watch." Michelle was alert to their body language. She said innocently, "You know, we're always looking for new acts for the Cabaret."

"I don't have a partner lined up yet," said Victor, with a sidelong glance toward Andy. "But I'm working on it."

"Well, it was very nice meeting you," said Michelle. "Hope to see you here again sometime."

"Thanks. Nice meeting you too." Victor turned to Andy as Michelle and Kenji moved away. "She's a knockout. And wasn't that guy a model?"

"He's a designer now. Does a lot of costumes for the troupe, stuff for the studios, ballroom costumes, wedding dresses."

"So where are you taking these lessons?"

"Where everybody here seems to. Shall We Dance, in WeHo. It's a hell of a hike from the Brewery, but it's a really friendly studio and the level of instruction is top notch. The owner is a friend of mine."

"I'll look it up. That's not far from where I live."

"True."

"Maybe I could meet you there for a lesson sometime."

"Maybe so." They looked at each other consideringly. Victor's gaze dropped to Andy's mouth for a second. Andy smiled, and shook his head. "I'd better go."

"I'll see you around," said Victor. He stayed behind, watching as Andy walked away, thinking, *is there a little extra swish there for me? This might be working.*

Rory got home from her stage-managing gig and said, "Andy's toast. I went to the bar during intermission and he didn't even see me."

Dana looked up from the novel she was reading. "Still that guy?"

"So much that guy. If that guy bails we're going to have to scramble the full rescue team."

Dana set down the book. "You think he's going to bail?"

Rory perched on the arm of the reading chair, frowning. "Not really. Michelle said she hinted they could do a number together for the Cabaret, that guy seemed to think it was a swell idea, and she's going to think of a way to drop an offer. If he goes for it and actually gets Andy to go for it I'm going to worry a lot less."

"If he's willing to dance in public? That would be huge." They stared at each other. "God I'd love to see that. I haven't seen him do anything since 'Chicago.'"

"If he does it, yeah. He can't look at anything else in the room. I've never seen him like this. If that guy wasn't acting the same way I would have taken him out to the parking lot and told him, hurt our friend and you're done."

Dana could relate. "You can be scary when you want to be."

"That's a big advantage to having all these tattoos. Everyone knows I'm willing to suffer to get what I want. And speaking of which, I have an appointment next week to do the next phase on my wings." Rory was in the process of turning herself into a cherubim.

Dana tugged Rory down onto her lap. "Then if I want you on your back, I guess I'd better get you there now."

Chapter 5

Andy got the email from 'Out' magazine a few days after seeing Victor at Chrome. It was a good interview. They wanted three pictures: a head shot (one that wasn't a generic portfolio image), a full-body candid (clothed, which went without saying), and 'something sexy.' Andy thought *Jesus catnip you are really laying yourself open*. He couldn't help but admire it. Victor was copied on the email. Andy left it for a day after making his selections, to give Victor time to reconsider that whole 'I don't need to see them' thing, but there was no message. He drafted his reply and gave it one more review.

The head shot was easy, he'd taken quite a few. The candid was one of the last photos from that first night, taken after they were dressed again. He couldn't help it if the picture had a distinctly morning-after quality. It had, after all, been the morning after. Victor was in that sleeveless undershirt with his denim shirt unbuttoned over the top. In his jeans, barefoot, lounging on the couch with a mug of coffee. Black hair looking as though it hadn't seen a comb for a while (which it hadn't). Unshaven, smiling, impossibly bright-eyed. Beautiful.

There were too many possibilities for 'something sexy.' It couldn't be one of the explicit photos, this wasn't actual porn. The final choice showed Victor lying on his front, propped on his elbows, in profile, bare. Framed from the waist up, with his forehead dipping to his fisted hands. It could have been taken during yoga, or waking up, or an actual sex act. The quilt underneath him could have been on a bed, instead of on the floor. Andy was fairly certain the

69

magazine would agree the image was sexy. Everyone who saw it would wonder if the next thing that happened was another man on Victor's back. Which, in fact, had been the next thing. Andy pressing him down, kissing that strong neck, then pulling him up onto his feet. Victor letting himself be manhandled, dominated, taken. *God almighty*. Andy pushed away from the desk. He sent his reply, and the pictures, ten minutes later.


July 2013

Andy's friend Dmitri had been pleased about the solo lessons. Andy didn't tell him exactly why these lessons, or why now. He hadn't done anything at Shall We Dance for years – ever since moving to the Brewery, in fact – and before, it had only been the Sunday community classes. Never a partner dance lesson. Andy was grateful for this friend's unusual ability to not ask questions.

The question was there, though, when Victor met him at the studio the first time. Unspoken, but most definitely there. Some kind of explanation was called for, especially since Victor was extremely well-behaved. Both of them were. A casual observer would have thought they were simply friends, or perhaps working on a show together, not two men so hot for each other that they might as well have been a pair of matches lying on a sheet of emery paper. Dmitri was not a casual observer.

Andy watched the studio door close behind Victor after the lesson, heaved a sigh, and turned back to Dmitri. "Do you have a minute?"

Dmitri said nothing, simply stepped back in a way that indicated Andy should go ahead of him to the studio office. He closed the door behind them. "Your friend," Dmitri said then.

"Oh my fucking God Dmitri." There was something very close to a laugh, from this friend who almost never laughed. Dmitri didn't speak, only raised his eyebrows. Andy said, "I promise to tell you everything as soon as I possibly can, but that may not be for a while yet. Can I say, we are doing these lessons because he wants me to learn Argentine tango so we can go dancing together. And the reason for that is so we can see each other without, you know." He didn't want to say 'without fucking like bonobos' to Dmitri.

Dmitri knew as much about body language as any scientist on Earth. Ballroom was a very 'don't ask, don't tell' sport. Men who loved men were never open about it. He and his partner Patrick had conducted most of their courtship, and a great deal of their relationship since then, hiding in plain sight. So he didn't ask for more. He simply said, "Will you dance socially only?"

Andy stared back at him. He hadn't thought about that. There was that comment from Michelle, at the club. There was Victor, sounding like he thought dancing with the Cabaret was a fine idea. And here was Dmitri, who didn't even know Andy used to be a dancer, because Dana and Rory had kept that in the vault for him all these years. "Maybe not," he said after a long moment, and with a pause between words. "It depends what Victor has time for." That was probably true. He tested himself for panic. *Not a Broadway show. Not a song and dance thing. Not the real thing. If it happens at all.* Then someone knocked on the office door, and he made his escape.

They managed two more lessons together without busting the deal. The dance studio was a safe place,

71

neutral territory, where they could touch while supervised. They worked together well, which Andy didn't consciously recognize during the lessons but thought about constantly afterward. Victor obviously didn't have years of dance training, but he had rhythm, grace, and a strong center. And he was receptive, open to suggestion, which was great in dance lessons but which Andy couldn't help remembering in a different context. He was spending a record amount of quality time with his hand.

Aside from dancing with Victor, Andy was working on setting a show of new photographs. He kept doing what he'd told Rory and Dana he would do, which meant he saw a lot of them as well as of other friends, including men who'd at times been more than friends. Staying home alone didn't hold its usual appeal, because every time he saw that goddamned couch he imagined doing things with Victor on it. He occasionally indulged in a scroll through those November photos, and a replay of that last kiss. Both had predictable results.


Victor was doing a local play while on hiatus from the TV series. He'd always enjoyed working on stage. It was a whole new experience this time, because there was another gay man in the cast, and they could actually talk. The women in the cast flirted with them both with abandon, knowing they were safe. They all socialized, getting coffee before rehearsals, or dinner before the show, or drinks afterward. The minute anyone figured out that Victor was open to advice, there was a flood of it. It was all well-meant, if not all useful. He let himself have a few minutes every day of resenting those thirty years of lies. It wouldn't serve any purpose to pretend it didn't bother him that he could have had conversations like this all along. So for a few minutes he'd run through it and acknowledge it, regret it, be mad about it. Then he'd put it away so he could appreciate what he had now.

One thing he had was every intention of meeting up with Andy again for a new show at Chrome. This time, he sent an email first.

Hey Andy,

Saw the finished article, your pictures are great. Thanks for doing that.

Wanted to let you know I'm going over to Chrome for that new show. Figured you'd probably be there. Maybe we could hang out for the after party?

Victor

Andy sent back a simple *See you there*, but Victor was satisfied. The new show was called Mating Dance: Romance. It was billed as a short set of ballroom numbers telling the story of a relationship from beginning to end to recovery. Victor was doing a lot of thinking about relationships these days. Wanted Andy to see that. Wasn't sure this was the way, but he'd try anything.

He got to the club first and snagged a table. When Andy arrived, they checked each other out, then made eye contact. "Why do you have to look like that?" Andy said. "I saw you out with that ho from E Online."

It made Victor laugh, diverting him from the comment he almost let slip. The one about Andy's long legs in jeans, and the long-sleeved purple tee shirt he was wearing. It fit really well. "He was trying

73

to get in my pants, for real. I had to invent an early appointment to cut it short."

"Not interested?"

"Well, you said it. He's a ho." He smiled in a way that said 'I'd rather wait for you.' "I've had a date here and there. How about you?"

"Here and there." *Mostly there*, thought Andy, trying not to positively stare at the man. He was in a short-sleeved collared shirt tonight, in a silvery weave, with black jeans that probably showed off his ass really well. "I've got a couple of old friends, we help each other out sometimes."

"Sometimes it's all about not sleeping alone, huh." Victor was living for the day he slept with Andy again.

"Yeah. Sometimes a guy just wants a hug." Andy wanted one right that second. Instead, he changed the subject. "You ever, you know, been with girls?"

"Once or twice, back in the day. It's … not bad? Only I know that ain't me. I felt like that wasn't playing fair." He'd felt guilty, waking up those two mornings and seeing how much the women wanted him to stay. He was glad he hadn't done that often, and glad those mornings were long ago. The best thing about them, for him, was the sleeping-together part. He'd felt like he paid for that with sex. It was hard to imagine Andy doing that. He wouldn't have had to, of course. "Did you?"

"Yeah. I tried it a couple of times when I was a teenager, to see if I could switch myself around, but it was a giant fail. I mean the whole thing." He made a face. "Now I have a lot of gal pals."

"Rory and Dana?"

"Among others.  You met them here, right?"

74

"That Rory is one funny chick. I love her. And I Googled Dana, found some clips from her old show. Had to laugh at how straight she played it."

Andy was pleased that Victor liked his friends. "You should come to my next show. I'm shooting now and planning to hang it in September. Rory and Dana are in it."

Victor wasn't about to say no to an actual invitation. "I wouldn't miss it." Then the lights dimmed, and a few minutes later the show started. Victor was thoroughly enjoying it, even though none of the performers were people he'd seen before. Not until the fifth number, a foxtrot to 'Cry Me a River.' "Hey," he said softly, leaning close to Andy. "Did you know Dmitri was in this?"

"Mm-hmm," Andy said, trying not to lunge at him. Being this close in the dark was a bad idea. He'd been thinking of how much he'd love to be dancing with Victor at this very moment. Now he felt the man's heat and scrambled for something to say, so he wouldn't simply grab him. He was barely aware that he'd turned toward Victor. "He and Michelle are gunning for a World Championship this year."

Saying that might have been a *really* bad idea, because Victor turned his head for a moment, as if to answer. They realized how close they were. They locked eyes; then Victor's gaze dropped to Andy's mouth, and he sucked in a breath. He closed his eyes for a moment, then turned to the stage again, exhaled through his mouth, watched the rest of the dance. Wondered if Andy had any idea what his voice – so low, so silky - did to Victor. Wondered if the other man was as violently turned on as he was.

Andy was cursing himself for that whole 'give it a year' thing. They were barely four months in. This

75

was torture. He was an idiot. The only consolation was that Victor – while demonstrably doing the work - showed no sign of losing interest. Quite the opposite, in fact.

They both sort of knew that the closing number was a bitchin' hustle to 'I Will Survive,' but neither of them really saw it.


"That was close," Dana said to Rory after the show. They were sitting at the bar, at the end right next to the stage. It was Dana's turn to stage-manage, but because of the lighting, and where Andy and Victor were sitting, she'd been able to see the whole thing from her station in the wing. As soon as she came out into the house and made eye contact with Rory, they were fighting giggles.

Now Rory giggled into her drink. "God I know. I honestly thought Andy was going to pounce on him."

"That was superhuman." Dana giggled too. "I feel like I should send a text saying good job not mauling that guy."

"Do it," Rory begged. "He needs to know someone appreciates his sacrifice."

"Jesus, and they're only four months in." Dana got her phone out and sent the text. Andy and Victor were still there, empty glasses on the table. Talking, not touching. She saw Andy react to something, possibly her message. He pulled out his phone, did something with it, looked at it. Bit his lip, tossed his head back and gazed around the room until he found her. He shot her the bird. Dana and Rory both laughed.

"I don't know if the after-party is a great idea," Andy said to Victor. "I feel like if I have another drink my resistance is going to be really low."

*Mine too*, thought Victor, though truthfully he had no resistance at all. If Andy closed the distance, if Andy touched him, there was no way Victor could break the contact. "But if we stay, we could dance," he heard himself say. And if they didn't, he'd be going home alone to abuse himself again. He wondered if it was anywhere near this bad for Andy. "I promise to leave first. I promise I won't kiss you." He said it very softly, so no-one else would hear, though with the house music turned up and dozens of people talking over it surely nobody could. "I promise I'm working on my shit."

"I know you are." Andy wasn't strong enough. Nobody on Earth was strong enough. "Okay. Get me another drink. I'll be back." He stood up, got past Victor without touching anything more than his shoulder, and headed down the hall to the men's room. *This is going to be funny someday*, he thought a minute later, cock in hand in the bathroom stall. Then he shut his eyes and imagined that perfect mouth, so close to his. He was grateful for the music piped in. It was loud enough to cover the sound he couldn't help making. He tidied up, flushed, went to wash his hands. Stared at himself in the mirror, ignoring the other man in the room. Nobody he knew, thank God.

He wasn't gone long enough for the next round of drinks to arrive. Victor looked up, started to say something, then stopped to study him. "You look more relaxed," he said. "Did you just …?"

"Yes I fucking did," Andy said. It might have sounded sharp if he hadn't been grinning at Victor's expression. "You might want to do that too."

Victor shook his head, putting his hands up, palms out, to say No. "I'm doing that every goddamned day already. I know I'll do that when I go home. So I'll wait." They stayed at the table, talking, until the shoveling-out procedure began. By the time the after-party got properly started, they were dancing.

Victor had a date – playing along with the deal – the next night. It was with Gino Corsetti, a man he'd worked with on a different play, a couple of years ago; a man who now said, "I always wondered."

"My mother didn't know," Victor explained, and got an understanding nod. He told the rest of that story. They shared some showbiz stories. Gino told him about his own coming-out experience. It was, Victor realized, fun. There was even a moment, after they'd walked back to their cars, when they looked at each other and he could feel 'maybe' quivering between them. "Do you mind if I …?" Gino clearly didn't mind. They kissed. It was pleasant. It could have been more so. Victor could tell, this would be all right. This would be good. He was tempted, so tempted. He hadn't been with anyone since Andy in November. But he stood away after a minute, because he wasn't going to do that to anyone else again. He said, "Gino, you're great. I really enjoyed this. Thank you. The truth is, I'm in love with somebody else. It's going to be a while till we can be together, but I want to wait."

"Well, damn," said Gino. "You don't want to take the edge off with me?"

He had to be honest. "I do want to. But I've already been unfair to him once."

"Walk around the block with me. Tell me." He wasn't touching Victor now. His voice was calm.

So Victor nodded, and they walked, and he told this near-stranger about what he'd done. Not about

78

Andy, not who he was. Only Victor's side of it. "So that's why," he said. "I didn't ask him not to see other people. He flat-out told me to. But someday this will be over and I want to go back to him and say, I met all these other great guys, and one in particular who made me want to do things, and I didn't. Because I love you." He stopped talking, hoping that was enough, or maybe not too much.

Gino seemed untroubled, if slightly regretful. "It's probably for the best. I'm about to go up to San Francisco for six months. I know I'll find someone up there. I always do. You're really sexy, though."

"Thanks. You're going up there for work?" And with that, they were back to a friendly conversation, as if the kiss had never happened. Victor thought about it all the way home, realizing that he might have just had his first truly adult encounter. *Not only sex*, he thought. *There's so much more to it.* And he might never have known he could do that, if not for Andy. He sent a text asking if he could see Gino again before he left. For lunch, as a friend. The answer was 'sure, why not.'

On that same night, Andy was home at the Brewery, working on his upcoming show, and listening to tango music because it reminded him of Victor. There was absolutely no point in pretending he wasn't in love with the guy. He'd practically said so to Dana and Rory, months ago, before he even really knew it was a done deal. He might be fooling Victor with all that smoke about the dates he was going on, he couldn't say. The thought of fucking somebody else was completely unappealing. "Well," he said out loud to the empty room, "this is what I get for being so hard to please." It was his own fault. If he were more tolerant about drugs or infidelity, he could have been happily cohabiting for decades already. There'd been someone waiting for him for years, if he'd been willing to move back to Miami.

He'd honestly never thought he would be alone at forty-six. When he met Dmitri and Patrick, and learned that Patrick had been forty-eight when they got together, he'd thought *kill me now*. And here he was. He would be forty-seven at the end of this ridiculous experiment. If this didn't work out, he didn't know what he was going to do. He didn't know if he could stand to stay in Los Angeles if this failed. *Stop thinking about it*. He went to get a drink, a hefty slug of vodka with a splash of cranberry juice. Stared at the monitors. One displayed the image of Rory and Dana he was having mounted for his show. They found love. Patrick and Dmitri found love. Michelle and Kenji. It wasn't impossible.

His phone buzzed. He went to pick it up. A message from Rory, as if thinking of her had summoned a demon: *Hey checking in. Does our picture look good?*

*It looks great*, he wrote back. *I'm putting it right up front*

*Coolio. How are things otherwise?*

*Considering options*

*Uh for what. Oh shit you mean if things go south with that guy? What options?*

*Miami, Las Vegas, or alcoholism*

*Did something happen last night??*

*No it was cool I'm having a little freakout moment that I probably shouldn't tell you about*

*Um Andy you know we love you*

He did know it. He blinked, took a breath, told himself to get a grip. *Yes I know and I truly appreciate it. Anyway did I ever tell you about my pal Sergei?*

*What's the short version*

*Trainer for a Vegas show, dance captain on one of my last tours, think Baryshnikov crossed with Tommy Lee Jones*

*ROFLMAO eye color and hair color*

*Blue and bald*

*LOL OMG Andy is this srsly one of your options*

*Better than alcoholism*

*Okay that's true but I think you need to get out more*

*Can't. Working*

*It's late. I recommend a sleep aid and some, you know, sleep*

*Thanks chica probably better not take a pill on top of this vodka*

*Yeah probably not. Try to sleep though. OXO TTYL*

*OXO.* Andy set the phone down, relatively certain he would not be sleeping.


A few days after seeing Andy at Chrome, Victor got a call out of the blue from Michelle. "I hope you don't mind, I got your number from Dmitri."

"Hi Michelle, no, that's fine. What can I do for you?"

"We were talking about themes for the next few Mating Dance shows, and decided to do the September show around the theme 'Milonga.' So I remembered you said you liked Argentine tango, and I wanted to see if you'd be interested in submitting a routine. It's two consecutive nights." She gave him the dates. "And just so you know, submission is basically a formality. It would be great for us if you would do it."

Victor was surprised and flattered. He hadn't truly taken her seriously at the club. "Wow, Michelle, thanks. Dmitri thought I could? I've only been doing tango for a year. That's really cool." She made an encouraging sound. He said, "I personally would love to and my schedule should permit. I'll have to find out if my dance partner is willing."

"Would that be Andy? Because I could work on him for you. You should know Dmitri's been trying to get him back in the studio for years. He used to take those Sunday classes. Rory says Andy is the only person she ever saw who got through the jive part of the Cardio Latin without getting tangled up."

Victor laughed. "I wish I'd seen that. All assistance would be appreciated. What's the protocol?"

"If you two can do it, then let me know ASAP what music you're using, and send me the track once it's edited, if you're editing it at all. If you need help with that, we have some contacts. Send me a video once you have your choreography blocked out. And turn up on show nights."

"That's pretty easy. I think I could handle that."

"I'm sure you could." They exchanged email addresses, Victor complimented Michelle on her most recent performance, and then she said, "Don't let me sweet-talk you into doing anything you don't want to do. Or that Andy doesn't want to do. He's been working with the Cabaret for a while now, and he's never shown the slightest interest in being onstage."

Victor could tell she wanted to know why he thought this might be possible. "There's some history," he said. "He doesn't like to talk about it because he's got this new thing now. He moves on."

"Okay, I get that. Me too. You have to know I'm dying of curiosity."

"Yeah, I don't blame you." She giggled. Victor said, "Look, I'm not promising anything. We're not even dating. He's like my sponsor. Helping me get used to being out, that's all." He knew his tone probably said 'unfortunately.' He wasn't really trying to act like it didn't matter. In fact, now that he thought about it, maybe it wasn't a bad thing to let these new friends know. "He made a deal with me. I take some time to figure myself out, on my own, and maybe someday we could ... ." He couldn't think of a way to finish that.

"Dance together?" Her tone was suggestive.

He laughed. "At least. I'll let you know what he says." They ended the call then, and he thought for a minute. He honestly didn't know if Andy was going to be receptive to this. He'd put a stake through the heart of his stage life seven years ago, from the sound of things. *Make the call and find out.*

Amazingly, it didn't take much convincing, though for a minute or two Victor thought he was striking out. Andy said, "You want to do *what*?"

"You said your kind of dancing was probably okay. We've had those lessons."

"I was thinking at most we'd be going out to a dance sometime." Something where everyone else there had other things to think about. Not where they'd be the center of attention. And they hadn't even *been* out yet, because that would have been too much like a date. Andy hastily amended that. "Meeting up. Have you been going out dancing?"

Victor wished he could say yes, but at least he had an excuse. "No, not yet. Too many nights committed to the play."

"This would be in September?"

"Yes."

It was plenty of lead time; he knew they could do it; he was not strong enough to say no. He'd already done a panic check. Nobody cared if a washed-up chorus boy got on stage once in a while. And God, did he want to. "Well, you have to know I'm dying to dance with you. This all feels like a plot."

Victor almost couldn't believe it. "Is it working?"

"It's not *not* working, let's put it that way." Every time they talked, Andy was grateful that Victor was playing by the rules, because his own desire to say 'okay all right just get over here' was nearly overwhelming.

"So you'll do it?" Every time they talked, Victor was grateful that Andy didn't play games. They were doing what they were doing for a reason, and it was a good reason, but it helped to know that Andy wanted him too.

"You pick the music. Talk to Dmitri about doing choreography. Let me know when to be there." He was probably being much too pliable. But *damn* he loved dancing with Victor, and that meant this was probably a really bad idea. On the other hand, "He asked me if we'd only be dancing socially."

"Dmitri did? What did you say?"

"I said maybe not. He has no idea about the whole chorus-boy thing, by the way."

"I won't mention it. Michelle is awfully curious, though. I only told her there was history and you'd rather not talk about it. I said, he moves on."

*You understand*, Andy thought. "What did she say?"

"She said, me too. Does anybody know?"

"Dana and Rory."

"Okay. I promise not to mention it to anybody else."

"You're making an awful lot of promises, catnip." Andy didn't intentionally make his voice soft. "Maybe you shouldn't do that."

"You kept my secret," Victor said. "I owe you." *And God I love it when you call me that.*

Chapter 6

September 2013

That call had come at the perfect moment. Andy didn't know quite where the anxiety was coming from, and he didn't like it. It was tempting – if unfair – to blame Victor. It was his own damn fault, as he kept telling himself, that they weren't together at this very moment. He could put an end to it with a word.

But he could tell, from the occasional calls or texts, and even more from their infrequent meetings, that this time was doing what it was meant to. He could see Victor growing, changing, maturing. He heard about friends, old and new. And it was impossible to doubt that Victor was still very invested in the experiment.

So Andy did morning class with Mandy, did his stretches religiously, and went hiking in Griffith Park when he needed to wear himself out. He talked to his mother on the phone and did his best to plan for the next year, whether 'next year' had Victor in it or not.

Doing this dance together gave him hope, though. They took four lessons to work out the choreography, then squeezed in practice at the dance studio whenever they could. Andy's space wasn't available because of his upcoming show, and Victor's apartment was too small. Those were the official reasons. In truth, neither of them trusted themselves to keep it professional without supervision, or at least oversight. It was going well. Dmitri gave them some twisty stuff that was fun to do.

Instead of a traditional Argentine tango track, Victor chose 'The Mating Game' by Bitter:Sweet. Andy looked up the lyrics and couldn't quite figure out what they meant, but the track itself was so infectiously danceable that he decided not to worry about it. He noticed that Dmitri treated Victor as a friend. As if he expected the younger man to be part of all their lives in the future.

A week before dress rehearsal, at the end of a practice session, Andy realized they hadn't even discussed what to wear. "I shouldn't have left it so late," he said. "Maybe I was thinking a dance suit would appear automagically."

"What about Michelle's husband? Let's see if he has something in stock. It's not like you're an odd size." *You're the perfect size*, Victor thought. They were learning to switch leads, something Victor hadn't done before, and he loved it. Loved that feeling of having Andy's arm around his back, his own hand high up on Andy's shoulder, their faces close together. It was almost as good as kissing.

Andy may have read his expression; he was smiling. "Yeah, okay." It took a second for Victor to remember what they'd been talking about. He mentally shook himself, and went to change out of his dance shoes. "You want to drive, or shall I?"

"I will." Going anywhere in a single vehicle was another first, another step closer to 'together.' They went straight to Kenji's design studio, begged for some ready-to-wear, and found black dance pants with a matching blazer that fit Andy perfectly. A black fedora and red shirt finished the look. Victor chose a dance suit in medium gray pinstripe and a matching red shirt, with a gray fedora. "We'll be like a couple of gangsters," he said. "Like in 'The Bandwagon.'"

"It's a good style for both of you," Kenji said. "I saw the video you sent Michelle. She's very excited about having you in the show. Especially you, Andy."

"Why me?"

"She said she suspected you were a performer all along, from the way you handle their photo shoots."

"Ha! Well, I guess you can take the chorus boy off the stage, but you can't take the stage out of the chorus boy." For a split second he'd thought of playing the 'who me?' card, but what was the point. There was always at least one journalist at the Chrome shows, and it wouldn't take much Googling to pull up Andy's history. He glanced over at Victor. Everybody was going to know how much older he was. People would wonder why Victor was wasting time with him.

Victor didn't say anything then, but when they were getting into the car he said, "Nobody's going to wonder once they see you dance."

Andy blinked. "How did you know that's what I was thinking?"

"I don't know." *Maybe because I pay attention, because I don't want to miss a thing, because there's so much there.* Victor knew he couldn't say those things. He couldn't say 'don't you know how fantastic you are' because he wasn't supposed to be mooning over Andy. He was supposed to be learning how to be himself. Then he realized that those things weren't mutually exclusive. The thought made him smile.

Andy glanced over at him. "You look like you're scheming."

"I'm thinking about our dance." It was almost true.


Andy had another brief panic attack after getting home that day. He really didn't know why. Yes, Kenji would certainly pass on what he'd said to Michelle, which meant it would filter through to Dmitri and

Patrick, which meant all of a sudden instead of three people knowing about the history, there were seven. There was no way seven people could keep a secret. Although Dana and Rory had done a stellar job of it all these years. Dmitri never told anybody anything he didn't have to; Andy didn't even know he and Patrick got married until he spotted the ring, more than a week after the fact. And Patrick followed Dmitri's lead. If he simply asked Michelle to not make a big deal out of it, she probably wouldn't. *Nobody cares*, he reminded himself. Even if the press picked it up for a second after the show, nobody would care. It wasn't like he was Tommy Tune. He picked up his phone to send Michelle a text: *Hi gorgeous, I have a favor to ask. This thing I'm doing with Mr. Garcia is probably a one-off. I prefer to remain the photographer for the Cabaret et al. Would much appreciate keeping conversation in the present*

Her reply came an hour later: *Message received and understood, I don't like talking about pointe shoes myself. Really looking forward to seeing you though!*

*Thanks sweetie. Give my regards to Kenji, he saved our asses with those suits*

*LOL will do*


Andy stood backstage with Victor on show night, watching the other dancers, thoroughly enjoying the experience. His anxiety had disappeared as soon as the adrenaline kicked in. Victor had some nerves. Andy gave him a nudge. "What are you nervous about? You look gorgeous, you're a great dancer, and half the people here came to see you." Victor's name had been featured on the show ads and poster.

"Well, that would be why." Victor glanced at Andy. "I'm glad we're doing this, though. I'm glad I can contribute to making you this happy."

Andy patted his back, then with a mental *what the hell*, slid his arm around Victor's shoulders and half-hugged him. "I am, actually. Really happy." He dropped his arm before he was tempted to do any more.

Their dance went perfectly. It was all Andy could do not to kiss Victor when they hit their ending position, faces close together. The next day, he saw a photo posted with an online review. In the picture, they were facing but slightly offset, upper bodies twisted away from their feet and into the circle formed by their linked arms, eyes intent on each other. NOW THAT'S CONNECTION, read the headline.

> '... Valentino lives: L.A. Vice's Victor Garcia, a ringer for the silent-film star, turned in a smooth and seductive performance with veteran Broadway dancer Andy Martin. Garcia credits Dmitri Vasko for the choreography and tells us 'Mr. Martin was a dream to work with.' Martin hasn't been seen on stage since 2006 ('Chicago,' click <u>link</u> for story). We trust that this return to the spotlight is not a one-time affair. ... Frankly, if the cast of this show were any better-looking, they would have had to slap a warning label on the posters.'

After indulging a moment of nostalgia by visiting the 'Chicago' link, Andy archived the review, then printed a copy and taped it to the wall by his bed. *Nice to know I've still got it.* He couldn't wait to do it all again that night.

The next day, after another successful performance and a lot of attention from other Cabaretadjacent people, Andy got a text from Michelle: *okay I said I wouldn't talk about it but I saw that article and OMG I WANT TO TALK ABOUT IT but all I will say is you were sensational. See you at the next photo shoot. You sneaky bastard*

Andy grinned, sending back *Thanks sweetie.* He was dying to talk to her about it, but he knew the urge would pass. He could get all that out of his system the next time he saw Rory and Dana.

The day after that, he got a call from a casting agent. An hour after that, he called Victor, whose voice mail picked up. "Well I hate to leave you a message about this, catnip, but it seems I'm getting a guest spot on a TV show and it's all down to you. See you at my opening next weekend."

Victor had been in touch with Gino off and on, so he wasn't all that surprised to get a text a couple of days after their dance went up on the Underground Cabaret's channel. The content made him smile, though: *Well Mr. Garcia I guess I know why you turned me down this summer. Nice job with that tango. That's the guy?*

He had a few minutes free, so he answered right away: *That's the guy. You saw the clip online?*

*Me and every other gay man on planet Earth*

*LOL I'm obsessed with him*

*You and every other gay man on planet Earth*

Victor laughed out loud for real. *Five point five months before I know for sure this is a go. I'm told it's big that he got onstage with me*

*Cultivating his friends are you? Good play*

*Speaking of plays how's your thing going?*

*Extended. By the time we have to exit this theater I'll be due over in Vegas*

*Did you decide to do the Sinatra thing?* For a minute Victor had thought about mentioning Andy's new TV gig. Now he thought he'd keep his mouth shut about that.

*Yeah I'm ready to put down some roots. It's been a long time. I might even rent an actual apartment*

*Whoa that's crazy talk.* Victor knew Gino was the definition of 'itinerant.'

*On the other hand if I keep living in hotels I never have to make my own bed*

*There you go. Oh FML just got the signal time to head back to the set*

*Keep doing your thing. Bring that showstopper to see me on the Strip sometime*

Victor knew it wasn't a done deal, but he liked that Gino assumed so: *You know it. All the best to you*

*You too. Ciao for now*


Victor was among the first to arrive for the 'My Pet' opening. The maze of display walls in the space set him back, but only long enough to realize that the oversized print facing the door featured Rory and Dana. Dana was scantily costumed as a bird of paradise. Her enviable body was draped face-up across a trapeze in an oversized gilded cage. Rory lay prone on the top of the cage, completely naked except for her feather tattoos, looking into the cage with an expression of covetous fondness. He made a sound of appreciation.

"You like it?" said Rory, coming up alongside him.

"That is *so* freaking sexy!"

"That's what I thought," said Dana. "Andy said it would be, and he was right."

"And that angle hides all my chunky bits poking through the bars," said Rory.

"We all have our better angles, but that is a righteous booty," Victor said with a smile.

Dana said, "Yes it is. Hey, that dance of yours was really good."

"Thanks. I have to check in with Andy. He said he got cast in something a couple days after the show."

"Yeah, we heard. Pretty awesome, right?" The women moved into the exhibit, exclaiming and laughing over images of people they knew. Victor followed along.

"Hey there," Andy said, behind him. Victor jumped and turned around. "Effective display?" He studied the younger man, not even trying to be subtle. He had the gray jeans and silver chain on again, this time with a blue sports tee. If they'd met in a bar, Andy would instantly have tried to pick him up.

Victor felt a little thrill at Andy's expression. *Apparently MY display is effective.* "If by effective you mean I'm feeling like I'm in one of those hamster things, yes."

"The Habitrail actually is the exact effect I was going for. Yay me."

Victor studied him, smiling. Andy was again in jeans, this time with a short-sleeved lavender shirt made of some kind of thin velvet. It was all Victor could do not to touch it. *My Pet*, he thought, *my God.* "Have you got a minute to tell me about this thing, or is later better?"

"Now is good. People won't start buying till later."

"Do you sell them right off the wall?"

"Yep, but they can't take them home till I take the show down. So it's actually on that show '10-31.' They're working on an episode set in a casino and they needed a cheesy entertainer. After last week's thing, they looked me up and decided I'd be perfect for it."

Victor studied him, trying to decide if a laugh would be appropriate. 'Cheesy' wasn't the word he would have chosen.

"Yes, you can laugh, Victor," said Andy, electing to ignore the expression that quite clearly (and satisfyingly) signaled disagreement with his word choice. "I did, I thought it was fucking hilarious. And I get to sing 'Delilah,' it's like a lifelong dream."

Instead of laughing, Victor hugged him. He didn't hold on long, though he let his hands linger on Andy's velvety sides for a second before stepping back. "Sorry, I couldn't resist. That's so great. I can't wait to see it. I'll set my DVR."

"I didn't even have an agent anymore. You know Julia from the 'Mating Dance' team, her boyfriend Ray just got on that show. His agent Raquel is repping me." Then, surprising both of them, Andy took Victor's head in his hands and kissed him. Not for long, but long enough that they both had to take a breath when he stepped back. One hand stayed on Victor's neck for a moment. His ring rasped against the chain and Victor shivered. Andy almost did it again to see if Victor reacted the same way. *Play fair.* He took his hand away with a reluctance that Victor could probably see. "Thanks, catnip. Stick around, we'll talk more later. If you can."

"Of course I can." Andy turned away then. Victor took a moment to settle himself, thinking about that touch, and that delay, before resuming his amble through the exhibit. He stopped at an image featuring another pair of women. "Wait a minute," he said out loud, and looked closer. Then he looked around for Rory. He caught up with her a minute later. "Is that Vicky and Sharon? From the space show?"

"Yep."

"I almost didn't recognize them. Was that their idea?"

"I think so. It really works, huh?" Vicky was in drag in a 1950s-style suit, Sharon dolled up like a magazine-ad housewife. Sharon wore a golden collar with a leash, and Vicky held the other end. A closer look revealed the real joke: Vicky also wore a collar, with Sharon holding the other end of her leash. And Sharon's collar had spikes.

"Vicky looks like, I don't know, Tony Curtis here."

"Yeah, with a better nose."

Victor looked again and decided she was right. "So, are you buying that big print of you and Dana?"

"Eh, Andy would give us a break on the price but it's still kind of high. We're saving up for something. You know how it is." He nodded agreement. She shrugged and moved on.

Victor went to find Andy again. "A moment, Mr. Martin?"

Andy excused himself from his current conversation. "Yes, Mr. Garcia?"

"I want to buy that big print up front. Present for Rory and Dana."

"Why is that?"

"Rory said they wanted it, I can afford it, and I want to butter them up because they're friends of yours."

Andy made an 'oh I see' face. "You scratch their back, they'll scratch mine, and I'll scratch yours?"

"Whatever works." Victor grinned at him. *Stop being adorable*, Andy thought, but went and put a SOLD sticker on the print. Then he went to mingle some more. The place was packed, and noisy, and that bird-of-paradise print wasn't the only one with a SOLD sticker after a couple of hours.

Toward the end of the open-studio period, Rory found Andy again. "You gonna tell me who bought our print?"

"Nope, but it's for you. I'll bring it over after I take down the show."

She was amazed. "Well that's awfully nice of someone. Gee, I wonder who that someone could be. But look, have you seen this?" She turned her phone around. Someone had found and posted a video of Andy dancing. He was in a tank top, hot pants and espadrilles, and looked about twenty-five.

Andy watched with interest, counting, then nodding approval when young-Andy stuck the landing, tossing back his hair and laughing. "Four fouettés and six pirouettes. Not bad. I remember that, it was after a Pride parade."

"You look like a young Billy Bob Thornton with a snootful of Ecstasy."

Andy thought back. "If I remember correctly, it was strawberry daiquiris." Rory snorted.

"Let me see," said Victor, who'd materialized behind them. Rory played it again. "Damn! I didn't know you could do that. Can you still do that?"

96

Andy smiled into his eyes, loving that expression. It said 'is there anything you can't do,' and at the moment he thought maybe not. "Haven't tried for a while. Maybe."

"We should put them into our next dance."

"Oh, 'our next dance,' huh?" Neither of them noticed when Rory rolled her eyes and walked away. She sent Andy a text later: *Having fun yet?*

He wrote back: *Amazingly, yes*

*He doesn't act like someone who's planning to disappear on you*

*No he doesn't. Trying not to get ahead of myself, still a ways to go.* Six long months.

*U R an idiot he wants to bang you like a screen door in a hurricane*

*LOL OMG I know but a deal's a deal*

*Also wow those arms*

Andy glared at the phone. *SHUT UP*

*Bahaha*


Victor didn't get any new work out of the tango performance, or at least not right away, but his agent said 'that was interesting' and made sure to link the video. Some of Victor's co-workers also said 'that was interesting,' in a way that seemed approving. The cast meeting following those comments from the LAPD consultant resulted in a slight change of chemistry on the set. The other regular supporting actors didn't precisely discuss it, but they all seemed to be watching Victor. He was approaching everything now from 'what do I want and how do I get it.' In real life, that seemed to be getting some results, so he applied it to Detective Alvarado too. He decided that

Alvarado wanted to make lieutenant. He didn't say so to the writers or anyone else. He simply took every opportunity to show initiative and creativity. He also tweaked a line of dialogue here and there. None of the actors ever got much direction on the delivery, but only the stars had dared change a word before. Nobody called him on it until mid-October, when they were working on the mid-season-ending episode. It had a cliffhanger, of course, to keep people interested for when the series resumed. Victor did his thing, and nobody said anything at the time.

It wasn't until the following week's continuity meeting that one of the writers said, "So, Mr. Garcia. You had a different reading there in the hostage negotiation. Any comment?"

He took a second, wishing he could look around for reactions. "Well, I've been thinking a little more about Alvarado's motivation. His goals. He's been with this investigative team a long time. I think at this point, he's ready to move up. He wants to close cases, and he wants to close them quickly, with minimum mayhem, at minimum cost. He's heard all about the overtime. He's worked a lot of split shifts. There's this script for how the team does things and it's effective, but it's slow. Some of the moves in that chess game, the bad guys know they're delaying tactics. Those moves don't accomplish anything. The bad guys are hip to it, is what I'm saying. The delay doesn't calm them down or change the outcome. If they're going to lose their shit anyway, I guess Alvarado thinks they might as well lose it fast."

A couple of his colleagues were amused. The head writer didn't appear to be. Victor thought, *well, it's been a good run.*

But the head writer didn't hire and fire. That line of conversation didn't go any further, and Victor didn't hear about it from the show runners. The word change he'd made in that scene was small; it didn't alter the meaning of the speech. All it did was help define Alvarado's character. The other actors had responded to it in character, which gave the scene some added energy. If he didn't get spanked about it in that meeting, there was a good chance he wasn't getting spanked at all. The rest of the season suddenly looked a lot more interesting.

Andy hadn't given a great deal of thought to the logistics of his guest appearance on that TV show. When his new agent Raquel sent him an email with the schedule he thought *fucking hell, really*? He wrote back to that effect and got a reply that made him laugh out loud.

Dear Andy,

I realize you are used to doing the stage thing i.e. rehearse till you know the number and then go up on stage and do the number. That is not how TV works, sorry. You will rehearse the thing on the soundstage which will probably take all the first day while they decide where to put the cameras, the lights, the extras, the stars, et cetera. They will probably shoot the thing eight or more times at the location the next day. They will record you live with the backing track. Your vocal will go to a separate track for mixing. They will then circle-jerk about it for a couple of days, or a week, before letting you know whether you have to go to the recording studio to loop it.

What that is, is standing in a tiny booth with the scene playing in front of you and being recorded while you sing along trying to perfectly match your vocal to the face et cetera on screen. It's a skill. They know you haven't done it before.

Nobody on this show has worked with someone who has musical-theater experience. They do not, in short, know that you can actually sing. So try to have fun with it.

Cheers – Raquel

p.s. take something to read

The first day was exactly as described. Andy got through most of a three-hundred-page book, because after watching the set-up and mechanics a couple of times he was over it. He didn't sing at full power; they played the backing track and said 'mark it through,' which he took to mean next-best-thing to humming, and which seemed to satisfy. The second day, on location, was much more interesting.

It was also deeply satisfying to let it rip on 'Delilah' and see the director's eyes go wide. He knew the creative team had seen his 'All That Jazz.' He didn't have any other solo performances online. His archive of audition tapes was private. Raquel had seen a couple of things, enough to say 'okay I'll take him on.' This whole thing had been – he knew – more about his look than how he would sound. He'd been to a vocal coach, told her he had a gig, and gotten a refresher. He was doing this as close to Tom Jones as he could. He'd been practicing. He knew it was a showstopper. *Gotcha*, he thought, suppressing a grin when he stepped off the casino stage after 'Cut.'

He was hanging out, sipping water, waiting for the crew to finish re-setting for the second take, when Ray sidled over to him. "Andy," he said, offering a hand. Andy shook it. "I think you surprised a few

100

people." Andy snorted. "When Julia saw you on the list for 'Milonga' she said, what the hell, he's the photographer. Then we saw that little thing about 'Chicago.' And you should know when they run it again I've got a P.A. taking a bootleg with my phone, because Julia is going to want to see that. So what the hell."

Andy giggled, he couldn't help it. "God that was fun. Look, it's no big mystery. I did Broadway stuff for twenty years. I don't really talk about it because it was hard to give that up, and I've got my new thing now. I am not Nostalgia Man," he added, to make sure Ray understood.

"So you'd rather if you do a Mating Dance show again, this is not part of the conversation."

"Yes please. I did that for Victor. And I shouldn't even really be telling you that." *Because it still might implode.*

Ray was staring across the busy room. "Okay. You know I only started doing ballroom because of Julia." They shared a glance of understanding, then Ray heard someone call him. He nodded to Andy and went away. A few minutes later it was time for take two.

He was tired, thrilled, and ready for alcohol when he got home. He was polishing off the first bottle of beer when his phone buzzed with a message from Dana: *We hear through the grapevine that you KICKED ASS on location today*

*OMG that was fun. The first three times anyway*

*Have you talked to Victor?*

*Not yet, only got home a beer ago*

*LOL glad you did it?*

*Hell yeah. Not sure I'd want to do it again mind you*

*Boring huh*

*OMG. Light a candle I don't have to loop that fucker*

*Looking for matches right now. See you soon OXO*

He stretched out on the couch with another beer, thought about some actual food to go with it, thought about who else he could talk to about that experience. Victor was the obvious person. Raquel might be fun. He'd talk to her tomorrow, he decided. For now ... maybe Victor was home.

Victor knew today was the on-location day for Andy's guest spot on '10-31.' He was hoping to get a report. His own day had been, for a change, not long. 'L.A. Vice' did a lot of location shoots too, and those were rarely less than twelve-hour days. This time he'd been on the soundstage, doing a couple of scenes in their police-station set. He got home, had some dinner, and settled down to read. He was trying not to be the one who called, this time. He'd been that one the last few times and was worried about looking too needy. When the phone rang and he saw the ID, he said a quick silent prayer of thanks as he picked up.

"Hi Andy. How'd it go today?" Then he didn't have to say anything for quite a while because Andy had a lot to tell him. Victor laughed, made encouraging noises, the occasional sound of understanding. He remembered his first experience on a TV set. "And I wasn't even singing, my first time," he said when Andy finally ran down. "What else was happening in the scene?" He knew the casino entertainer wouldn't be the actual focus of it.

"There's this whole suspense thing happening. I haven't been following the show so I'm not sure exactly what the story is, but it seems like their new guy Ray is undercover at the casino, some kind of money-laundering operation, and this is the night the team swoops in. They were taping a whole lot of stuff in addition to my song. God knows how it will play when they put it together." He finished that second bottle of beer, held the phone away so he wouldn't belch at Victor, then added, "It was sixty percent total fun and forty percent mind-numbing boredom."

"That's TV for you. Any idea when it's going to air?"

"Not a fucking clue. Raquel said she'd let me know. I'm setting the DVR though. On the off chance somebody wants a comment it would probably be a good idea to sound like I've actually seen the show." Victor laughed again. Andy was smiling; Victor could hear it in his voice. "Ray said he was getting a P.A. to take a phone video. I don't know if he made it off the set with that."

"If he does, I want to see it." They talked a little longer, about Victor's work this time. After a while he forced himself to say, "I'll bet you haven't eaten yet. Go do that, and get some sleep. Call me sometime."

"I'll do that." Andy might have wanted to say something else. After the briefest pause, he said, "Good night."

"Good night, Andy. Welcome to TV Land." Victor disconnected, wishing they were in the same room. Wishing 'good night' was face to face, skin to skin, switching off the light, kissing. *Less than six months to go.*

Chapter 7

After cleaning up his fourth-quarter calendar and trying not to literally count the days left to 366, Andy called his mother. "I have news," he said. "Well, sort of about that. You remember the dance video I sent you? God I *know* wasn't he great? I got a TV gig out of that. Taped it a couple of days ago. I'm still waiting to hear if they need me back to fix the vocal. Say what? Oh, sorry. I'm singing! Yes!" He giggled, listening to the burst of Spanglish excitement on the other end. "They wanted a casino entertainer for this big scene on this cop show. They saw the dance with Victor and looked me up. I got to sing 'Delilah.' It was hella fun. The show is called '10-31' and I don't know exactly when the episode is airing, but if you set your DVR now you won't miss it." He listened for a minute. "You know, I think it's because those cop shows are always trying to top each other. The show that called me, and the show Victor's on, they're not on the same night. They're trying to pull the same audience. So I get the idea they keep an eye on each other and if someone does something interesting, they'll try to find a way to capitalize on it. That's based on nothing, you know I don't watch cop shows." A pause, smiling, while she laughed her way to another question. "Yeah, it worked out for me. That was two days and it paid more than doing two weddings would have. Uh-huh. So how's Pop doing?" He got his mother talking about their life in Miami. She always had a ton of gossip, some of it about people Andy actually knew. After winding up the call, he had another of those moments of feeling bad for Victor, who didn't have this anymore. Who maybe never had, because he couldn't talk about his real life. *Hang in there, catnip*, he caught himself thinking. *My mother's going to love you.*

Andy didn't have to loop his scene, which was good because he found himself slammed with business. First there were baby pictures for two of the Underground Cabaret principals; then there were glamour shots of Michelle and Dmitri, who won a world championship in November. He shot three weddings and got several calls from publications wanting to use photos from the 'Cut Open' exhibit. A charity he'd supported before asked if he had anything for a silent auction; he gave them the last unsold print from the empty-theaters exhibit. None of the 'My Pet' photos were going into his stock portfolio, so he dug through the archives to add some fresh material from earlier collections. He had a photo session for the Cabaret principals for their January show. With all his usual business, he had no time for rehearsals or lessons. He did, however, take time to go watch his episode of '10-31' with Dana and Rory when it aired right before the mid-season break. He also forwarded that on-set phone video to Victor after he got it from Ray. Victor's reply was *You probably do not want to know what I did after watching that.* He did want to know, of course. Maybe someday he'd ask for the details.

They didn't have a plan for more dancing, but Andy got to work reviving his fouettés and pirouettes. He also went out on dates, glad he had enough friends that he could call the dinners, shows, and movies 'dates' without actually doing - or wanting - anything more. It felt like he was in a holding pattern, but one accompanied by a growing sense of possibility. He and Victor continued to touch base regularly. It was more and more difficult for him to sign off, or to end a call. He couldn't help noticing that Victor was no good at it either.

Meanwhile, Victor wrapped up the first half of his season on 'L.A. Vice' and sorted through offers for fill-in work. He took a four-day shoot doing a Latin lover for an R-rated comedy feature. It was a lot of fun, and another straight character for his resumé. He missed doing the dance lessons, but from the sound of things Andy was swamped. At least they were still talking.

Victor's agent checked in with him after Andy's episode of '10-31' aired, asking if Victor was open to singing gigs. He hadn't done anything since that play, but he was up for it. The result was a set as a guest vocalist for a swing-and-salsa New Year's Eve event. It started to give him ideas. He had dinner again with Janis, who'd just wrapped up a ten-date local tour for her album. They talked music for an hour. Then she asked him about the Andy situation.

He could have talked about Andy for hours. The dance, the photo exhibit, that TV guest spot. He didn't know if Janis had seen that, and didn't ask. He could send her the video later. For now, he'd keep it about himself. Andy wasn't really his to talk about, after all. "It's still a situation," Victor said. "I'm doing what I said I would do. I'm figuring myself out."

"I like your new look," she said. "You've got a very slinky thing going."

"I was inspired by my villain in the play we did. I bought that suit, you know, from the wardrobe mistress. When I was going through my stuff to find what Victor Garcia looked like, that was the one thing that really rang my bell."

"I suppose," she said thoughtfully, staring at him over her glass, "you weren't ever in a position to be yourself, were you? God, I was lucky. I remember the first time I said 'fuck' in front of my mother. I thought I was going to be in so much trouble."

"What did she say?" Victor was half-laughing already.

"She said, well now you know how that feels. Did you like it?" Janis giggled at Victor's expression. "And I said fuck yeah."

He laughed out loud. "How old were you?"

"Oh, I was twelve. It was so inappropriate. But she said, you know, it's only a word. As long as you're talking to us, we're good."

"God I wish I could have really talked to my mother." Victor was quiet for a moment. "She loved me, she truly did. She wanted the best for me. But she never got to know me."

Janis patted his arm. "Well, another thing my mom told me. She said, it's not your job to be anything for us. Obviously Dad wants you to be a musician. But it's our job to give you the tools, and your job to figure out what you want to do with them. What *you* want."

"It wasn't even about what I wanted," Victor said. "It was about who I *was*." She nodded, and he changed the subject. "What did you like best about touring?"

"Oh my God *everything*." That subject lasted until the check came.

Victor checked his phone when he got out to his car, read a text from Gino, and had to sit there giggling for about five minutes. Every time he tried to start a response he cracked up again because he could totally hear the exasperated tone: *The motherfucker sings too?* When he finally composed himself enough to type all he could say was: *I KNOW*

Victor was still thinking about music when he took a date to Chrome for the Cabaret's December performance. He knew Andy wasn't going to make it but he also knew Andy would hear he was there, and he wanted to prove he was playing the game. It was another casual thing, this time a friend of a friend. Someone he liked, who found him attractive; someone who could have been a lover, but understood Victor was only out for a pleasant, friendly, low-demand evening. The guy had an early flight and left right after the show, wishing Victor happy holidays. Victor watched him go without regret. Then he looked around for Rory, intercepting her when she came out to the club from the green room. "Hey chica. Loved your number. Got a second?"

"Whatcha need?"

"Is the owner here? I wanted to ask him something."

Rory noticed that Victor was holding a printout. "What's that?"

"It's from the website, about booking for the club. I was thinking about doing a little concert here."

"Oh hey, that's cool. Tyrone's usually in his office about now. It's past the bathrooms, down the hall, all the way to the end. Oh and by the way, thanks for the picture."

"What picture?" He grinned at her and she silently enunciated *whatever*, waving him away and going to join Dana at the bar. A few minutes later he knocked on the office door.

The next day, he made a call to the director of last year's play, looking for some contacts. "Hi Tanith, how you doing? Still hanging out with that cute detective?" He'd heard through the grapevine that they'd started dating.

"Well hello Mr. Garcia. Yeah, I figured I'd keep him around in case I get another maniac on a job. What's up?"

"I'm putting together a vocal set to perform at this club in Hollywood. Wondered if you could put me in touch with the music producer from our show." Within a few minutes he had all the information he needed. "Fantastic. One more thing."

"Jesus, Victor, I don't hear from you for a year and then you have all these *demands*," she said. He could tell she was smiling.

"You're right, I owe you dinner, at least. But first, can I do my two songs from 'What Went Down'?"

"Oh! Well, yeah. Sure, that'd be great." Tanith sounded pleased now.

He told her the date. "I'll put you and Detective Cutie on the list."

"How did you know I call him that?"

"Doesn't everybody?" He disconnected, smiling, and started thinking about his set list. *Blues*, he thought, *and some standards. 'Knock me a Kiss,' for sure. And how to say what I want to say?*

When Andy heard about the New Year's Eve thing, he was strongly tempted to go. His all-too-vivid recollection of the last time he'd been to a New Year's Eve thing was telling him not to. "I won't get to see him except for the however many minutes he's on

109

stage, it's expensive as fuck, it'll be loud as fuck, everyone there will be drunk and stupid, and I'll feel hateful about it the next day," he told Dana on the phone.

"Andy," she said, "this isn't about you."

"Eh?"

She snorted. "He told you he's doing this thing. It is a thing you could go to. Do you honestly think that he won't be standing up there looking for you in the crowd?"

Andy thought about it. Victor had not said 'I wish you would come.' On the other hand, he hadn't said 'I'll understand if you can't come.' They were not officially boyfriends yet, if they were ever going to be. On the other hand, if it were Andy onstage, he would want Victor to be there. *More hearing loss,* Andy thought with resignation, and said, "What should I wear?"

Everyone there was drunk and stupid. Andy had a drink or two himself, to get with the program. It was loud as fuck. But the swing band was surprisingly capable of playing more than swing. The salsa band had a surprisingly good singer and a surprisingly reticent horn section. Andy had to admit he was enjoying himself. There were plenty of people looking for someone to dance with; he was happy to oblige. He wasn't an expert in any of the partner dances, but he could fake it well enough. Then it was eleven o'clock, time for the swing band to come out again. This time he knew Victor was supposed to be singing with them. They hadn't checked in with each other. Maybe Victor didn't want to know if Andy wasn't going to be there. Andy wasn't sure why he hadn't texted to say he would be. *Passive-aggressive bitch*, he scolded himself, and pulled out his phone to send a

110

message: *Can't wait to hear you sing, catnip. Right down front in my dance suit.* There was a good chance that Victor didn't have his phone turned on, that he wouldn't have time to check it, or that the message would get bounced around to satellites over Latvia or Lesotho. But at some point he would see it, and know Andy was there.

Then he was onstage, looking straight at Andy, clearly happy to see him. *Oh I am so totally fucked*, Andy thought. He didn't even look for someone to dance with, simply stood there watching for the half-hour set. Watching and admiring, because Victor was more than a good singer: he was a good team player. He was working the crowd, interacting with the rest of the band, sharing the mic, obviously having a blast. He also looked like a million bucks in his gray dance suit, with a white shirt and striped gray tie. As the swing band left the stage, he blew a kiss in Andy's direction. Some girl standing nearby squealed to her friends. *That wasn't for you, chica.*

Now he had another decision to make: wait till midnight, or GTFO. The salsa band was coming back out. Andy had no idea what Victor's agenda was. He was edging toward one of the bars when he felt his phone buzz. He pulled it out of his pocket: *God it was good to see you out there. Fun set. They say I'm free to go. Want to ring in the New Year with me?*

Andy knew what that meant. That meant a kiss. He couldn't stand next to Victor at the turn of the year, and say 'Happy New Year,' and not kiss the man. But they'd be in public, with about three hundred chaperones, and two cars so they couldn't possibly accidentally end up going home together, and this wasn't a hotel so they couldn't possibly accidentally end up going to a room together. To confirm, he wrote *Here? Because I'm over by the Pull-up Bar*

The reply was immediate: *I'll find you there.* Andy got himself another drink, put his back to a convenient wall, and waited. The salsa band was into their second number, and he was accepting that he would initiate that kiss because Victor had promised not to, when he heard his name and turned. *You beautiful thing.* "You were great," he said. "A real crowd-pleaser. This girl standing next to me thought you blew her a kiss."

"I didn't even see her." Victor was gazing at him, faintly smiling, telegraphing 'please kiss me NOW' with such intensity that Andy very nearly did.

Instead he handed over his almost-untouched Manhattan. "I've already had a couple of these. It'll be good for your throat." Then he wished he hadn't said that because 'throat' made him think of a lot of things he shouldn't be thinking of. Judging from the way Victor was staring at him over the glass, they were thinking the same things. He held up a hand like 'wait,' returned to the bar, and got an egregiously overpriced bottle of water. Went back to Victor, who was halfway down the cocktail. Took the glass out of his hand and replaced it with water. "Hydrate."

"You're bossy," Victor said, twisting the cap off. He drank about half the water. "But smart." He blew out a breath. "That was such a rush."

"It's a good band." They had to almost shout to hear each other. "Better with you up front." Victor smiled again, and edged closer. Close enough that their shoulders were touching. Andy didn't move away.

Victor said, "I like your tie." A candy-cane-striped bow tie, courtesy of Rory and Dana. They

112

shared the rest of the cocktail, then the rest of the water. Andy chucked the bottle in the general direction of a trash bin, heard Victor laugh, shrugged. They didn't say anything else, not even at the end of the set, when the salsa singer turned into the countdown queen. As she called out the numbers, they turned to look at each other.

"Happy New Year," they said with the rest of the crowd. Andy still had that goddamned cocktail glass in his hand. Fortunately it was plastic. He threw it at the trash bin and pulled Victor in. *Oh God this mouth.* Three months since the last kiss, the kiss he'd cut short because of ten thousand reasons, the way he should cut this one short. He couldn't. Victor had both arms around his neck, mouth open, body pressed tight against his. He tasted of maraschino. Andy was half out of his mind.

They were rudely returned to reality by a surge of traffic toward the bar. Someone banged into Andy's back, he lurched forward, Victor stumbled backward, and then they were gripping each other by the arms, getting their balance, checking in. "Fuck," Victor said after a moment, when they were in two separate spaces again. He touched his mouth.

Andy wanted to touch it too. "Shit, I'm sorry. My snaggle tooth got you." His canine, the one that never had quite conceded the fight when he had braces.

"Your fang." Victor was smiling, even though his lip was bleeding a little. Andy dug in a pocket for his bandanna. Victor took it with a nod of thanks. The DJ was playing now, not as loud as the bands. They could talk without yelling. "I suppose this means the party's over."

"Do you have to get anything from backstage?"

113

"No, I came in clean."

Andy was fairly sure it was a mistake to say, "I'll go down with you." That choice of words was totally a mistake. "To the parking garage." Victor gave him an amused sideways look. He pressed the bandanna to his mouth again. They didn't say anything else as they went out.

At this point Andy wasn't sure whether he was relieved or disappointed to find they weren't parked on the same level. Victor's was first. "I'll be in touch," he said quietly, wanting to say a lot of other things.

"Happy New Year," Andy said, with heroic restraint. Victor got out of the elevator; they waved to each other; the doors closed. Andy slumped against the back of the car and watched the numbers until it stopped again.

January 2014

Andy wasn't expecting to get to sleep easily after that kiss, but maybe it was exactly what he needed. He texted Victor after he woke up: *Slept surprisingly well. How's the injury?*

A reply came back before the coffeemaker was done doing its thing: *Worth it*

Andy nearly sent back *Yes it was* but settled for *Hope you don't mind I'm planning to go drink mimosas with Dana and Rory and talk about you for an hour*

*No worries, I'm going to do the same with Janis. She's touring and it sounds complicated. Someday soon I'll introduce you two*

*Look forward to it. Happy New Year*

Andy then texted the girls to make sure they still wanted to see him (they did), to ask if he needed to bring anything (he didn't), and to give them an ETA. He drank some coffee while he did his first-quarter calendar. Then he flipped back to the previous year and thought about what was different.

"So different," he said to the girls, when he was over there a couple hours later. "Last January I was seriously considering moving out of L.A."

They were all in the yard, stretched out on loungers, enjoying the cool sunny day. Dana nudged his ankle with her foot. "Aren't you glad you didn't?"

"I will be glad in slightly less than three months. Or else I'll be planning to leave L.A. in three months."

"Still considering your options, huh." Rory slurped some of her mimosa, watching him. "You would really leave? You've been in Los Angeles a long time."

"Longer than I've lived anywhere since I left Miami," he agreed. "I don't truly want to move away. It's fear talking."

"You should have said six months." Dana made it dry. Andy laughed. "Seriously, a year?"

"But he needed it. I promise you. He's been doing the work."

"You talk a lot."

"We talk often," he corrected. "Someday I hope we'll talk a lot. But basically, I tell him about all the people I'm fictitiously dating. He tells me about the people he's actually dating, or I find out about it online. He tells me about his friends. He's made a lot of friends. I don't ask if he's fucking anybody, he doesn't ask if I am."

"Do you think he is?" Rory hoped he wasn't. That guy might have been new to being out, but he surely hadn't been a virgin. Those pictures had been of someone at ease with intimacy. Or maybe he'd simply been at ease with Andy. She hoped he'd learned there was more to being out than having an open sex life.

Andy thought about it for a minute. He hated the idea, of course, but better now than later. "I don't know," he decided. "The way he is with me, I'd say not. He wants it. I kissed him at midnight and Jesus Christ." Both women laughed. "It's a good thing we were in public, is what I'm saying. But for all I know he's like that with everybody." He shrugged uncomfortably.

Dana wanted to reassure him. There were enough press mentions of Victor's dates, and most of those dates were with people in the industry. If anything more than dating were happening, somebody would have said so. But she didn't want to push any buttons, so she topped up their glasses and turned her face up to the sun. After a while she said, "How do you like our kitten?"

"This furball on my chest?" Andy's voice was amused. "Are you sure he's still a kitten? He's gotten big since the last time I saw him. He's an actual cat now."

"Spike's not even a year old yet. He's going to be a bruiser. He's so cuddly," Rory said. "He gets in between us and he's like a hot water bottle."

Dana snickered. "A fluffy orange hot water bottle that purrs."

Andy looked to the left; Dana had her eyes closed, smiling. He looked to the right; Rory was watching him. He had one hand on the cat. He reached over with the other and picked up his glass. "So what are you doing for the Cabaret this month."

"For 'Stayin' Alive?'" Rory sipped her mimosa. "Striptease to 'She Blinded Me with Science.' Starting out in nurse's outfit, et cetera." She smiled, listening to him giggle.


"This is better?" Victor said to Janis. They were at her parents' house in Glendale, because it was a gorgeous day and neither of their apartments had outdoor space. Her parents were stretched out on another pair of loungers. They all had mimosas in hand. Ed and Deborah were talking quietly about something, probably music; Ed was a composer. Janis and Victor had been talking – again – about her fall tour, and the album experience, and what she wanted to do next. That had led into their not-quite-settled love lives.

"It might be better," she said. "Stefan's a musician. We don't have a lot in common otherwise. But he's good-looking and really smart. I'm interested, he's interested. We'll see. How's your situation going? I've had bruises like that before." She touched her own lip.

Victor stifled a laugh, because he didn't want to open up the cut again. "That was an accident. Midnight, kiss, mob at the bar."

"How'd you like singing with the band?"

"Oh *damn* that was fun. I had no idea. I need to send my agent a thank-you note." They talked about that for a while. How many songs, what songs, what Victor liked most about doing it. Which led him to the moment of looking out and seeing that gorgeous man, knowing the only reason he was there was to see

117

Victor. "Andy sent me a text right before we went on. I wasn't sure he was going to be there. I was afraid to ask."

"But he was there." Janis was smiling. She thought this whole deal was ridiculous, and said so frequently. She freely admitted to being in the 'fuck first and figure it out later' camp.

"I didn't ask him to come. The whole point is I'm supposed to be learning how to be me under my own power."

"I think you're doing pretty well at that."

Victor was starting to think so too. He'd done a lot of new things in the past year. "What did you think of that video I sent you?"

She sat up, excited. "That sneaky *fucker*." Victor laughed, cursed, waved off her sputtered apology. "Did you have any idea he could sing like that?"

"I knew he could sing. Wasn't expecting that. Who knows what else I'm going to find out about him." Andy was responding, reacting, replying. It was a damn sight better than nothing, but one day Victor hoped he'd really learn what made the man tick.

Janis watched him think for a minute. "Three months to go, right?"

Victor blew out a breath. "Thank God I'm going to be busy."

Chapter 8

Andy geared up fast for his spring show. He was calling it 'Mirrorball,' seeing a lot of dance people, many of them connected with the Cabaret. He'd done a dozen subjects and booked a dozen more before he thought *hey wait a minute*. He had to sit down with a glass of something and interrogate himself about it. Was this some pathetic way to re-live the thrill of dancing on stage, or was he simply using the available resources in an almost-certainly crowd-pleasing way? He liked what he was doing. These weren't conventional portraits; you couldn't even tell who the subjects were unless you already knew. They were all motion and color and sparkle. *Okay*, he decided. *This is actually art.*

But between that and his regular poster shoots, he couldn't avoid hearing about the next Mating Dance show, set for February. He liked the theme, and it seemed like a good excuse, so he called Victor. "Remember what you said about our next dance?"

"Well hello stranger.  Had any good dates lately?"

"So many and so good, I can't even tell you," said Andy, lying like a pro. Or not; he heard Victor make an amused sound. "How about you?"

"All of that. What's this about dancing?"

"Michelle, Chrome, Assassins."

"Tango?"

"What do you think?" Andy gave him a second and then said, "Mr. and Mrs. Smith."

"Oh yeah, baby, let's do that."  Victor's tone was suggestive.

"Only let's not really bang each other into the walls."

"Not yet."

*Yikes, walked right into that one,* Andy thought, stifling a laugh. "I've got a pretty clear schedule right now. Why don't you set up some lessons for choreography and let me know?"

"You're gonna do those spinny things, right?"

"Wait and see." He disconnected, smiling, before he could lose his head and tell Victor to come over.

Unfortunately, Victor got an email the next day from his producers. The show was sending him out of town for two weeks for location shooting, so the opportunity to prepare a new dance fell apart. "I'm sorry," he said when he called to break the news. "They just now decided to wrap this two-episode arc around Antelope Valley. We're going to be shooting mostly nights and getting back into town during normal hours is not going to happen."

"Oh well. The idea won't go away. We can always do it some other time." *Shit,* he thought immediately, *that was a little overconfident.*

But Victor sounded pleased when he replied. "Yeah," he said. "We'll do it another time."

He was back in town for the 'Assassins' show, and met Andy at Chrome for the second night. Afterward, they hung out behind the curtain with a few of the dancers, chatting about other upcoming events, including Victor's mini-concert. Andy showed off his revived turn series, just for the hell of it, then turned to Victor. "You remember that shit we did in September?"

Victor would have agreed even if he didn't remember any of it. Andy was killing him tonight in the pants from his dance suit, spectator shoes and a crisp white shirt. The top three buttons were undone

120

and his sleeves were rolled up. He had to know how sexy he looked. "Maybe? Let's see." They got into position and started working through it, egged on by the others. By the time they figured most of it out again, and danced it through, it was time to call it a night. Except pretty soon they were alone on stage, and couldn't make themselves leave. "This was fun," Victor said. "A crazy good time."

Andy was so very strongly tempted to suggest they jettison this ridiculous deal. Victor was dressed to kill in a slim-fitting black silk shirt and tuxedo pants. That same chain glinted against the smooth skin, saying 'bite here.' He mentally shook himself. "You're dancing crazy good, too. Too bad you're wasting yourself on TV."

"Eat me," Victor invited, with a wicked smile.

"Not yet."

"So cold."

"The coldest." They were staring at each other, half laughing, half 'give me one hint and I'll be all over you,' when Michelle saved the day by tapping each of them on the shoulder.

"Guys," she said when she was sure she had their attention, "Tyrone says everybody get the hell out, he doesn't serve breakfast." She herded them offstage.

On the way out, Andy picked up a table talker promoting Victor's upcoming set. "It doesn't have your set list on here."

"It's a secret."

"Guess I'll have to come see it." *Like I wouldn't have anyway*.

"You'd better," said Victor, more seriously. "I want you to tell me if I'm actually good at it."

"What are you talking about? You're a great singer."

"Thanks, but … well, I've never done a solo show."

Andy gave him a look. "All you have to do is stand there and look like you do and not sound like a crow. Well, and remember the lyrics. You'll be fine. Trust me."

"Great, now I'm going to worry about forgetting the lyrics." *I wonder if he's noticed the date.*

He had. *I wonder if that date was intentional.* At this point, he couldn't imagine that it wasn't. Andy whipped the promo card out of the table talker and stuck it in his back pocket. "You'll be fine," he said again, pretending he didn't know Victor had seen that little operation.


Andy got a text from Rory the next morning while he was doing a portfolio: *I hear Michelle had to physically separate you and that guy after the show*

He wrote back as soon as he had a break: *NOT TRUE but a little too close for comfort*

*Almost to the finish line now. Sure looks like he's heading there with you*

*From your lips to God's ear*

*How's the chastity?*

*I am SUCH AN IDIOT*

*LOL I also hear that you looked like pre-coital James Bond last night*

He smiled. *Licensed to thrill*

*Did he like it?*

*Oh yes he did, no thanks for reminding me. Gotta go I have another client coming and oh fuck me I can't even use that word right now HELL that one either, help me Jesus*

*ROFLMAO*

Andy put the phone down, sincerely cursing the chastity, and the next few weeks. At least he had 'Mirrorball' to distract him. He was hanging it that week and opening on the weekend. It occurred to him that he had somehow scheduled the thing so that it would be down by the time Day 366 arrived. He would have sworn that wasn't a conscious decision.

March 2014

Janis was being sent on another ten-date tour in NorCal, but she'd immediately agreed to play for Victor's midweek mini-concert at Chrome. He was glad she was there. The stakes were high, and he was nervous. Between friends, co-workers, Chrome regulars, and fans of 'L.A. Vice,' the club was packed. He peeked out from the stage door, and nearly panicked.

"You're okay," said Vicky, who was acting as stage manager. "The musicians are set, the sound check is done, you know your shit and you look like a million bucks. Now breathe, for fuck's sake." She straightened his satin lapels and bow tie.

"Right." Victor breathed. "Right, thanks."

"Lights are down." Victor walked out on stage, nodding to the musicians – Janis gave him a thumbs-up - and then to Vicky. The curtain went up, and a spotlight came on. He waited for the polite applause to fade. The set began with 'Knock me a Kiss' and progressed to some blues and jazz standards that suited Victor's Nat King Cole-adjacent voice. The arrangements were spare, swingy and light. Tanith's two songs fell in the middle. Both got a good response, even though most audience members had never heard them before.

He closed with a torch song.  The club was silent as he sang the final lines:

> "Someday if all my prayers are answered
> I'll hear a footstep on the stair
> With anxious heart I'll hurry to the door
> And maybe you'll be there."

The musicians played a lingering finish, and Victor's gaze found Andy, sitting near the stage. Victor set his mic in the stand and walked to the stage steps. Andy stood up and stepped closer. One step up from Andy, Victor laid a hand on his tear-streaked face, then bent close and kissed him. The room exploded with applause.

"Come home with me," Andy said, hand wrapped around Victor's wrist. "And make me scream."

Victor smiled. "Count on it." He tipped his forehead to Andy's for a moment, then went back up on stage to take his bows.

It seemed to take forever to get out of the club. Andy fled the scene early. "Don't even call me before you start over," he said. "I don't want to be sitting there counting the minutes any worse than I already will be." *Way to act cool*, he thought, mentally rolling his eyes at himself.

"What are you going to do?"

"Knowing me, I will either clean the place from top to bottom, or pour a large drink and pace and stare at the walls.  Odds favor option two."

Victor wanted to grab him, haul him backstage, do things to him. "Weren't you going to start planning your next show?"

"Yeah, that'll probably occupy me for a minute." Andy looked at him ruefully. "I'm no good at being cool."

"You don't have to be cool. Just be there."

"I'll be there." Andy sketched a wave and bolted.

Victor had to mingle for over an hour. He had a few words with Janis. "Where's your guy? Didn't you say Stefan was going to be here tonight?"

"He was here," she said, looking cranky. "He took off already. He lives in Claremont. How long are you staying? Because I have to say, if somebody kissed me like that after a concert I would not be hanging around the venue."

Victor did a half-shrug, half-smile thing. "He's gone home. I'm going over there as soon as I get done here. But I have to say thanks, you know. All these people came out. For all they knew I was going to suck."

"You do not suck," she told him. "Good singer, good set, and Jesus do you look good. Fuck Stefan anyway." She kissed Victor and headed back to the bar. Victor deduced that her last phrase was her way of saying 'good night,' and went to get properly caught up with Tanith and her partner, Detective Sid Palacio.

Tanith wanted to know all about the Andy situation. "Did you two know each other before he did the photos for my play?"

"No, that's when we met. I ran into him at the Brewery that fall and he had these shorts on. I don't know if you've ever seen his legs. Never knew I was a leg man." She laughed. Victor didn't blame her; he was grinning like a dog himself, and Sid was looking at the ceiling like one more word was going to crack him up. "Anyway, I had some personal stuff going then and we haven't been together. However, we have a very important date tonight so I'm going to say thank you for being here."

"And now you're getting the hell out, I see. Okay. Well done tonight. Keep in touch."

"You too, Tanith." He kissed her cheek, shook Sid's hand, and headed out.


It felt like forever before the knock finally came. "That wasn't fair," Andy said as he let Victor in. "That song! Jesus!"

The main space was dark; Andy had a light on in the kitchen, and one in the loft, but nothing else. He was barefoot, but otherwise still dressed. Victor started undoing his tie. "A year, that's what you said, that's what you got. Did I pass the test?"

"Did you *pass*? Are you *insane*?" Andy seized him by the shoulders and shook him a little. "I think that yeah you possibly are insane. But I don't care. I can't care. I'm too in love with you."

Victor heard the words and stopped thinking. He put his hands on Andy's ribs and slowly walked him backward to the nearest wall. He leaned in and put his mouth on Andy's throat. "Oh God," Andy said faintly. Victor said nothing, only tasted, kissed, explored, and touched until they were both breathless and shaky. Then he stood back a little. Andy pushed the tuxedo jacket off his shoulders and Victor shrugged out of it, tossing it in the general direction of a chair.

He bent down to untie his black patent leather shoes, stepped out of them, and looked at Andy. "Bed. Now."

"Upstairs." Andy missed a step but made it up intact, Victor right behind him. They stripped without speaking, eyes on each other. Then Andy took Victor in his arms, going in for another of the kisses they'd

126

both been craving for months. Neither of them could have said who made the move that took them down to the bed. All they knew was that they were finally skin to skin again. Long delirious minutes later, Andy took his mouth off Victor's throat long enough to say, "I have a confession."

"Ego te absolvo." Victor pushed him onto his back and started kissing his way down Andy's body.

"I haven't been with anyone else."

"Good. Neither have I."

"Goddammit, Victor." Andy started to say something else, then caught his breath because Victor's hand was wrapped around him. His other hand was groping on the nightstand for condoms. Andy let him take care of that, glad he'd done it without prompting. There was one more kiss before Victor headed south again, and then it was lips and teeth and tongue. "Jesus!" Victor made a happy sound. Andy got a hand under his knee and pulled him closer. "In my mouth." Another, even happier sound as Victor adjusted his position.

Andy had no idea what time it was. He'd seen and touched and tasted almost every inch of Victor's body and he still wanted more. He'd had his mouth on the gecko, the stag, and the rattlesnake, listening to – and seeing - Victor's breathless response. They'd done even more kissing than they had on their first night. This time, it was Victor's turn to lie back and take it, face to face. Andy would never forget the sound he made into Andy's mouth when he was all the way in. Or how it felt to see him come. It was good he'd had time to think things through before Victor got there. Everything they needed was up in the loft, so they could tidy up and then relax together. "I'm exhausted but I can't stop touching you," he murmured.

"You don't hear me complaining." Victor opened his eyes, smiling lazily because Andy's hand on his hip and Andy's leg between his were what he'd wanted for so long. "How long has that been there?" He was looking at the taped-up review.

"Since the day I found it."

"It's a good picture."

"Yeah, it's got you in it." Andy pressed his body close to Victor's back, burying his face in the other man's hair. "I'm so glad you're here."

"Me too." He wrapped his arm over Andy's, hand to hand. "I wasn't really sure I'd make it."

"Huh?"

"I mean every time I saw you, it got worse. If Michelle hadn't come backstage that time I think I might have put you up against the wall."

Andy laughed softly and kissed his neck. "Can you stay?"

"I'm not called tomorrow. Told them I had an appointment. So yeah," he said softly. "I can stay."

"Thank God."

Victor turned around to face him, fitting their bodies together, brushing his hand across Andy's cheek. "I love you." He was almost afraid to say it, but Andy smiled.

They kissed again, soft and light. Andy said "I love you, too." He reached up and switched off the lamp.


When it was undeniably morning, or rather broad daylight and edging toward noon, Andy dug out the

'Chicago' disc. "I said you could see it," he said, dropping it on the bed next to Victor. "So if you still want to, here it is."

Victor turned from his study of the books up in the sleeping loft. Dozens of them, about theater and dance. He was glad that Andy kept those close. There were a few pictures, too, framed snapshots of what had to be friends and family. One day he would ask about those. "You said tape."

"Because I grew up with videotapes, yes, I said tape, whatever." Andy didn't really mind that Victor was snickering. "Coffee, food, and screen are downstairs."

"But I like it up here. We're naked up here."

"We can be naked downstairs," Andy pointed out. He pulled on sweatpants and a tee shirt. "It's happened before."

Since that was true, Victor threw his pants and shirt over the railing and followed Andy down the loft stairs. It was cooler down there, and he got dressed. "If I was thinking, I would have brought something else."

"My stuff would probably fit you all right. But bring something to keep here, next time you come over," Andy said, setting up the coffeemaker. *Ugh, overconfident again.* "I mean, you know."

Victor stood beside him and ran a hand up his back. "Do I need to say I love you in the light of day? Because I'll say it all day. I love you."

Andy turned to make eye contact. "Thanks," he said quietly. "It might take me a while to get used to. I love you too." Victor slid his arms around Andy and they stood there, holding each other, getting used to it. After a while, and after another kiss, Andy stepped back and opened the refrigerator. "I blew the budget at Bristol Farms."

Once they were on the outside of some food, Andy loaded the disc and pulled the couch into comfortable viewing distance from one of his big monitors. "This should be interesting. I haven't watched it for a while." He sat back with the remote and pressed 'play.'

"I almost went looking for it, but I waited." Then Andy came on as Velma Kelly, and Victor said, "Holy shit." Fringed, very short flapper dress; long gloves; a sleek bobbed wig; fully made-up; fishnet tights and high-heeled T-strap shoes: pretty much as imagined, but even better. "Andy, those *legs*. God almighty." Andy barely had time to hit 'pause' before he was underneath Victor, half-laughing and already breathless.

They didn't get through the whole show until late in the day. Victor felt like he'd been steamrollered. "Jesus. Was that what they call an orgy?"

"An orgy generally has more than two people, but close enough." Andy rolled off the couch onto his hands and knees. "I can't walk." He giggled, and pushed himself to his feet using the couch as a prop. "We need more food."

"And a shower." Victor sat up slowly. "Holy wow. Hey, I just thought of something."

"What's that." Andy had made it to the kitchen and was plundering the refrigerator again.

"I hope I didn't screw up your schedule today."

"That's exactly what you did. But don't worry, there wasn't anything on my schedule except screwing."

"Oh har de har." Victor tottered into the kitchen and leaned on the counter.

"I didn't schedule anything but you." Andy brushed his fingers over Victor's jaw, then his own. "We need a shave. If you'd said, well, that's the year and thanks buh-bye, I would have taken the day to marinate in vodka. Since you didn't say that, it's been a much better day. " He shoved a couple of sliced bagels in the toaster oven and turned it on. "Smoked salmon for you? How about some of this chicken salad?"

"All of the above." They stayed in the kitchen till they'd eaten again, at which point they had enough energy for the shower. "I wish I could stay here tonight," Victor said once they were clean and dressed. "I have an early call."

"Action scene?"

"No, thank God, it's a stakeout. I get to spend the whole day sitting in an unmarked car." He lifted his jacket off the chair where it had landed the night before, made sure he had his phone and wallet and keys, located his shoes and put them on. Then he leaned on the door, because he didn't want to open it, and gazed at Andy. "When can I see you again?"

"I'm not in the mood to be moderate. Text me whenever you're free. We'll see who can go where."

"Perfect. I have to open this door and I don't want to."

"I don't want you to. You look like the best morning after of all time." Victor smiled. Andy took his hand. "It sucks being a grown-up."

"Yes it does." He gazed at Andy for a minute, wishing he didn't have to go. "You've got whisker burn."

"So do you. Put some olive oil on that before you go to sleep." Andy leaned in and kissed him lightly, then moved him off the door so they could open it. "I don't want to say goodbye. So I'll say good night."

"Good night." Victor stepped through the open door. "I love you."

"I love you. Text me when you get home."

Victor smiled. "I'll do that. Good night." He turned and walked away. Andy let the door close behind him. Then he leaned against it himself with a sigh. He knew this thing could still go pear-shaped. Victor could get over him, or tired of him. Life could get in the way. The odds were against long-term success.

So he'd have to make the most of this while he had it. Make the kind of memories he could live on if he found himself alone again. The past twenty-four hours could last him quite a while. He went to pull the slipcover off the couch.

A half-hour later, the kitchen was clean, the washing machine was working, and he was contemplating a cup of decaf. Ten minutes after that, the text came in: *Andy, thank you for an educational year. I learned a lot about myself. Now I'm looking forward to a year of learning about you. Dancing with you, kissing you, loving you. I hate this apartment because you're not in it. I love you. Good night XOX*

Andy read the text about ten times before writing back: *Victor, I think you're going to teach me a few things too. Get some sleep. I love you. Good night XOX.* He was unbelievably tired. After their first night, maybe he should have expected this, but it wasn't exactly something you could get in the gym and train for. He laughed at himself as he went to wash up.

He wasn't expecting any more texts that night, so when the phone pinged on its charger he looked over at it with a frown. Then he smiled and picked it up. The message was from Rory: *So????*

*So what?*

*OH DON'T EVEN WE SAW THAT KISS AT THE CLUB HOLY SHIT*

Andy was giggling now. *You don't have to yell @%#$&!*

*LOL Okay so he got here about 1:00 and left about 20:00 and OMG tired*

*Happy?*

*He said he loves me*

*Guess we'll let him live then*

*Yes please I am out of my head can't believe it's real and generally on the verge of tears*

*Me too. We love you. Get some sleep OXO*

*OXO Zzzzzz.* Andy switched off the kitchen light, put the phone down, and crawled up the stairs to bed.


He had to tell someone, and there weren't all that many people he could tell. Janis was in Marin that weekend, Victor knew; it would be a good crowd, and someone would probably take her out after the concert, and she might not want to hear about this after a late night. But he didn't want to tie her up during the travel and rehearsal part of things, and she'd told him she was booked solid right up to the flight, so he held onto the news till Sunday: *Hey gorgeous ping me when it's a good time to talk*

Apparently noon-thirty was a good time, because she texted right back: *Now is good. Conscious, caffeinated, and don't have to go anywhere for three hours. Full report plz was that year worth it?*

*So worth it OMG*

*Best thing?*

*I told him I loved him and he said he loved me too*

*OMG Victor that is AWESOME I'm so happy for you!!*

*Thanks. It helped so much having you to talk to*

*Happy to oblige. What's next? Aside from a lot of fucking I presume*

*LMAO*

*I swear to God I almost had an orgasm when he kissed you at the club*

*LOL stop*

*Does he do everything else like that?*

*STOP*

*Hey, I don't get to see mine very often and frankly he doesn't kiss like that, you can't blame me for imagining how yours does everything else*

Victor was giggling so much he couldn't type for a minute. Once he settled down, he wrote *Let's say he is thorough*

*Oh goddamn you and your hot boyfriend, it's a good goddamned thing I don't have to leave this room for a while*

*LOL well maybe I'll let you get on with whatever. Catch up soon in town tho right?*

*Yes plz go away now*

*ROFL TTYL.* Victor disconnected, giggled some more, blew out a breath and texted Andy: *I've been talking about you. Any chance you're free?*

The reply came back instantly: *Your place or mine?*

Chapter 9

April 2014

*I'm shooting the Cabaret girls tomorrow. Have something else to show you. Any chance you could come over?* Andy sent the text and sat at the desk, waiting for a reply. He'd said he didn't feel moderate, and that had proven to be an understatement; 'insatiable' was more like it. Only after sending that message did he see the innuendo. No doubt Victor would see it too.

The reply that came back definitely seemed to be in the same spirit: *I have something to show you too. And glory be, not called tomorrow. I won't be a distraction?*

*Of course you will be. That is not a problem*

*LOL okay what time?*

*The girls will be here about 11:00. I would be delighted to see you at any time basically starting now*

*I could come straight from Burbank*

*Yes please*

*See you soon XOX Love you*

*Love you too, drive safe.* Andy set down the phone, already turned on. They'd been managing an average of three dates a week, nearly all sleepovers. Andy would go over to Victor's place a couple of times during the week; Victor would join him at the Brewery on the weekend. They were fucking like bonobos. They hadn't been near the dance studio; neither of them had seen any of their other friends; as far as the world knew, they had fallen down a well. He was sure this phase wouldn't last. He had no

135

intention of doing anything to hasten its end. *Get the place ready*, he told himself, because once Victor arrived nothing practical would get done for a while.

Victor showed up with a bag full of provisions from a fancy deli, his overnighter, and a smile. "I got some good news," he said, as soon as the door closed behind him. "Let's put this away and I'll show you."

Andy thought *show me?* but didn't question it. Instead he kissed Victor for a few minutes, helped him put away the food, and then kissed him some more. "Do you keep that bag in your car now?"

"Yes I do." Victor went to retrieve the overnighter. He'd dropped it by the door. "I do not ever want to miss out on a night with you because I left my script or my phone charger or some other bullshit at home." He dug in the bag and pulled out a folded sheet of paper. "Got the report." He handed it to Andy.

Andy was already scanning the page; he glanced up at Victor with a smile. "I got mine too." He finished reading the report. It was everything he'd hoped for: clean, across the board. He handed it back and went over to the desk, found the printed email from his doctor's office, gave it to Victor and watched him read it. It was the same.

Victor laid the paper on the desk. Then he set both hands on the surface and leaned over, head down. "Oh my Lord. I just thought of getting you in my mouth naked and I almost passed out." He knew he was flushed. "I can't decide what I want to do first."

Andy was right up against him, unbuttoning his shirt from behind, mouth on his neck. "You could do that first. Then I could do that."

"Jesus, Andy." His shirt was off. Then his undershirt, Andy's tee shirt, and their jeans. "God *damn* you're gorgeous."

"You are." Andy was walking backward toward the couch, one arm around Victor's waist and the other hand buried in his hair, pulling his head back so he could kiss that perfect mouth. "Or we could do that at the same time."

"Maybe that," Victor said, because he was on fire, he was in Andy's hand now, and then he was on his back. "God, yes, that. Please." Andy moved down his body, got a mouthful, made a sound only slightly less loud than Victor's. "Jesus *Christ*, get around *now*, now Andy –"

Andy kept his mouth on that beautiful naked cock while he rearranged himself. He couldn't wait to feel this. He'd been hoping for this, dreaming of this. "*God*," he said indistinctly when Victor's mouth closed on him. He had his arm wrapped around Victor's thigh, holding it up, listening to the stifled reaction. His own topmost foot was braced against the arm of the couch. The sensation was so intense he couldn't move, could barely remember what he was supposed to be doing. Victor's hips were moving. Andy held still, let Victor fuck his mouth, knowing this would be fast. *Please don't bite*, he thought hilariously. Then a louder sound, something that probably wouldn't have been a word even if Victor didn't have his mouth full. He thrust hard, coming deep in Andy's throat, moaning. He didn't bite. He was breathing fast. He twitched and whimpered as Andy swallowed. Andy let go of him. Braced his hand on the back of the couch and laid his head on the gecko and said "Holy fucking *hell*" because Victor had him in that hot, wet mouth. Giving the task his

137

full attention for a few delirious minutes until Andy bucked against him. "*Fuck!*"

Victor swallowed, slowly drew off. Licked once more, then rested his head on Andy's thigh. Andy was so motionless Victor might have been worried, if it weren't for the soft sounds he was still making, a faint note at the end of every exhalation. His foot was resting on the top of the couch; his head was flung back, dangling off the seat. One arm was under Victor's leg, hand gripping the back of his knee. The other arm was folded, hand lying limply on his ribs. "You should see yourself right now," Victor said after a minute. "Good thing I've got my arm around your back."

"Uh-huh." Andy lifted his head to consider the situation. The upper arm went behind Victor's hip; the upper foot went behind his head. Andy levered himself up as Victor scooted down. A moment later they were sitting up, turned toward each other, both leaning against the back of the couch with one leg folded and the other foot on the floor. Close enough that their knees were almost touching. "I think we set a speed record. You taste good."

"So do you." Maybe someday they'd talk about the history, talk about how they'd both managed to make it through to each other without any dangerous baggage. *We've got plenty of other baggage*, Victor thought. At the moment it didn't seem important. "I was a little out of control there."

Andy smiled. "I liked it." He leaned closer, reached out, touched Victor's face. Swept a thumb across his mouth. Victor closed the distance for a kiss. "I love you."

"I love you too." Victor wanted to say more, wanted to say 'you know I've never said that to a man before, you are the first, you are the only.' Maybe one day he could. When they were both sure this was forever.

It was a good thing the Cabaret girls weren't coming in until eleven o'clock. Andy woke up at eight, but didn't get out of bed because Victor was in it. Somehow everything they'd done the night before did not add up to 'ho hum you again maybe later.' They were putting the freshly-laundered slipcover back on the couch at ten forty-five. Then Andy had a few minutes to arrange his props for the photo shoot. The theme for the June show was 'Going for the Gold,' in honor of two couples who trained at Shall We Dance and were heading for the Dance Sport events at the Gay Games. All four principals were there: Michelle and Rory, Stacey and Kim. It was the first time Victor had seen that process, and he thoroughly enjoyed it.

Dana had come with Rory. She kept Victor company while Andy was busy with the others. "First time you've seen him work?"

"Yeah, it is. I was lucky I didn't get called today."

"Me too." Dana had recurring roles on two series for different networks. Victor thought her management must do an awfully good job with avoiding conflicts. She pretended to watch what Andy was doing. "So how's it going?"

He knew what she meant. "I'm completely in love with him." He glanced over at her. She looked pleased. "You've known him a long time, huh?"

"Eleven years. We met one summer when I was on hiatus from the sitcom and went back East to do a theater thing. He's one of my favorite people in the world."

"Mine too. What show was it?"

"Footloose. He still looked like a teenager. I barely squeaked by."

"Gimme a break, you still look like a teenager." She snorted. Victor smiled. "Okay, twenty-three, max."

She stifled a giggle. Rory shot her a look from the 'awards podium' (three plywood boxes), where she was doing something sexily gymnastic. Dana blew her a kiss.

"What the hell were you giggling about with Dana?" Andy asked later, when they were alone.

"Talking about you and how cute you are." Victor leaned back on the couch. "Told her I'm completely in love with you."

Andy knelt on the couch facing him, straddling his lap, and bent down for a kiss. Victor wrapped his arms around Andy's back, eyes closed, mouth open, drinking in one of those moments of uninhibited passion that kept catching him by surprise. Andy pulled back a little, hands on Victor's face, and waited for his hot, sleepy eyes to focus. "I love you," he said.

Dana and Rory invited Andy and Victor over for dinner soon after the Cabaret photo shoot. Andy noticed that Victor was a bit nervous on the way. "What's going on, catnip? I've known these girls forever. They know you. They know all about you. All about you and me," he amended, because Victor's history wasn't his to share.

"I think it's because this is our first time doing a thing that feels personal," Victor said after a few seconds to think about it. "I know they're cool, but

140

they've been your friends a long time. They probably had ideas about who you should be with."

"Are you fucking kidding me?" Andy glanced over from the driver's seat. "The minute they found out about you they were lighting candles. I mean yes, they love me and they care about me. Which is why as soon as they knew I was in love with you, they wanted you for me."

Victor was staring at him. "When was that?"

Andy glanced over again. "That day last March. Last year. I owed them an explanation for that night at the club when I took you backstage. Went over there for dinner after you left, and told them everything."

"Last *year*? And you still made me wait?"

"Tell me I was wrong."

Andy hadn't been wrong, and Victor knew it. He'd needed that time to settle into being himself, on his own, without leaning on anyone. "Did you really want me to fuck other people?"

"No, but if you were ever going to, I wanted it to be when you weren't fucking me. I don't like to share."

Victor huffed out a laugh. "I don't either." After a minute he said, "I was tempted a few times. I got frustrated, and there were opportunities. But I remembered what it was like with you, and I didn't want to mess that up. I thought it was important to be tempted, to be frustrated, and still be faithful. That seemed like something a grown-up would do."

Andy had to take a moment. "I would still love you. But that means a lot to me." They were almost to West Hollywood.

Victor waited until Andy pulled into the driveway at the cottage before he said, "I woke up in the middle of the night after we talked in the green room that time. You were asleep, you had your arm across me, and I thought, this is all I'll ever want. I didn't think I deserved it."

Andy turned off the car and set the parking brake, then draped his left arm over the steering wheel and turned to face Victor. "Well, are you over that now?"

Victor's eyebrows went up. "Yeah, I am. I earned it. You made me wait a fucking *year*, you vicious bastard." Andy made a half-apologetic face. Victor leaned over and kissed him. Then they got out of the car.

The cottage door opened as they walked up. Rory stood in the doorway, tilted her head to one side, and said, "So about that whole year and a day thing."

Andy rolled his eyes. Victor said, "Worth it."

"Do you agree with that, Mr. Martin?" She couldn't help noticing Andy had his arm around his lover.

"I'd like to answer that with a glass of wine in my hand," he said pointedly. She stood back to let them in. "Where's that red menace of a cat? Oh. Victor, that is Spike."

He looked up at the top of the stairs. "Jeez, that's a big cat. This is a cute place. Do you sleep up there?"

"Yes we do." Rory had a full glass in each hand. She gave one to Victor and one to Andy, then looked over her shoulder at Dana, who was leaning on the kitchen counter next to her own wineglass.

"Victor, you should know we've been following this story for going on fifteen months," Dana said. "I got to talk to you at the photo shoot but Rory kind of didn't. So apologies for this and any other interrogation."

"I am not *interrogating*," Rory said with a scowl. "I asked *one question*." Dana snickered.

"The answer is yes." Andy sipped his wine. His free hand was still, or again, on Victor's hip. "Worth it. Come on, catnip. Let me show you how these ladies set the scene for seduction." He led the way to the dining den.

For those first few weeks, Victor barely spoke to anybody he didn't see at work or at home. Janis obviously knew the Andy situation had progressed. Valerie would know soon enough, if Janis hadn't already told her. Tanith was there at Chrome that night, so everybody she knew would know by now; Victor certainly hadn't asked her to keep it quiet. The past few months, he'd been practically skywriting 'I am chasing Andy Martin.' But after they came up for air, he thought about Gino, who by now should be in a groove in Vegas. So when Victor had a day off from the TV show that didn't happen to overlap with a free spot on Andy's schedule, he decided to check in: *Hey Mr Corsetti according to the internet you're catching on there in LV. How do you like it so far?*

He'd apparently chosen a good time; a reply came straight back: *Had to get a humidifier for my room this fucking desert air but generally good. Getting a nice crowd at the lounge most nights. How's things with you?*

*Mission accomplished*

*LMFAO does that mean you're getting laid?*

*And how*

The next text was slightly delayed: *Sorry had to laugh for a minute. Won't ask for details because I haven't found one here yet and don't want to get all worked up. Any travel plans?*

That sounded like a hint. Victor hadn't been thinking of going anywhere. *Nothing yet. My agent hooked me up with another play this summer*

*Good for you. Haven't decided if I'm going to look for side gigs. This one's pretty mellow*

*Sometimes it's nice not to hustle. That's me while Vice is in production*

*You're doing good. Keep me posted esp if you want to come out here. I've got some connections now*

*I'll bet. Take care of those pipes*

*Will do. Thanks for checking in.* Victor disconnected, wondering if he should show this to Andy. He should at least mention it. He wasn't really sure what the rules were. But he liked Gino, and he liked the idea of going over to Las Vegas sometime with Andy to see him perform. So the next time they got together, he asked. "A friend of mine has a new gig in Vegas," he said, after dinner and before they went to bed. "He saw the video of 'Mating Game' and said I should bring you over there."

"Oh he did, huh?" Andy leaned back in his chair, smiling. They were at his place, where they always ate at the big desk before transferring to the couch or the sleeping loft. "How much does this guy know about me?"

"A lot," Victor confessed. "I knew him from a few years back when we did a play together. We had a date last summer. It was a really good date, but you know I had my own agenda." Andy snickered. Victor smiled. "Anyway I didn't want to give him the wrong idea so I told him what was going on. We've been friends since then."

"And he's in Vegas now. Doing what?"

"Sinatra tribute show in this high-class lounge. I think it's a long-term-contract kind of deal. He said he was ready to put down some roots."

"Well, good for him. I've got a friend out there myself." A friend who, it seemed, might be in the same category: someone who'd been a possibility, if this hadn't worked out. "Maybe we should introduce them," he suggested. "My guy is a trainer for a show. He's got a house and everything."

"Maybe we could have a double date."

Andy was grinning. "Let me ping Sergei. Tell him to go see this guy. What's his name?"

"Gino Corsetti." Victor watched while Andy sent the text, admiring the ease of the whole conversation. No jealousy, no bullshit, only this sense of 'hey maybe our friends will like each other, maybe we'll all be friends now.' He had no idea if this kind of thing happened with other guys. It seemed to happen all the time with Andy. "Want to see his message?"

Andy swooned a little. "Oh sweetheart. I don't need to verify anything. I trust you."

"I trust you too. I love you."

"I love you too." Andy scooted his chair closer so he could get a kiss. "Let's clean this up and go to bed."


Midway through May, Andy finally brought his mother up to date. She knew about Victor's concert, about the successful conclusion of that Year of Maybe. Andy had promised to fill her in when he had a minute. Their usual time for a phone rendezvous was Saturday morning, unless Andy had a shoot

145

somewhere. He debated making the call, because Victor was with him. *Use your words*, he reminded himself. "Is it okay if I call my Mom? This is sort of our usual time."

"I don't mind." Victor stretched luxuriously. He was almost done shooting; all they had left was clean-up for the season-ending episode. No more locations, no more late nights. He'd come straight from Burbank again, and he didn't have to be anywhere until late Monday morning. "Want me to bring some more coffee up here?"

"That would be great. Thanks sweetness." Andy accepted a kiss and watched his lover exit the loft, gloriously naked. He sat up, reached for his phone, and placed the call. His mother picked up on the second ring. "Hi Mom. What do you mean, late? It's seven o'clock in the morning here in La La Land. Considering how I spent the night you're lucky I'm calling at all. Victor's here."

Victor heard that, down in the kitchen, and had a moment of vertigo. *That's how his life is*, he thought. *No wonder.* He filled the mugs, added half and half, and started back to the stairs, listening.

"Yes. He's sensational. Best ever. For God's sake, Mom, do your church ladies know you ask about my sex life?" He laughed, watching Victor finish the climb and set down his mug, then go to the other side of the bed and sit cross-legged, watching him. Andy listened to a question, then put the phone on speaker. "You want details? You dirty old lady. You saw that picture, you know exactly what he looks like. I think that's as much detail as you need."

"That tattoo of the deer, that's so beautiful."

Victor looked startled. Andy said, "Mom, you're on speaker. Victor, this is Eva. Say hello to Victor, Mom."

146

"Hello Victor!"

"Hi Eva." Victor knew his face was saying 'what;' Andy was grinning. "Nice to meet you."

"I've been dying to talk to you! Ever since last year, no, since before. Oh, Andy said some bad things about you."

"I'm sure he did."

"Not anymore. He's so happy he doesn't even make sense."

Victor glanced at Andy, who rolled his eyes. "I'm happy too. I'm glad he gave me another chance."

"He made you work for it!"

"Well, yeah." Eva laughed. Victor said, "It was a very educational year. He's worth it. I really love him." Andy patted him in a 'me too' kind of way.

Eva said, "He loves you too. He told me. We're both so happy, Ronnie and me. It's too bad he already left. He'll be mad he missed you."

Andy said, "Is he out on the boat?"

"Yes, what he calls fishing. He sits out there with his cooler, Victor. Bait and sandwiches and beer. Old men in Miami, *pfft*." Eva's tone was so resigned that Victor laughed. "We'll take you fishing when you come visit. Can you swim?"

"Yes ma'am, I grew up in Puerto Vallarta. We swam all the time. I'd love to go fishing with you." It had never occurred to him that was a thing that could happen. Going to Miami with Andy. Meeting his parents. Being part of the family. He swallowed hard.

Andy noticed. He patted Victor's thigh and took the phone off speaker. "It's just me now Mom. Yes, we'll talk about when we could come out. His series is about to go on hiatus but he's doing a play here in

147

town over the summer. We're probably going over to Vegas for a minute, we've each got a friend out there. I've got all my usual bullshit." He listened for a minute. Victor set down his mug and stretched out with his head on Andy's thigh. Andy set his coffee aside so he could put his hand in Victor's hair. "Did Pop do anything about the driveway? For God's sake, Mom. Last time I was there it was like a flow chart made of potholes, it's a wonder you can even get your car in and out. Yes, tell him I bitched about it again. You know if it's money I can help. Okay, whatever." Another pause, Andy caressing Victor while he listened. "Well, yes. Completely. God, yes, if I weren't doing photography we would never have met. I'd probably be out in Vegas with Sergei training showgirls, not here in L.A. falling in love with a TV star. Oh, he'll be a star." A full-throated laugh. "No, I'm not going to show the world that picture. He might let me take some more, though. Yeah, something he could publish without getting invited to a porn convention. Yes, I'll call you next week. I love you too." He disconnected, set the phone aside, looked down at Victor. Brushed his fingers down the side of his face, down his neck. Circled his throat, letting his ring scrape against the silver chain, watching Victor shiver. *God you're gorgeous.* Visible arousal, triggering his own.

"What picture?" Victor could hardly remember any specifics, but he knew there had been quite a few that were borderline porn. Or straight-up porn. He still couldn't quite believe he let Andy take those, much less keep them. "Which one did you send her?"

"I'll show you in a minute. Or ten. Jesus, Victor, you're irresistible. Kiss me." He didn't, though. He tugged the sheet down, put his mouth on Andy's

148

naked thigh, then on his erection. "Holy *hell*." One hand between Andy's legs, then his whole body. The other hand on himself, making the sounds that meant he wasn't going to be moved till he was satisfied. Andy wanted to close his eyes and concentrate on the sensation, but he couldn't bear to not see this. He was breathing through his mouth, hearing himself. Breaths getting faster, harsher, more vocal, and then actual words. "God almighty, Victor, you're so fucking gorgeous, Jesus *Christ* that mouth, oh my *God* I'm going to have that cock later I swear I want to taste that –" He came hard, thrusting up into Victor's mouth, barely conscious of the satisfied grunt or of his own exclamation. Eyes closed for a moment as Victor swallowed, then open again because he knew what happened next and he couldn't not see it. "Yes, Jesus, do it now, come for me, *now* Victor, fucking *yes*." Victor's mouth was on his thigh again, open, panting. Andy tipped his head back against the wall, thinking *I need to get a headboard. Something I can tie him to.* He laughed softly.

"What."

"For some reason I keep thinking of porntastic pictures I want to take of you." Victor snickered. Andy curled down onto the bed, running a hand down Victor's leg. "I love you."

Victor shifted, reorganizing himself away from the wet spot, and cuddled close. "I love you too."

Chapter 10

June 2014

After a quick trip to Vegas (where interesting things were happening) Victor decided to do a second mini-concert at Chrome, to fill an empty night in August. This time, he wanted to go with a slightly longer set of Latin-inflected songs. He got in touch with his arranger Valerie, and she lined up the same musicians. A text came in from Janis: *Glad you're doing it again. Is Andy going to sing with you?*

Victor had thought of that too. He wasn't sure Andy would want to; getting back out on stage did not seem to be a goal, much less a priority. But the thought of doing something together had a lot of appeal. He wrote back *I'll ask him.* The next time he went over to the Brewery, he brought a first draft of his set list. "I was wondering," he said, "if you'd like to do a number."

Andy glanced up from the list. "You talkin' to *me*?"

Victor gave him a look. "The whole world knows you can sing."

"One little bit part."

"Gimme a break, you're a fucking meme machine."

Andy leaned back, grinning. "How long do I get to decide and or come up with a suggestion?"

"Only till we get dressed again."

"We aren't even *un*dressed."

"Yet." Victor started unbuttoning his shirt.

Andy tilted his head to one side. "You know once you get your clothes off you can talk me into anything."

"Can I really?" Victor took off the shirt, and unbuttoned his jeans. The zipper went down with that nasty little *zzzzzt* sound that, these days, always got Andy's heart rate up. He stood up and pulled his tee shirt over his head. Victor watched. "You've gotten some color."

"That's because you keep dragging me to the beach on your days off." Andy untied the drawstring of his shorts. They fell to the floor a moment later.

"And your legs look even more amazing than last year."

*They should*, Andy thought, but said, "Quit flattering me, you seducer you." Victor came close, in undershirt and briefs, and pressed up against Andy's bare back. He let his hands wander, his mouth on Andy's neck. Andy rubbed his cheek against Victor's hair, and stood there doing nothing else, eyes closed, while Victor got them both warmed up. Then he turned around. "Get this thing off," he said against Victor's mouth. "Get both these things off."

"You do it," said Victor. "My hands are full." That was actually true, but one way or another the clothes had to go. Andy disengaged enough to pull Victor's undershirt off, kneel and tug down the briefs, and put his mouth where it wanted to be. "Damn! You feel good."

"So do you. Stand still."

"Uh-uh. Couch. Now." They stumbled over to the big couch and stopped talking.


Later, Andy said, "'Miss Chatelaine.'" He was on his back with Victor in his arms, lazily stroking up and down the arm across his chest. They'd both fallen asleep for a few minutes. It felt like such a luxury,

151

every time. Waking up together was the best thing in the world.

"Huh?" Victor sounded drowsy.

"I want to sing 'Miss Chatelaine.' It's a samba, you know."

Victor laughed for a long time, while Andy listened with growing vexation. Then he said, "Whatever you want, baby."

"It's a *metaphor*," Andy snapped, half-pissed. The other half didn't blame Victor for thinking this was funny. "Listen." He sat them up. Victor settled against the back of the couch, watching and listening as Andy sang it, soft and low, jazzier and slower than the original. His supple baritone never sounded so right.

Victor was stunned. "You're right. Jesus, you're right," he said humbly. "That'll kill."

"Don't you forget, sonny, I was making a living on stage when you were still mooning over lounge singers in cheesy tourist hotels." Andy was looking around for the coffee mug he could have sworn was on the desk.

"I'm sorry."

"I forgive you," Andy said grandly, and got up to go to the kitchen. He gave his ass an extra twitch, and looked over his shoulder to make sure Victor noticed. Then he whipped around, aghast. Victor was sitting forward on the couch with his hands over his face. "Honey, what's the matter?"

"It's just. I know, you're a better dancer than me, you're a better singer than me. I get it I get it I get it."

*Jesus, fuck, no.* "No. No, honey, stop." He went back to the couch, sat beside Victor, and gathered him

152

into his arms. For a moment there was resistance, then he let Andy pull him close. "Catnip, I am *ten years older* than you. I was studying music and dance literally before you were born. I'm not *better*. I'm simply more experienced."

Victor didn't say anything. Andy asked, "Have you ever even had a voice lesson?" Victor shook his head. "So you're this goddamned good from natural talent, and probably being a smart listener. Do you know how rare that is?" Still no response. Andy kissed his forehead. "I feel like such a prick right now. I'm sorry."

Victor sighed. "No, I'm … overreacting, I guess. All this is still really new, you know?"

"And I don't help when I forget it's new to you. Look, I can hook you up with a voice coach if you're really feeling insecure. I went to see her before my casino thing, she's great. Two, maybe three sessions, but you're really seriously good already. You do know that, right?"

"Eh."

"You made me cry with that torch song, and I'm a cynical old bitch." He gave it a few seconds. "Also I really hate to cry." That got half a smile. "You know I was a chorus boy. And I mostly loved it. But."

"Yeah?"

"Being in a chorus is … you're in this insular little world for weeks, sometimes months at a time. You go everywhere together, you do everything together. If there's a threat from outside - whether that's a bad review or a gang of rednecks or AIDS - everybody bands together. But on the ordinary? It's competitive. It's a new pissing match every day, and every other sentence is 'fuck you.' We're a bunch of shit-flinging gibbons.''

Victor laughed a little. "No."

The laugh was a relief. "I assure you. And I still go there because so many of my friends are from that world. But I should never do it with you, because I love you and because it's stupid. So don't let me do that. Tell me, Andy, you're being a shit-flinging gibbon.''

"I can't say that," Victor protested, finally smiling. "How about, hey monkey. *Monito.*"

Andy nodded. "That's good." He regarded Victor for a moment. "I really didn't mean to be mean. I'm sorry. We okay?"

"Yeah, we're okay."

"Besides, you know you're ten times a better actor than me. It's like Laurence Olivier versus Shia LaBeouf, not even a contest." He'd forgotten all about going to the kitchen. Instead, he kissed Victor again. After a while they had something to eat, and watched a movie. Andy was realizing that he wasn't quite the relationship expert he'd thought. He was glad Victor didn't have to go home tonight. He had a few hours to settle them both down.


A couple of weeks later, Victor called to ask if he could come over again. They hadn't seen each other during the interim because of work commitments. Two weeks felt like another year; Andy's imagination immediately ran wild. He said, "Duh, of course. What's up?" *Aside from me.*

"Aside from me?" Victor heard Andy laugh. "I've got something for you to listen to."

"Bring it, sweetness." Andy disconnected and got busy cleaning up his latest mess, preparing the scene for seduction.

Victor showed up about an hour later. After they kissed hello, he handed over a CD with a hand-printed label reading 'VG Aug14 no15.'

"What's this?"

"The arrangement for the last song I want to do. Valerie automagicked some sheet music on here too, so I could show it to you."

"Okay. Cool. You want something to drink? I made some coffee."

"You read my mind. We had a late shoot last night."

"I figured, when you didn't text till after midnight."

"You weren't waiting up, were you?"

"Not exactly," Andy hedged. Victor was not deceived. They went over to the computer and Andy loaded the disc. He went to get their coffee while the track played, a rumba arrangement of 'La Vie en Rose.' "It's like the Tony Bennett - k.d. lang version, huh?"

"You like it?"

"It's nice. Great one to close the show."

"Well, it's actually pretty much exactly that version."

"Eh?" Andy set his coffee on the desk and sat down to open the sheet music file. "Oh! It's a duet! Who are you going to do it with?"

"I was hoping that would be you."

Andy looked up, a smile dawning. "Well, I'm going to be there anyway."

"Super convenient."

"You sure? The gossip mags are going to be all over that."

"You've been to my place, you know I got a print of that snap from the other show." Someone in the audience at Victor's March set had taken a photograph of the moment they kissed, and it had made the rounds online. "I tell anyone who asks that we're together."

"Come here." Andy tugged him over and down to sit on his lap. "Give me that mouth, you gorgeous man." A few minutes later he said against Victor's throat, "I didn't think this through."

Victor snickered. There was no way that task chair was up to this task. He stood up and backed toward the couch. "I think we'll be more comfortable over here, don't you?" Andy had his shirt off in a few seconds, Victor's shirt joined it on the floor a few seconds after that, and then Victor was underneath him on the couch and they were kissing as if they were getting paid for it. "Jesus, Andy," Victor said when he could. "I love you."

Andy moved off enough to unbutton Victor's jeans. "I love you too. Tell me you don't have to leave here tonight."

"I don't have to leave." He had spare clothes at the loft now. "I wish I never had to leave." Andy looked up, tugging the jeans off and tossing them on the floor, running his hands up Victor's bare legs. "Put your hand on me."

"This hand?" The one with the ring. Andy knew Victor liked it. He skimmed it up that perfect body, all the way to Victor's throat, around into his hair, then back down. Ever so lightly, right down the middle. Cupping, fondling, then skimming up again. Brushing over the stag. Thumb running under Victor's jaw, the ring rasping against the silver chain.

"More. Please." He blew out a breath as Andy's hand swept down and closed around him.

"Like this?" Andy stretched out alongside him, hand busy, one leg in between Victor's, mouth on his chest. Then, after a few minutes, "Or like this?" He shifted over, face against Victor's, hand curled around both of them.

Victor surged against that hand. "Sweet Jesus yes. Oh *God*," and they both lost their minds.

August 2014

Andy was still thinking about that a couple of weeks later, when they met up with the musicians and Valerie for a rehearsal of the Latin set. Victor might have been too, though he didn't have as much time for daydreaming. They kept glancing at each other like 'any minute now.' Victor could tell Andy was about to have a fit of the giggles. "Get a grip, Mr. Martin," he said, and then Andy did crack up. Victor pinched the bridge of his nose and tried to keep it together.

Valerie rolled her eyes and waited for them to settle down. When they eventually did, getting through the song with an appropriate degree of seriousness, she was satisfied. "You realize you guys could take this show on the road," she said, when the musicians had packed up and gone.

"Oh, come on," said Victor. "You're kidding, right?"

"I'm serious. There are not a million clubs that would book an act like this, but you could easily get a gig every month right here in town. Re-work a few more numbers as duets. It would run."

"For real?" Andy hadn't even thought of something like that.

"Adult love songs performed – really well, I might add – by an out gay couple? Whether geared to the queer audience or not, there is not a ton of competition out there, but in that space I think you're unique. You should talk to your agents about it." She finished packing up her gear. "Anyway, break a leg. I wish I could be there but I've got this session in Portland."

"Thanks, Valerie. I'll be in touch." Victor held the door for her, then turned and looked at Andy. "Bet you never expected that, huh? I sure didn't."

"It's like ... dancing well together, that wasn't such a surprise after that first night we had. Singing well together is a whole 'nother critter. Let's listen to the playback." They reset the rehearsal recording and listened to the duet, looking at each other throughout. Victor raised his eyebrows, with a little tilt to his head. Andy shrugged. "We do blend. It is ... professional."

That was, to Victor, the highest possible compliment. He reached over to dig his hand into Andy's hair, pulling him close for a kiss, wishing they could go home together. But Andy had a thing he had to get to early the next day. They kissed goodbye in the parking lot, said 'I love you,' and parted. Victor hated it every time.

When he got home, he sent a note to Janis: *Valerie said she thinks we could take this show on the road*

The reply came about a half-hour later: *You probably could. You guys should definitely cut an album sometime. Although for the record (HA) parts of the process are a giant pain in the ass*

*Are they sending you on tour for the new one?*

*YES meant to tell you but you were too busy flirting with Andy. Out of state this time, so excited, EEEK. I'm moving out of this apartment in west bumfuck. All my shit's going back to Mom and Dad's very soon*

*Let me know if you need a hand*

*Thanks maybe I'll put Stefan to some use*

*LOL okay. Is he coming to the show this time?*

*Grrr no*

*Oops*

*Getting him out of Claremont is a fucking TASK*

Victor laughed out loud for real. *Thanks for all your help chica*

*Glad to be part of it. See you soon!*


They both wore their dance suits for the Latin mini-concert, with white shirts. Victor wore his silver chain. Andy watched him under the spotlight and thought *Still cannot believe it*. Victor finished his first seven songs, and after the applause introduced Andy. They passed each other as Andy went on; Victor made sure their hands brushed. Andy couldn't help glancing over at him, standing in the wing, as he sang 'Miss Chatelaine' to close the first half. He put his heart into it, deeply happy to be back on stage, loving Victor even more for giving him this moment. The applause was loud and long. When the curtain closed for the intermission, Andy and Victor grinned at each other, then turned to thank the musicians.

"Everybody good? Anybody need water?" Rory was stage-managing and mama-bear-ing. "You both sound amazing."

"Thanks chica. I have to stretch for a minute." Andy went to the green room and threw one leg up on

159

the barre. "Ay caramba." He switched legs. "Urrrrrrrgh."

Victor had followed him in and was doing some upper-body stretches. After a while he said, "I feel better about it this time. That coach was great. And it's nice having you up here with me."

"You could do that jazz set again some time. Pretty sure you'd sell out again."

"Would you do a number with me?"

"Well you know, you could *probably* talk me into that. I'm easy." They were smiling at each other, possibly wondering whether they had time to make out a little, when the two-minute alarm pinged. Andy made an irritated sound and Victor patted him consolingly. They had to check the mirror and get ready to go back on.

Andy stood offstage watching again while Victor did his seven songs alone, approving of his confident stage presence. Then Victor said, "And now please welcome back the lovely and talented Andy Martin." There was laughter and applause as Andy went back onstage, carrying the second mic. They hit their marks, waited for the music to cue them in, and sang together.

After the encore, the bows, and the requisite post-show mingling with an amazing number of friends who'd shown up, Andy and Victor sat down with Tanith for a nightcap. "That was really good," she said. "Even better than last time."

"Andy hooked me up with a coach," said Victor. "Made a world of difference."

"Well, you know. Remember the difference in Madonna from before and after 'Evita'?"

"Yeah. We should do 'What Went Down' again," Victor suggested.

"I'd have to write you some more songs."

Andy made a *pfft* noise. "You'd have to make him the star, are you kidding?"

"Now you know, the bad guy cannot be the star unless you are making a Tarantino movie." Tanith watched Andy laugh into his drink. "But that said, when we did it before I was already like 'if I knew he was going to be this good I would have written more for him.' So, you know." She shrugged.

"Maybe you should write a whole new show."

Victor said, "Maybe you should stop! Obnoxious."

"Hey, nothing ventured. It would have to have chorus boys, though," Andy said, very seriously, and Tanith cracked up. "But I hear you're doing a thing here that has, like, no script at all."

"Dance concert," she said briefly. "End of September. Based on Beowulf. Want to do promo pictures for us?"

"Just tell me when."


After Victor's concert, between the end of his play and the beginning of his new season with 'L.A. Vice,' he and Andy made it over to Miami. Victor wasn't sure what to expect; he'd never been to the city before, and had only the vaguest idea of what it might be like. As their plane came around for a landing, he was watching through the window. "How is this place not underwater?"

"Some of it already is. Mom and Pop live in Shorecrest, and high tides wash up on their street once in a while. It's down there." Andy pointed past Victor.

"Mom found an eight-inch blue crab on their front step one time. She claims they had it for breakfast." He was close to Victor, so he stole a kiss. "We will *not* be staying in their house. Pop and I get along great, and you know what Mom is like, but we wouldn't get any sleep there. He's up early and she's up late. I made us a hotel reservation."

"I could have taken care of that."

"You got the flight." Another kiss. Then he spoke softly, close to Victor's face, where no one else could possibly hear. "I'm so excited I can't stand it. I know you're nervous. This is new for me, too. Do you believe that?"

By now, Victor did believe it. He still didn't know how it was possible, but everything in the past five months supported that conclusion. Everything Dana and Rory said, or any of Andy's other friends. They were all now Victor's friends, and each one of them said, in their own way, 'he's never been like this before.' The friends that Victor brought to the table said, 'he's perfect for you.' He gazed at Andy and said, "Janis says we make her believe in love songs."

"We make me believe, too." They held hands without talking until it was time to exit the plane.


Nothing about that visit was anything Victor could have expected. The way Andy was with his parents – exactly the same way he was with everyone else – blew his mind. As did the way Eva and Ronnie were, both with their son and with Victor, as if they couldn't imagine anything better than for them to be together.

Eva was short and curvy and cute. When she hugged Victor, her face was right against his chest.

Ronnie was Victor's own height, and bulky. Andy had Eva's eyes and Ronnie's nose. God only knew where the willowy height came from. In the afternoon of their second day, after dropping Eva and Ronnie at home following a leisurely brunch at the hotel, Andy took Victor out onto the beach. They walked all the way up, and all the way down, hand in hand. The water was warm. They were both tanned; it was the most Latino Victor had ever seen Andy. "You are amazing," he said after a mostly-quiet hour. "I can't believe I'm here with you."

*I can't either*, Andy thought. "Ready for the fiesta tonight?" Eva and Ronnie were hosting. Andy was hoping it wouldn't all be too much for Victor. The family (a very loose term) was a lot even for someone who was used to that kind of thing, and he knew Victor wasn't. "If it gets to be too much we can bail."

Victor glanced over, frowning a little. Bailing out of a family thing was the last thing he wanted to do. Before he could say so, he got distracted. He'd been trying not to stare at Andy this whole time, because all they had on was shorts and flip-flops. If Victor looked for too long – like, five seconds – he started thinking of getting his hands and his mouth on that brown body. Started imagining the way it would feel and taste. Remembering it, with undiminished hunger, as if it had been days since their last time and not hours. *Fuck*, he thought, almost laughing. "What was that again?"

Andy was cracking up. That look had started with one sort of intention and then quickly derailed. *Never fails*, he thought. "Let's get in the water for a minute." Waist deep, at least. He wondered if Victor would let him do anything under the water, there in plain view of the beach. A lot of people were out there. Better not conduct that experiment. Not till it was dark, anyway.

"Good idea." Victor stepped out of his flip-flops, stuck them in the waistband of his shorts, and waded out. Andy was right behind him. "What happens if I kiss you out here."

"We probably commit some kind of indecency," Andy said. "I'm already a little indecent."

"Me too."

"So let's talk about something else for a minute. Party tonight. Totally casual, but everybody's going to be all over you because I haven't brought anybody home for a really long time. Like, kids were born and grew up and graduated from high school since the last time. So what will help you get through that?" The subtext was 'are you sure you want to do this.'

Victor heard it loud and clear. "I can't wait to meet everyone. I hope they feel like you made the right choice."

"Jesus, Victor, are you even serious? For me to bring you home is like I won a Tony award or something. God I want to kiss you right now."

Victor wanted that too. "Could we go back to the room?"

"I think we'd better." They waded out, not touching, both going into low-voiced commentary on everyone else out there so they wouldn't look at each other or think about what they were going to do up in the room. Not too much, anyway.

About an hour later, Andy rolled over onto his back, stretched, and sighed. "That is the only reason I didn't kiss you on the beach, you know."

Victor huffed out a laugh. "I know. Me too. Every goddamned time, it's like hello. Those shorts were not going to get the job done." Andy was giggling. "Besides, now we're all relaxed." He rolled onto his front and studied Andy for a minute.

"What?"

"Checking for evidence." Andy made a yummy sound that was almost enough to get Victor going again. "You wouldn't mind, would you, if I marked you."

"Not one bit. Go right ahead."

"Later." Victor leaned close for one more kiss. "Time to get cleaned up."

Midway through the fiesta, Victor realized he wasn't worried anymore. Maybe 'worried' wasn't even the correct word; maybe 'uneasy' was better. The approval of all these people meant so much; it felt so consequential. He wasn't sure he'd successfully hidden that from Andy. Probably he hadn't. In any case, it didn't seem to matter now. The gathering was so much like a big family party in Jalisco.

The only thing really different was the fact that Victor was there with someone. With Andy, with him in every sense of the word, and everyone there knew it. They could look at each other, smile at each other, touch and hug and hold hands and even kiss, and nobody minded. Everybody was happy. Maybe Victor would ask later, were there people who wouldn't have approved, people who couldn't handle this kind of relationship. Was this everybody, or was there someone you didn't get to see, because I was here.

Or maybe he wouldn't ask. Because the mere fact that he was here meant Andy had made that choice. He'd planted his rainbow flag long ago. Bringing Victor was a message to everyone: if you want to see me, this is who you'll see me with. Victor wondered if

Andy had any idea how much that meant. How hopelessly, thoroughly, endlessly in love he was.

He realized Eva was standing beside him. She patted his back. "He's so happy," she said. "It makes me happy. He waited so long for the right one."

Every time someone said something like that – he'd heard it many times tonight – Victor got a little choked up. "You're sure I'm the right one?"

She made a dismissive sound. "No doubt about it. You've got it all." Victor waved that off, pleased. Eva was looking across the room at her son. "I'm sorry about your mother. Andy told us. He said that was why your first date didn't end so good."

"Thank you. I should have told him everything then."

"Yes, you should!" She patted him again, looking up to make eye contact. "It's okay. Sometimes it's good when we have to work for something."

"It was good for me. I only wish I could have gotten all that work out of the way before we met."

"Maybe not," she said, surprising him. "This way he saw you do it. Nobody ever worked that hard for him before."

Victor turned toward her. "Now see, this is what keeps blowing my mind. He is so, so *everything*. I can't believe no-one else ever thought so."

"One or two came close." She shrugged, as if none of that mattered now. "You know how to dance bachata?" Victor tuned into the music, made a 'maybe?' face. Eva took his hand, smiling. "I'll teach you."

Andy watched his lover dancing with his mother and fell in love all over again. It kept happening.

Waking up together, dancing together, laughing together. Everything felt so perfectly right, he almost didn't trust it. Not because that feeling had betrayed him before, but because he'd never had it before. New and scary.

The whole house was still full of people. Relatives of various degrees, friends going back for years. Victor had been uneasy at first, Andy could tell. Maybe he'd thought this was some kind of test he had to pass. But he looked happy now with Eva, more relaxed. She was always good at settling people down. It was a talent Andy usually shared, though he clearly hadn't said or done quite the right things with Victor. Or maybe he had, and Victor's history got in the way. It was hard for Andy to imagine going to a family gathering and not being wholly himself. That must have been Victor's entire experience up to now. No wonder he still hadn't quite figured it out.

They made eye contact across the room. That kept happening, too. Keeping track of each other. *Jesus, he's beautiful.* Andy wondered what his lover saw in his face right now. Wondered if Victor could tell how completely, irretrievably, irrevocably in love he was.

Chapter 11

A month later they were at Chrome again to see another Mating Dance show. This one was called 'Bandstand' and featured a number of performances inspired by World War II. "It's nice of them to do these on Sundays," Victor said. "Otherwise I would have missed it." It was the one day of the week that he reliably had off. The next day, he was doing a night shoot.

"I don't know how they landed on Sundays and Mondays, but it must be working for the club. These girls have been running shows here for at least four years."

"When did you start doing the posters?"

"Three years ago." The lights dimmed, signaling the imminent performance. Andy moved over to the bar. Victor leaned against him, thinking *I wish I'd known you then*. A few minutes later the room went dark and the curtain opened.

Rory and Dana were there on the same night as Andy and Victor. They knew both men wanted to perform again, but Victor had been out on location a lot and the schedule didn't work. During the final number, an adagio by Dmitri and Michelle set to 'I'll Be Seeing You,' Dana looked over to the bar and nudged Rory. Their friends were standing there, Andy holding Victor back to front, Victor's arms wrapped over Andy's. They were watching the dancers, but their heads were tipped ever so slightly toward each other. At the end, they didn't applaud with the rest of the audience. Victor turned his head and Andy kissed him.

"You know it takes a lot for me to miss a piece of Dmitri dancing," Rory said after a moment.

"I know. Good thing we've already seen it before."

"Yeah, just as well. This one always makes me bawl." Rory got her phone out. "Have to bust their chops."

"I know you do."


Andy's phone buzzed, but he wasn't ready to let go of Victor. It buzzed twice more before Victor started laughing. "That thing is not helping." The phone was in Andy's front pocket, right up against the base of Victor's spine.

"Or maybe it is," Andy said, and kissed him again. Then he let go of his lover and fished out his phone. The messages read: *Hey schmoopy*. Then: *Clap for your friends you jerk*. Then: *GET A ROOM*. He was giggling. Victor read the texts, then looked around the room. He spotted Rory and Dana. Another text rolled in: *Quit grinning like that you better be ready to say something nice to Dmitri*

Andy texted back: *Already saw it and already did and we'll be going now*

*GOOD IDEA.* Still giggling, the men waved to the women as they made their way to the stairs. They were holding hands as they went outside, thinking about what they were going to do next. They weren't paying much attention to the people around them, but couldn't help hearing someone say "Mr. Garcia?"

Victor turned to see a stringer from Pop Quiz, one of the entertainment sites. Her handheld camera was on. He gave her a professional smile. "Hi Sherry, how are you tonight?"

"I'm good, thanks, and you?" He did a 'we're great' thing and she smiled. "I was hoping to see another dance from the two of you. Any plans?"

"My schedule's been a little difficult this year," he said. "Mr. Martin's being very patient. We're hoping to get to some milongas after I'm done shooting out of town."

"Mr. Martin, I read about your last show but didn't have a chance to see it. What's next for you?"

He glanced at Victor, who was still holding his hand. "I have a new show going up next month. I'd be delighted to see you at the opening." He dug a business card out of his jacket pocket with his free hand. She took it with a nod of thanks. "Send me an email and I'll give you the date."

"Thanks very much. Look forward to seeing you both again."

"Thanks Sherry." Victor nodded to her again, and stepped away. Still holding onto Andy, who squeezed his hand. "I really do want to get to some milongas."

"Me too." Andy had the idea Sherry was still watching. "Want to give her a little preview?" He didn't wait for Victor to answer, simply turned toward him, wrapped his right arm around Victor's back, and starting tangoing toward his car. Victor was smiling. Sherry got a picture of that. What with one thing and another, they didn't see it till the next day.


"They're sending us all to Barstow in a couple of weeks," Victor was saying to Andy as they went toward the elevator in his building, a week after 'Bandstand.'

"For how long?"

"Supposed to be five days."

170

"Five?! Fuck! Oops, sorry Mrs. Cohen." Andy made an 'eek' face at Victor. They parted, so as not to run over the old lady with the walker.

Mrs. Cohen didn't seem to have heard the swear word. "I'm so slow with this thing. You boys go on ahead."

"We'll hold the elevator for you." Victor had been in the building so long, he knew all the old people, their caregivers, and the family members who visited regularly. There were a few other residents his age, but they tended not to run into each other often enough to get acquainted. He and Andy summoned the elevator. It came before Mrs. Cohen reached them.

Andy flipped the stop switch. "You don't see these in every elevator," he remarked. "It's a very humane feature."

"Some of us take forever to get on and off. You should have seen Mr. Levinson when he was in his wheelchair." Mrs. Cohen made it into the car and sighed. Andy flipped the switch again and pressed the button for her floor, then Victor's. "Thank you. Where have you boys been this evening?"

"We had a dance lesson," Victor said. "Andy's friend runs a studio down in West Hollywood."

"Oh? What kind of dancing?"

"Argentine tango. When my job shuts down for the holidays, we're hoping to get out to some milongas."

"Milongas," she said, as if tasting the unfamiliar word. "I used to go out dancing. We all did, in the fifties. Out dancing, or to the drive-in. Those were the days. I should have kept dancing, maybe I wouldn't be stuck with this." She looked at the walker with hatred. "My physical therapist says I could get rid of it if I tried hard enough."

"Tell you what," Andy said. "You may have noticed I'm over here a lot. If you want, I could come up sometime when your therapist is here. We could do a little dancing. Maybe you could come out with me and Victor."

She looked startled, then delighted. "You would take an old lady out dancing?"

"Why not?" Andy dug out his wallet, found a business card, and tucked it in the carryall attached to the side of the walker. "My number's on there." The elevator stopped at her floor. He flipped the switch again after the doors opened.

"Thank you," Mrs. Cohen said. "I'll see what he says. You have a good day."

"You too." They made sure she was all the way out, then re-started the elevator. Victor glanced at Andy. "That was awfully nice."

"I like old ladies." He shrugged. "She'll probably never call. Tell me more about fucking Barstow."

"It's for the mid-season ender. This whole Breaking Bad kind of thing. They've got a big-name director and honestly, it's likely to go more than five days."

"Fuck," Andy said again as the doors opened. "Sorry Mr. Levinson." He and Victor stifled laughter as they went down the hall. Victor opened the door to his apartment, they stepped in, he closed the door and they cracked up. "My mouth, my God."

"Your mouth is perfect." Victor kissed that perfect mouth. Andy had his back up against the door a moment later. "Jesus!" Andy unbuttoned his shirt, getting his hands on Victor's body. Then his pants

172

were open, and then Andy was on his knees getting his mouth on Victor's cock. "Fucking hell, Andy."

Andy took his mouth away long enough to say, "I wanted to do this in the elevator. In the car. In the dance studio." Back to work, Victor's hands in his hair.

Victor was swearing under his breath, leaning on the door. Lost in sensation. The heat, the pressure, the sounds Andy was making, the feel of his hand at Victor's groin. The other was on his ass, that leather cuff against his skin. "Holy *God* you are good at that, mother *fuck*." A low growly sound from Andy, and then he did a thing with his tongue and Victor lost it. He said something really loud and really filthy, shoving himself hard into Andy's throat.

Andy swallowed, heard another fervent curse, and smiled. He took his time releasing Victor, bringing his right hand around slowly, letting that ring run over the crest of the hipbone. Another whimper, another twitch. Andy indulged in another lick. Then he got to his feet and tore off his clothes. "My turn. On your reading chair. So every time you sit there you're going to remember me in your mouth."

"Oh Christ, I already do." The reminder made Victor twitch all over again. A second later Andy was sitting there, one leg draped over the low arm of the chair, ringed hand on himself, staring up into Victor's eyes. "I need a drink," Victor said, voice husky.

"So do I." Andy didn't move, simply watched as Victor went to the kitchen and made them a drink. Rum and Kahlua on the rocks. He swallowed some, made a sound, brought the glass to Andy. "You give it to me." Voice low, eyes hot. Victor took another mouthful, leaned down, put his mouth on Andy's and fed it to him slowly. Then another open-mouthed kiss, taking his time. "Jesus, catnip."

"More." Victor did all that again. Then he opened the side-table drawer and took out the lube.

"Oh really." Andy was smiling. They hadn't yet done the particular thing he thought they were about to do. Victor's eyes were sleepy, his face was flushed. Half-hard again, and breathing through his mouth. Andy took the lube from his hand, slicked himself, heard Victor make a sound that echoed his own. Then his hand was between Victor's legs. Victor put a knee on the arm of the chair, eyes closing, letting Andy fondle and caress, readying him. *This had better be a strong chair.* Victor had his hands on the back of it, legs apart. Then he shifted his weight and the other leg went over one side of the chair. His foot could barely touch the floor. He moved closer, putting his chest in kissing range. Andy did some of that, mouth on a nipple, hand still doing things. Victor started to lower himself. Andy held still, ready to help with the angle and the speed of descent. "God almighty. Careful, sweetheart."

"Mmm." Victor couldn't believe they hadn't done this. Why hadn't they done this? This was great. He had all the control. Andy was there waiting for him, he was taking Andy, Jesus *Christ* this angle was perfect.

Andy's face was pressed to Victor's throat, arm tight around his back. Both Victor's feet were on the floor now, he had Andy all the way in. He was moving, vocalizing, erection hot against Andy's belly, fucking him with complete abandon. Andy was barely breathing, trying not to come. Not yet. Not till Victor went over again. He wasn't going to make it. He put his free hand on that cock, fingers wrapped around to

174

bring the climax, surging up as Victor cried out. "Jesus, Victor, Mother of *God* I love you."

Victor collapsed forward, arms giving out, legs shaking. It took a minute to catch his breath. This position was … he didn't even want to know what it looked like. He started laughing. "That was … wow."

"Yeah." Andy patted his ass. "Okay?"

"I'm okay. I don't know how to get out of this situation." He considered it. "Ay caramba. Give me a hand here." Andy put his hands on Victor's ribs, lifting up, giving him some support as they disengaged. Victor made a muffled sound, biting his lip. More support from Andy as he transferred weight to one foot, got the other one over to the same side, and rested against the back of the chair.

Andy reached for the cocktail glass – miraculously intact – took a drink, and handed it to Victor. "Time for a shower."

"Definitely. And then some food."

"You earned it." Andy stood up. They shared the rest of the drink. Then he put an arm around his lover and they staggered toward the bathroom. He kept an eye on Victor, noting the wince as he bent to dry off his legs after the shower. "A little sore, honey?"

"Yeah."

"Go lie down. I'll fix you some food." He cooked, served dinner in bed, cleaned up. Kept Victor off his feet. Put him on his front and gave him a slow, gentle leg massage, working into the muscles of his hips and lower back. Victor was half asleep when Andy said, "You were quite the bronco buster there."

A drowsy giggle. "I don't know where that came from. Did you ever do that?"

"Ride 'em cowboy? Once or twice. Not everybody has the right chair." Another giggle. "It's easier in bed. Or should I say safer. I was praying that chair would hold up."

"Maybe we'll do it in bed sometime." Victor was quiet for a minute as Andy moved up to his shoulders and neck. "I don't know how I'm going to read in that chair now." Andy cracked up. He leaned down to kiss Victor's shoulder. Victor turned his head a few degrees. "I love you."

"I love you too. Go to sleep." Andy stretched out beside him, one arm over his back, in contact all the way down. He watched Victor's eyes close, listened to his breath even out, and sent up a prayer of thanks for another night together.

October 2014

After several weeks of seeing each other regularly, a week without Victor was intolerable. Andy had to get out of his too-empty place for a minute, so he called Dana to see if he could invite himself over for dinner. "Well sure," she said. "Always happy to see you. Is the boy toy out of town again?"

"Yes, I hate that fucking show." His tone was pleasant but the sentiment was sincere.

Dana made a sound of amused sympathy. "Rory's doing chicken marsala with salad, want me to see if she can drop some pasta for you?"

"No need, I'll pick up something carby on the way. And some wine. And some dessert. That work?"

"That works. See you when we see you." She turned to Rory. "You got all that, I'm assuming."

"Yep. I hope he doesn't get a dessert we like."

"You know he will. Back to the gym for me." Rory snorted. Dana went to the gym almost every day, but she'd recently celebrated her forty-first birthday and was discovering that metabolic change was a real thing. They both disapproved, but they were coping. "I wonder if his burn rate will ever slow down."

"Not if they keep doing what they're doing."

Andy said as much when he got there. "I know it's cruel to show up with fettucine alfredo and a bucket of chocolate mousse, but my body thinks I'm out on tour. I can't believe how much I have to eat to keep my pants from falling off."

"Maybe the problem is your pants keep falling off," Rory suggested. He made a 'that could be' face while Dana laughed. "I mean, it's a theory."

"Every time I see him, oh my God." Andy leaned against the counter, accepting a glass of wine. "Can't get enough."

"So I guess compatibility has not been an issue." Dana sipped her wine, enjoying the dreamy look on her friend's face. "Anything he doesn't like?"

Andy started to say something, nearly giggled, held up a hand like 'wait.' Then he set down his glass and performed an elaborately stagey sequence of gestures that said 'brace yourselves.' Finally he said, confidingly, "He is a filthy motherfucker." Both women cracked up. Dana's wineglass was at risk; Andy took it out of her hand and set it beside his. He was laughing too. "I thought *I* was depraved. Up, down, top, bottom, you name it. I'm like, let's do this! And he's all, yeah baby. Then he goes how about this and I'm like, why didn't I think of that! It's a good thing I don't have a trapeze at the loft." Rory couldn't stop giggling. "Going through lube by the gallon." Dana was leaning on the counter, wheezing. Andy took a deep breath. "But enough about me. What did you think of Tanith's Beowulf thing? Was that fun to work on?"

Rory and Dana had stage-managed Tanith's big dance concert. Once they composed themselves, they had a lot of stories to tell. By the time they got to dessert, Andy was fully envious. "I would have loved doing something like that, twenty or so years ago. It was a great-looking cast, totes fun doing the photos, but damn."

"You know if you wanted to, you could," Dana said. "Between the Cabaret and Dmitri's, there's a lot of people who'd love to work with you."

Rory nudged him. "If you'd come out of your dance closet."

"Eh. I'd rather spend time with Victor when we have the chance." This wasn't a hundred percent true, and he knew they knew it. Andy still missed dancing, and he probably always would. But he'd moved on, and there was so much good in his life now that asking for more seemed greedy. "If that means a dance or a song occasionally, that's a gift. Thanks for indulging my TMI."

"That was way too much information," said Rory. "I'm never going to be able to look at that guy the same way again."

"Or you either," Dana said. "It was my own fault. I should never have asked that question."

"You knew I was filthy, honey." He gave her his best 'I'm so nasty' look. "What were the odds the man of my dreams wouldn't be just as rank?" She snorted. "Gee, I wonder if he's done for the day. I'm kind of inspired."

Rory said, "Get out now," and they all cackled again.


Victor was still out of town and not at all pleased about it. When he got Andy's text late that night it made him smile: *Told the girls what out of control love monkeys we are*

He wrote back: *Wish you were here there is not a damned thing to do in Barstow and even if there were I'd rather be doing you*

*All things considered it might be just as well we're forced to take a break from time to time*

*The hell it is, we've got a year to make up for. You could fuck me raw and I'd take it with a smile.* Victor was smiling right then, imagining what he'd do to Andy the next time they got together.

Andy was imagining that too. *Mr. Garcia if the tabs get a hold of your phone there's going to be a scandal*

*Did that turn you on Mr. Martin?*

*You know it did. What time do you start tomorrow?*

*Four in the fucking morning, if you were here I wouldn't even bother sleeping.* He was hoping Andy would change modes; there was one way they might both have a chance of getting to sleep. A second later the voice line rang. Victor picked it right up. "Hey baby. I'm thinking about going for hours with you and it's got me hard. Want to help me settle down for the night?"

"Well since I'm all worked up too, maybe we could help each other." Andy's voice was in the low, silky register Victor loved, beyond suggestive. "Put a hand on that beautiful cock and imagine my mouth is on your sexy neck, about to take a bite."

"I'm there," Victor said, his own voice low. "Now imagine we're in that new chair of yours, face to face, and my other hand is on you."

They were both really good at talking dirty. With all the location shoots, they'd had lots of practice. Not very many minutes later, Andy blew out a breath and said, "Tell me you're back in town soon."

"Two point five days. Can I come straight to you?"

"Jesus, yes. I love you."

"I love you too. I think I can sleep now." Victor couldn't help smiling.

Andy said, "Dream of me."

"I always do. Good night, sweetheart."

"Good night." As usual, it was difficult to end the call, but somebody had to. Andy disconnected, set the phone on his chest, congratulated himself for having brought a hand towel over to the couch before he called, and sighed.

Two point five days later, Victor wasn't the only member of the cast who was tired of being out of town. Everyone else was married, or in some kind of other committed relationship, and they'd been away for eight days straight, which was a record even for this series. They were counting down the hours when the episode's director floated the idea of re-staging a scene. There was a minor mutiny at the prospect of extending their desert shoot for another day. All the necessary coverage had been shot, plus a lot of alternate takes. "You've got great footage," said one of the stars. "You had this all storyboarded three months ago. It's going to be great, one of the most cinematic things we've ever done. Why in hell do you want to re-stage it?"

The director looked around at the three co-stars, at Victor and the other three supporting actors, at the hot, hungry, dust-covered extras, and at the location producer. That person had a face that said 'I will not throw myself between you and the angry mob.' The director wilted. "It was just an idea. We're a little over budget anyway, aren't we?" A cold stare from the producer. They were very over budget. "Okay, never mind. That's a wrap." Nobody gave him a chance to reconsider. The background coordinator had the extras processed out in record time. All the trucks and trailers were packed and rolling within two hours. Victor sent a text to Andy to let him know he was finally on his way.

The text came in the nick of time; Andy had thought 'two point five days' meant the time before he would actually *see* Victor. Four long hours of wondering if there had been some kind of disaster – traffic on the I-15 was almost as bad as on the I-10 - would have been stressful. Four extra hours to prepare were actually not. He went out to get food, having let that go while he finished hanging his new show. Then he tidied up his desk, and set the scene in the sleeping loft. When the knock finally came, he scampered past the display walls and opened the door. "You look good enough to eat."

"We could start with that." Victor stepped inside, set down his bag, and hooked an arm around Andy's neck. A few minutes later he opened his eyes, took a breath, and looked past his lover to the picture facing the door. "What *is* that?"

"That is a pair of Stacey's acrobat friends, doing something acrobatic. Recognize the prop?"

Since that implied he ought to, Victor studied it for a second. "Is that the same cage thing you used for Rory and Dana's picture last year?"

"Yes it is, well done. How do you like the show title?" That was on the same wall, in peel-off vinyl letters: BENT. Victor laughed. Andy kissed him again. "God it's good to see you. Give me that." He took the weekender out of Victor's hand. "Come through the maze. Make yourself at home."

Victor took that at face value, kicking off his shoes before detouring to the bathroom. When he came out, Andy put a glass of chilled pinot noir in his hand. Then he caught Victor's other hand, and put something in that. Victor glanced down. It was a key. He blinked, and looked back at Andy. "Is this a key to your front door?"

"You are not required to use it," Andy said. "But I wanted you to have it. So if you want to –" The wine splashed a little as Victor seized him. When they came up for air Andy's back was against the wall. Victor's eyes were wet. He dropped his head to Andy's shoulder and didn't say anything. Andy rubbed his back. "I love you, catnip. Mi casa es tu casa. I know with all my shit there is barely room to swing a mouse much less a cat except in the main space which I don't actually inhabit. But I was thinking the other day, the day you were supposed to be coming back, before those shitheads said hey it's fun here in fucking Barstow let's go another three, if you ever got done early and wanted to come here and I was in Pasadena or something shooting a wedding, you could come. If you wanted to." He said all that very fast.

Victor was smiling long before Andy finished. He straightened up, got another kiss, and said, "Thank you." They hadn't ever discussed living together, and he knew that wasn't what this was. They were only six months in, and there truly wasn't space for two here, not with the need to keep the working area open. What he heard was 'you don't need to knock, you can open that door anytime.' He was fairly certain that this was not a thing Andy had offered to many lovers. "I'll always text first. But I'd love that. I will love that. I love you." One more kiss. The splashed wine had dried on his hand. He stood back, glanced at the sealed concrete floor. "It's a good thing this floor is easy to clean."

"Yeah, I won't bother doing that until after this show comes down. Speaking of which, I was thinking of having a little party." He put his arm around Victor and they went to the kitchen to see about some food while they discussed that.

Chapter 12

November 2014

By the time BENT closed, all of the prints had sold. Andy put his display walls back in storage, dropped all the leftover promotional cards in a bin that hung on the wall outside his door, and borrowed chairs from friends around the complex. He and Victor were expecting nearly all of their particular friends for the closing party, along with the photo subjects – mostly acrobats, gymnasts, and aerialists. As the room filled up, Andy's circle of Chrome contacts was well-represented. Victor had gotten friendly with many of them over the past few months. He hung out with Rory and Dana while Andy mingled. "So, one of my good friends has upped stakes," Dana said. "I'm sad."

"What happened?"

"She fell in love with somebody who needed to move home to Washington State to take care of his mom. So she's moving up there too."

"They're expecting," added Rory. "We're probably going up there next spring to see the baby. It ought to be a stunner."

"Why, are they good-looking?"

"Charlene looks like Cleopatra. She's Ray's sister. And check her guy out." Dana got her phone out and pulled up a photo. "She took this picture of Juan when they were up there this summer. I made her send it to me."

"Wow." The subject clearly had Native American blood. He was standing with a horse in front of a forest. "Has Andy seen that?"

"I don't think so. Why?"

"Seems like he could do something with material like that."

"Material like what?" Andy said, circling around to them. "Oh, *hello*," he said, when Dana turned the phone so he could see the picture. "Yeah, that's pretty fucking good material."

"You want to go on a trip?" said Victor to Andy. Then, before he could answer, he turned to Dana. "Where are they, exactly?"

"Up on the peninsula, like right at the top. Little town called Sequim. Whale country."

"Have you ever been up that way before?"

"Never."

"Me neither," said Andy. "It sounds very not-L.A."

"Pretty much the opposite of L.A., from what Charlene said," Dana agreed. "If you really want to meet them, I can put you in touch. I have a feeling they'd be glad for some company from the city."

"Next summer, maybe," said Victor. "Once the show is on hiatus again. I'd love to see what it's like up there."

"Me too," said Andy. "I've never seen that part of the country at all, except for a few tours that landed in Seattle. And that's just another city, really. A trip up there sounds kind of great." *Going anywhere with you sounds kind of great.* He glanced at his wall clock. "Oops. Gotta make sure all these bendy people have enough to drink!"

He mingled again for a while, finally got to Vicky and Sharon, and did a double take. For one thing, they were both drinking Pellegrino instead of champagne.

185

For another, Sharon seemed to have changed shape. He'd last seen her when he did their wedding pictures the month before. "Sharon, are you, um?" He indicated a belly. She nodded. "When did that happen? *How* did that happen?"

"If we can hang out for a while after the crowd thins out, we'll tell you all about it," said Vicky, an arm around Sharon's waist.

"Well, shit, I'm going to start shoveling people out the door *right now*," he said, and walked away to do that. Not too much later, he and Victor sat down with their friends to find out what was up. "Tell all," Andy demanded.

"Not quite all," Victor amended. "I mean, there are some details we probably don't need."

"Men are such wimps," Vicky said to Sharon.

"But still, occasionally, useful. My biological clock went off about a year ago. Vicky and I talked about it, a lot, and started thinking of what we could do."

"What kind of compromises. What kind of strategies."

"It was one of those things, you know, back in the day I always just assumed I'd get married and have kids."

"Both of us did," Vicky said.

"But it never seemed like a *necessary* thing until recently. Those hormones, boy. So anyway we talked a lot. And ultimately we both thought we'd like the father to be someone who we're already close to, you know? So we started thinking through the list."

"At first we thought of asking Vince," said Vicky, referring to one of the Cabaret regulars. "But he and Kelli are going to have their own kids, and we didn't want to complicate that. He'll make a terrific uncle."

"We're going to have so many fabulous uncles! Including Uncle Andy."

"Better watch out or I'll teach the kid to tap-dance. Why not me?" he asked. "Not offended, just curious."

"Well, you were a strong contender," Sharon said. "You're tall, good-looking, and talented."

"And we like you," added Vicky. "Which is not the case with every tall, et cetera guy we know."

Andy laughed as Sharon said "Nooooo. Anyway, we thought about it. I mean, you even have acceptable hair. But you guys are so new, and it was kind of like with Vince and Kelli: we didn't want to complicate things. The counselor at the clinic told us some horror stories."

"Apparently the conversation can send some relationships into a death spiral," said Vicky.

"Anyway, it was tricky. We didn't want to, like, *embarrass* anybody."

"But eventually we thought, what about Dmitri?" Vicky said. Andy sat back, astonished all over again. "We've been out with him and Patrick plenty of times, and we got the story that years ago, they really wanted to adopt. But they weren't married then, and Dmitri was working crazy hours, and Patrick's kind of a big deal at his firm; it wasn't like either of them could be a full-time parent. And they decided they didn't want a two-career family with nannies and shit. They have a god-child, and a few nieces and nephews, and that's where that is. But we knew that at one point, at least, they'd wanted a child. So we girded up our loins and took Dmitri into his office and asked him."

"What did he say?" asked Andy, fascinated.

"Well he was all formal and gruff, you know how he is, but his eyes got all shiny. And that set me off," said Sharon. "It was a mess."

"It got pretty sloppy," Vicky agreed. "Anyway, he said he would be honored. So we all went to the clinic for tests."

"And Dmitri passed inspection, then they told me 'you're fertile as a turtle, when do you want to start,'" said Sharon. "So after we got home from the Games, we went back to the clinic and did the thing. And it took right away."

"That's really fantastic," said Victor. "What a great story. Are you going to stay in the same apartment?"

"We looked into buying a house," said Vicky. "But prices being what they are, we'd need about four roommates."

"Yeah. We have enough savings for a down-payment, but the mortgage would be … well, it would mean we basically couldn't do anything except pay for the house." Sharon shrugged. "It's okay. There's enough space."

"Well, you never know," Andy said. "A friend of mine who runs a dance studio, she and her husband bought a house and it was like you say. But an instructor at their place who they're really friendly with moved in with them. It's working out great."

"We'll see. One thing at a time. Anyway, so that's the story!" Sharon said. "And thanks for the party and everything, but us pregnant ladies have to get our rest."

"Yeah," said Vicky. "We're gonna head out now. We'll see you soon."

"Good night, ladies," said Andy, walking them to the door. Victor walked with them, and they all hugged goodbye.

"Incidentally, Victor, thanks for making our boy happy," said Vicky. "We expect great things from the pair of you." She grinned as she stepped out the door. It closed behind her.

Victor and Andy looked at each other. "What in the hell did she mean by that?" said Andy.

"You're asking me?"

"I mean, I *am* happy."

"Me too."

"But now if I don't win a Pulitzer, and you don't win an Emmy for best actor, we're going to feel like a couple of underachievers."

Victor shook his head. "She didn't say the *two* of you, though. She said the *pair* of you."

"Oh." Andy thought about this. "There is a difference."

"Yes there is."


They made it to the last three Cabaret shows of the year. All of Victor's location shoots were done and they finally made it out to some milongas, too. They took Mrs. Cohen out dancing a few times – first to the studio, for a little practice under Dmitri's expert eye - which made Victor the hero of his apartment building because she told *everybody*. They weren't trying to get attention, but couldn't help noticing at least one journalist or paparazzo every time they turned up somewhere. "Are you okay with all this?" Victor asked one night. They were out for dinner at Musso and Frank before heading to a dance.

Andy knew what he meant. "It doesn't bother me. Any rustlings from your show?" Being out was one thing, being out and with someone could potentially be another. Victor shook his head. "That's good. We're getting the hang of this. I'd hate to give it up."

"Me too." Victor loved dancing with Andy. Because he was known, people tended not to cut in on them very much. When either of them did dance with another partner, there were selfies, handshakes, and hugs. "I think it's good for us. Good for the community, too."

Andy thought so too. It was that whole being-represented thing. He changed the subject. "I can't wait to see the January show. When they set that Broadway theme, it was all I could do not to jump up and down and go me me me!" Victor laughed. "But they've got you going right back out, haven't they?"

"Yeah." Victor sighed. "If it wasn't the same for the rest of the cast, I'd be paranoid about it."

"Cheap bastards don't want to build sets. Though I will say that desert stuff looked great. Very cinematic."

"Too bad the plot was so predictable."

Andy snorted. Victor's show, like many primetime dramas, tended to recycle plotlines. "Getting dessert tonight?"

"You're my dessert. I'll have coffee." Victor couldn't eat the way Andy did unless he wanted to spend way too much time in the gym. He watched, only slightly envious, while his lover mowed through a serving of brioche bread pudding.

When they went outside, there was a photographer waiting. *Again with this*, Victor thought, then caught himself. So far it had been nothing but good to have these little bits of press. Andy said, "Hi Steve. Fancy meeting you here. Seems like old times."

The photographer wasn't crowding them. Maybe he could see they weren't going to be cranky about it. "Hi Andy. Mr. Garcia. You're both looking swell tonight. Mind if I get a picture?"

"No, go ahead." Victor linked arms with Andy. They did look swell, in three-piece dance suits. Victor's was his favored gray and Andy's was chocolate brown with a pink pinstripe.

"Where are you headed?"

"Going to a tango thing at the Fonda," Andy said. "Getting a few more dates in before Mr. Garcia gets sent off on location again."

"Everything good with you?" Steve was taking pictures. "Anything to say to your fans?"

*Do I have fans?* Andy thought hilariously. He glanced at Victor, who said, "We wish everyone happy holidays. So far this is looking like my best Christmas since I was about six. Mr. Martin is the greatest gift I could have."

Andy swooned a little. "Same goes," he said, voice soft, suddenly remembering a years-ago moment when he stood right here with Dana and Rory and Steve. "Mr. Garcia is the love of my life. And you can print that." It might be indiscreet, it might come back to bite them. *But goddammit, it's true.*

Victor was looking at him with such love that he couldn't resist. One of Steve's photos from the next minute or so was everywhere the next day, with quotes. Dana sent Andy a text: *That sounded familiar*

*You gave me the idea*, he wrote back. *Thanks OXO*

The week after Christmas, neither of them had much to do and both of them were happy about it. Andy was at his computer going through another set of photos of Victor – always a rewarding subject – when an email notification popped up. He glanced at his other monitor; the message was from his agent Raquel. He hadn't heard from her for a long time. This was the last thing he ever expected.

Hi Andy -

This is coming out of the blue, but you seem like a flexible guy so give it a thought before you ping me back.

You probably know L.A. Vice has been working a storyline where our mutual friend VG goes undercover. I got a thing from their head writer, countersigned by the show runner, asking me to feel you out about taking a multi-episode role.

The part would be a bartender working in a gang-run club that is one of VG's targets. It would be a love interest part, working with VG. They have never done a LGBT storyline before and are shitting bricks but with the positive press about you two they are wondering if this could grab them some new audience.

Potential to go into a recurring character if the storyline works. Otherwise the bartender character probably gets killed off. Either way - let me know what you think.

If you happen to see VG, sound him out too. I don't know if his rep has heard about this.

Cheers – Raquel

> p.s. the love interest thing is only a thing if you say yes, otherwise bartender is just another gangbanger

"Well ain't that a kick in the head," Andy said out loud. Victor was over on the couch reading a script. He looked up when Andy spoke. "Catnip, come and look at this." Victor came over to the desk and read over his shoulder. "Did you know about this?"

"No, honey, it's news to me. I mean yeah, the undercover thing. But the other thing is, wow, that's pretty big."

"That's *hella* big."

Victor's head was full of all the good – and bad – possibilities. The last time his character was featured in a prominent storyline, he'd been on the outside of an undercover operation that went wrong, a multi-episode arc that was written expressly to help an actor exit the show. But that actor's character hadn't been in a relationship. So far, all the main characters' partners had survived, though their screen time was barely enough to remind the viewers that they existed. "Quick reactions?"

"Terror," Andy said. "Amazement. Hope." This was so far beyond anything he'd ever thought of doing that it wouldn't have been accurate to say he wanted to do it. It also wasn't accurate to say he didn't.

"Me too." It was so huge. Victor could see his lover's ambivalence; he felt it too. If they did this, it would change both of their lives. Victor's career would never be the same, whether the experiment succeeded or not. Andy would be thrown out of his well-managed, *self*-managed life and into a largely uncontrollable situation. Victor wondered if he realized that if this happened, if the series took the storyline seriously, he would be instantly famous.

They stared at each other for a few silent minutes, both thinking hard. Then Andy said, "Check your email. Maybe Parker got this shit at the same time." Victor went to get his phone, opened his email, and a few minutes later nodded.

"It's here." He brought it over to Andy so they could both read it, both verify that what they thought it said was actually what it said. "Maybe this is our great thing, baby." He wanted to do it, wanted to see where this could take them.

Andy heard it. He thought of all the men they'd met out dancing, who'd said 'thank you' when all they'd been doing was something they wanted to do for themselves. He opened a reply window to Raquel, copied in Parker and Victor, and typed WE ARE IN. Before he hit 'send' he looked up for confirmation. Victor nodded. Andy pressed the button. "You'd better give me some tips," he said after they both exhaled. "I don't know how to act on camera."

"Just be you. That's who they're hiring." Andy gave him a look. Victor pulled up the other chair and sat down. "Okay, okay. If you're in a gang club and I'm going to fall in love with you, there's the possibility we get you out of the club. Or the gang gets shut down and the club goes legit. Either way, if you're a good guy –"

"Which I pretty much have to be, right? Otherwise you wouldn't fall in love with me."

"Obviously." They were close enough to kiss, so Victor did that. "So you're a good guy, which means

194

you're not thrilled to be working in a gang club, but you have to seem like you are."

"I have to be down with the hoodlums," Andy said, throwing a gang sign. Victor would have laughed except even that looked sexy to him. "I'm going to need some bartending skills. And a much, much better poker face."

"Think back to that night I came to Chrome and you brushed me off." Andy hissed; he hated to remember that. Victor stroked a hand through his hair. "You were justified. And that was perfect. So cold."

"My heart was *pounding*. I felt nauseated." Andy thought for a second. "Oh crap, that has to be there, huh? I'm afraid all the time. Fucking hell, what did I just sign up for?"

"Well, you haven't signed anything yet."

"I have to, though. I mean, even if they end up killing us both, nobody's ever done this before in primetime." He stood up, pulled Victor out of the chair, and steered him over to the couch. "Let's see what the contract says and what the scenes are like. Then you can help me work this out. Right now I want to forget about it."

"I can help you do that." Victor turned around and slid his hand into Andy's hair, lifting his face for a kiss.

The contract arrived two days later, with script pages for four episodes. The scenes went the direction they were half-expecting, a direction that was both exciting and scary. Andy stood firm, signed back the contract, and started thinking about the character. He also got in touch with Terry, one of the bartenders at Chrome, and asked for a crash course. "I found a school that looks good but I don't have weeks to prepare," he explained. "Will Tyrone let me come in and do this? Obviously I'll pay for your time, plus booze and any breakage."

Terry promised to call right back, and they were at the bar the next morning, prepped and ready to go. He looked Andy over. "I would lose the jewelry. Your hands are going to be wet all the time."

Andy didn't argue. He'd been wearing the ring and cuff for years; he was due for a new look, and the show probably wouldn't let him wear the stuff anyway. He took both off and stowed them in his messenger bag. "Okay?"

"Cool. First lesson: no drinking."

"Goddammit," Andy said, which got the intended laugh. "Fine. Beer, wine, cocktails, let's get going."

At the end of their second three-hour session, Terry looked down the bar at Andy, polishing glasses like a pro, and said, "You want a job?"

Andy gave him a sidelong look. "I'm afraid you can't afford me," he said grandly. When he got home that day, he sent a text to his mother: *Hi Mom remember when I did that TV thing? Well I'm doing another one. Four episodes!! If you don't already have the DVR set for Victor's show, set it now*

He and Victor worked on the character some more the next time they got together. Victor wasn't surprised to find that Andy assimilated the new technique quickly. "They'll have some direction for you," he said once they'd gone through all the scenes. "Here's hoping it's not the exact opposite of what we're doing."

Andy shrugged. "You would think they would give me a heads-up if they wanted something specific. I'm guessing you're right, they want me to play me. But I've never been a bartender in a gang club, so what the fuck."

"I know. I'll bet they're counting on the storyline itself to keep people watching."

"Oh, so it doesn't matter if I'm crap? Or maybe they think if I'm no good they can wind up the storyline and nobody'll question it. Get all the credit for breaking the taboo and then run away." They stared at each other. "I really am a cynical old bitch."

"No," Victor said. "You're smart. That would seriously piss me off, if that's what they're thinking."

"No way to know." Andy thought about it. "We need someone to watch me do these scenes."

"Dana. Let's ask Dana. I'll ping her, see if we can go over there." They were at Victor's, not far from Rory and Dana's place in West Hollywood. He found his phone and sent a text: *Hey gorgeous, we're having a fit of paranoia about something. Can we consult?*

The answer came back almost immediately: *At your service*

They rolled up to the cottage about twenty minutes later. Andy was second-guessing. "If the producers find out about this you're going to be in so much trouble." The storyline was supposed to be kept under deep cover.

"They won't find out. Hey Rory." The door was open and they were going inside. "Sorry to land on you like this."

"No worries. Everything okay?" She glanced back at Dana, who was standing in the kitchen, one hand on a bottle of wine, eyebrows up like 'should I pour.'

"Yes please," Andy said to Dana. "We need some professional advice. Or rather, I do. And this isn't just in the vault, it's in fucking Fort Knox."

"Have you eaten? Because we got done a minute ago and there's plenty left." Rory joined Dana in the kitchen. "Beef stroganoff."

Victor perked up. "God that sounds good. We were in the middle of something, lost track of time."

"Something fun, or something that sends you running over here?"

"The other thing. We'll have some fun later." Victor glanced over at Andy, who made a 'definitely' face that earned him a smile.

"Where's your ring and thing?" Rory was looking at Andy's naked hand. "You've been wearing that stuff forever."

"Well, that's part of this thing that's freaking me out."

"Whatever, okay. Go back in the den, I'll bring you some eats in a minute, you can tell us what's going on."

"Yes ma'am. Thanks." Andy moved into the kitchen to kiss both women, leaving it with a glass of wine in each hand. Victor followed him to the back of the cottage. Dana and Rory joined them in a few minutes, carrying steaming plates. "That smells amazing," Andy said. "I need a wife."

"You can't afford me," Rory said, and he cracked up. Once he got hold of himself, he told her why. Then while he and Victor ate, they told the whole story and defined their concerns.

Dana said, "That's legit. I mean, that they might be thinking a marginal performance gets them off the

198

hook if the response isn't good. I hope that's not why they're giving you radio silence. I hope they're just so scared they don't know what to do."

"That could be it," Victor allowed. "Our agents both said the contacts they've had were in the 'shitting bricks' category." Both women laughed. "But we'd like to make sure Andy goes in with some good stuff in the tool box. What we've been doing is what I thought was true to my character, in the context of the years I've been on the show. Who that character would fall in love with, and why."

"You know I like a challenge," Andy said. Both women nodded. "But this is on a different level from learning to dance in heels. This is me producing something that's going to work for a show that I basically hate." Rory snorted. "I wouldn't even watch the goddamned thing if he wasn't in it. I cannot tank at this. Me fucking this up could mean me fucking up Victor's career."

Victor took his hand. "Not gonna happen. So what do you think?"

"Let's get going." Dana refilled their glasses. Andy pulled the script pages out of his messenger bag, and they all got comfortable. As written, all the bartender's scenes were going to be shot on a set at the soundstage. The character would be introduced in a brief scene with various gangsters before Victor came in for their first scene together. The other three episodes would have scenes where both men were in the bar but not interacting, as well as scenes together. Dana read all the pages first, passing them to Rory as she finished each one. Then she thought about things while the men reviewed them, quietly discussing what they'd prepared. "Those are awfully thin pages," she said, when they seemed ready to proceed. "They

199

haven't given you *any* sense of how they want you to approach this stuff?" Andy shook his head. She muttered something that sounded like 'assholes.' "Let's see what you've got." At the end of two hours, having listened to the men read the scenes and then watched what they'd come up with for business, Dana said, "If they don't like that, they're crazy. It's really subtle, but you're making it so clear."

"Well, we've both been afraid for our lives," Andy said. This wasn't a thing he'd ever said to her before. She and Rory both looked startled. "I'm not super thrilled about reliving it, but," he paused for a moment, "this wasn't the time to go easy, was it? We're not doing this only for ourselves."

Victor took his hand. "No, we're not. Thanks for taking the time with this." Dana and Rory both made 'don't mention it' faces. "I'm glad you think we're on the right track."


After the men left, Rory and Dana cleaned up the kitchen, both thinking hard. When they went to bed, Rory said, "Is it just me or is that guy kind of awesome?"

"He's kind of awesome. Fifty percent of guys would have said nothing but no. Another thirty percent would have said not with someone who's never really done TV. Another nineteen percent might have said okay, but would not have helped."

"And out of the last one percent, ninety-nine percent would not have come up with stuff that's going to make the new guy possibly look better than the regular guy. He's like Dmitri."

Dana looked over, thinking about that. "You're right. God I hope the production company doesn't screw this up. If they'll let those guys do it the way they've worked it out, this could be so, so big."

"It could also get scary. In the real world." Rory pulled up the quilt. "Come here kitty. What do you think he meant, they've both been afraid for their lives? Oh *shit*."

"What?" Dana was alarmed.

"You didn't see those pictures Andy took that time. Victor has scars. Like, knife scars. Oh my fuck. Something bad happened to him. Do you think something like that could have happened to *Andy*?"

"I've only seen him naked in that picture from 'Oh! Calcutta,'" Dana said after a moment. "I didn't notice anything there. Well, I didn't notice any scars." Rory couldn't help giggling. "He doesn't act like someone with PTSD. Neither of them do. But Andy's been around the block a few times. It's possible some monsters were waiting down an alley once or twice. Jesus. I hate to think of that."

"I know. Ugh. Come here and hug me." Dana did that. The cat purred between them.

Chapter 13

January 2015

Victor caught up with Janis for a minute before she went back out for the second leg of her tour. He didn't tell her about the TV show – he was following the directive with everyone except Rory and Dana – but he gave her a full report on every other aspect of the Andy situation. "He gave me a key to his loft," he said at the end. "So I gave him keys to my apartment."

She slapped the table and hooted. "You gave each other keys?! Holy shit, I have *never* given someone a key! I was always, you know, stay away until I call you." He laughed for about a minute. She drank some wine, watching. "If you hadn't worked it out with Andy, I would introduce you to my tour manager. He is adorable. Let me tell you all about him." Victor didn't get another word in until it was almost time to go. Then he asked about Stefan. "Oh my Christ, Stefan." Janis rolled her eyes. "I got some acceptable sex out of him. He doesn't much like me touring. He will never go see me out of town, because he hates to travel. It's better than nothing."

"Chica," Victor said after a moment, "that is not a ringing endorsement."

"Easy for you to say. You're getting laid left right and center by a guy who looks like *that*." She drained her glass. "Are you doing any more singing?"

"Not for a while," he said. "Both our schedules are fucked. We did a lot of dancing last fall, though."

"Well, that's something. We'll catch up when I get back to town, right?"

"Yes we will. We should both have some good stories by then." They fake-argued over the bill. Janis let Victor get it, eventually. He gave her a hug and a kiss, told her to say hi to the tour manager for him, and sent her on her way. "I think she's got a crush on him," he told Andy later.

"Who, the tour guy? Did she have a picture?"

"She had a ton of pictures. He's tall, with red hair and dark eyes."

"Sounds like somebody else we know. Same type?"

Victor shook his head. Their mutual friend Red Warner was tall and red-headed and basically a beast. "According to Janis, this Niall guy went to Oxford and has two primary modes. One is a diplomat and the other is the kind of bastard who will take you to pieces so smoothly that you don't even realize you're bleeding until you try to walk away and can't locate your feet."

"Ooh, very interesting." Andy tugged him down for an unhurried moment without words. "Thanks for coming over tonight."

"Super convenient from Glendale," Victor said with his mouth on Andy's neck. "Much better than Hollywood. And you're not in Hollywood." A few kisses later, he said, "Ready for tomorrow?"

"Ugh. Thank God you're going to be there."


At first, the on-set work was sufficiently novel to be entertaining. Before long, Andy was prodigiously bored. "Two days for that casino thing was fun," he complained about two weeks in. "This shit is *so slow*!"

Victor sympathized. "When you're used to going to the theater, playing something through in two hours, and going home - yeah. I know what you mean. That's why I like doing plays too."

"At least it's not every day of every week. Jesus wept." He couldn't imagine being stuck there full time. "They won't even let me take pictures on the soundstage."

"Poor baby. And we can't entertain ourselves or we'll have to go back into makeup."

"Ha! Serve them right if we did. At least I'm working with you all the time." He lowered his voice. "The rest of these guys, eh." Victor stifled a laugh. "Hey, and if this ends in tragedy, we'll always have Pico-Union." He watched with satisfaction as Victor cracked up.


Working on the scenes and the character at home was interesting; seeing it all come together on the soundstage was a revelation. Victor was standing off set, behind the camera, watching Andy do a take. There were a couple of day players, a dozen extras, mostly heavily-tattooed guys who looked like authentic gangsters (a couple of them had been, years ago), and the guest star who was playing the main bad guy. Andy had only a couple of lines in this scene – his introduction - and those were only bartender lines. The extras had all been given business about going to the bar for drinks. Most of them chose shots, or bottled beer. Then the bad guy went over and tapped the bar. Without saying anything, Andy reached for the bottle of Courvoisier and poured a couple of ounces into a snifter. He slid it across the bar with his fingertips on the far side of the base, where he couldn't possibly touch the bad guy's hand even if he reached for the glass.

The bad guy stood at right angles to the bar, one elbow resting on it. He wasn't obviously watching the bartender, but there was a flicker of a glance down to the glass, and then a flicker of a glance up. A moment of eye contact; neither character gave anything away. Andy's hands were back on his side of the bar; he picked up a towel and wiped the edge. The bad guy nodded, lifted the glass, and turned away, going to talk to a day player about some criminal enterprise. Andy angled his body, not quite turning his back, watching the whole room in the mirrored back bar, inhaling visibly and non-obviously wiping his hands. The entire exchange took less than a minute. *Jesus, he's good*, Victor thought with delight. The direction had been 'give him a glass of brandy,' and nothing more. "Cut. Good. Re-set for one more."

Someone spoke softly. "You ever think getting him in here was a mistake?"

Victor turned to study his longtime co-worker. "Not for a second."

"We're all, shit, better step up." Victor grinned. They both took a few steps away. "What did you think when they floated this storyline?"

They were still walking, moving toward the craft services area. Victor would be doing another scene on the schedule that day, but until a production assistant called him, he could roam around. "We mostly thought about representing."

"He's really never done this before?"

Victor shook his head. "We're working on it together. I've had to think about why I do things. I got into a groove a while back, you know. I get on the set and I'm Alvarado and I don't have to think about why I move a certain way. It's been great for me. Even if they end up killing us off, I'll be proud we did this first."

"I don't think that's going to happen." The other actor was sipping coffee, not making eye contact. "The grapevine says you're going to be big next season." Victor didn't say anything; this was news to him. He'd been an actor long enough to be superstitious about 'what if.' They heard 'Cut. That's a wrap for the scene. Take twenty while we re-set for the next one.' Victor's co-worker sighed. "Guess I'd better get to the station set. Later."

"Later," Victor echoed, and waited for Andy. A minute later he was there, rolling his eyes dramatically. Victor smiled. "Nice business with the towel."

"Eh. Getting into this character is freaking me out sometimes. That guy gives good gangster."

"Yeah, he does. If they actually take this through to trial, he's going to give people chills in the courtroom." He didn't mention that if the show runners took the storyline through to trial, there was a very good chance they'd ask Andy back.

Andy picked up a bottle of water, twisted off the cap, and drank half of it. "Fun stuff next."

"We get to do some eye-fucking." That wasn't in the script. Their dialogue was innocuous. Victor's undercover cop was casual, almost dismissive; the bartender was brusque and efficient. This was their third of seven scenes together. Victor knew Dana and Rory were going to love it. He certainly did. Andy was watching him, smiling, eyes promising some real fucking later. Victor had to look away again for a second. *Every time.* Every look, every move, every touch. He was using this. Letting that desire bleed through, reaching for ways to mask it in front of the bad guys but still allow the bartender to see it. Ways to let the audience see the difference, without it being so obvious that they'd think, this guy will be shot in the head in five seconds. They had to be afraid of that, but it couldn't seem inevitable. "God, I love you."

Andy's eyes looked darker than usual. His lips were parted as if he couldn't get enough air through his nose. "I love you too. My guy would have your guy bent over a table the second the doors were locked."

Victor swallowed. "Jesus, Andy."

"Wish I could clear the set and bend you over this table right now." Andy really meant it, but the way Victor's face flushed, the way his weight shifted, made him step back. He shook his head, smiling. "Sorry. Didn't mean to say that. Taking a walk now." A walk straight to the restroom, pulling out his phone on the way and turning it on. Then into the stall, setting the phone to play some random music, turning the volume up. *Never fails*, he thought a few minutes later. Someone would probably write about this later, about the notorious Andy Martin and his musical interludes in the men's room. If there weren't so many goddamned people around, he'd have taken Victor in there with him.

When Andy's shooting days finally wrapped, he was relieved. There had been no sign of discontent from the producers concerning his performance, and no direction that went beyond what they'd covered on their own. The rest of the cast was welcoming and helpful. He thought there was a good chance the big experiment would be a success, by their own measure.

They'd been warned to brace themselves for the viewer response.

He spent the next few weeks catching up with photography jobs, and kvetching about not having time to do his regular spring show. Before he knew it, their first episode was on the schedule. "Want to have a viewing party?" he asked Victor. "Or do you want to watch it alone?"

"Let's have a few people over. What do you think - Rory, Dana, Vicky, Sharon? Sharon ought to be taking up a little more space by now. Anybody else?"

"Let's get my pal Jim. And Ray and Julia, let's see if they can come. Tanith and Sid?"

"Definitely Tanith. Gimme the contacts for Jim and Julia, and I'll send an invite."

"Thanks, sweetness."

Eleven people filled up the studio space nicely. Andy borrowed comfortable chairs from friends around the complex, and served popcorn, pigs-in-a-blanket, and s'mores, along with drinks. Only Rory and Dana knew the full story. Everyone knew Andy was playing a bartender. They all wanted to watch him make fancy cocktails. "We had to add this whole thing so I could practice," he told them, indicating the new bar shelves outside the kitchen. "I have broken a phenomenal number of glasses." He didn't break any that night, though. The group was getting noisy by the time the episode came on, and was positively rowdy at the end.

"Guys, you were right on target. The best thing about it," Tanith said sincerely. The writers had produced a scene in which the characters' mutual distrust was tempered by instant attraction. Because they were both in risky situations, the attraction was conveyed almost entirely through body language, with a breath of innuendo in the dialogue. It had played like a dance. When Andy passed a drink across the bar to Victor – their fingers brushing for an instant – and their eyes met, it had all the impact of a kiss. Tanith, who really only watched the show out of loyalty to Victor, couldn't wait to see what happened next. "How much of that did they give you?"

"The words," Victor said, smiling at her. "They threw Andy in the deep end."

"They fucking did, those lazy fuckers." Andy polished off his cocktail. "At least I learned how to tend bar. So Vicky, you think this is our great thing?"

"It could be," she allowed. "We'll see how it goes. It's certainly not a *small* thing. How you doing, sweetie?" Sharon was performing a 'standing up now' maneuver and made a 'the usual' face.

Victor helped her up for another trip to the bathroom. "Everything well with you, Sharon?"

"Aside from feeling like nine tenths of a manatee, yeah."

"You're gonna let Andy do baby pictures, right?"

"Well who the hell else would we ask? Our parents loved the ones he did after the Gay Games. They loved the wedding pictures. Vicky told her mother see, if we hadn't started this crazy dancing stuff, all you would have gotten was a bunch of phone pictures." Sharon turned to look at Andy. "Stop being so talented. You're making the rest of us look bad."

"It's impossible for you to look bad," Andy said. "You're the prettiest little blonde manatee in all the land." Vicky laughed. Sharon waved a middle finger as she waddled away.

The next day, Andy scoured the internet for reviews. When one popped up from the Hollywood Reporter, he called Victor and read it to him. "'The chemistry between real-life partners Victor Garcia and Andy Martin lends some much-needed electricity to an otherwise formulaic episode.' Oh snap!" Victor snorted. Andy went on. "'It's to be hoped that the show runners will make the most of this energy boost for the long-running and slightly tired 'Vice.'' Yeeeee-ikes."

"Wow," said Victor. "There's gonna be some mixed feelings about that at the office."

"Well, the guy has a point." Andy heard Victor laugh, and wished he was in the same room. "I guess we'll wait and see what happens."

The first thing that happened was a media shitstorm. 'L.A. Vice' had, by means of a strict lockdown on the set and scripts, and plentiful threats to the cast and crew, kept the new storyline under wraps. Once it broke, everyone had something to say, and everyone wanted the inside scoop.

It wasn't as bad for Andy. He was - rightly, he thought - viewed as the less-newsworthy half of the couple. There were regular press visitations, but he was able to come and go from the Brewery more or less as usual. Victor, on the other hand, was besieged. It got worse week over week as the other three episodes in their arc aired.

The characters' situation grew more and more dangerous as their attraction deepened. Private moments – sometimes conducted in plain sight of the gang - put the whole undercover operation in jeopardy. The storyline built up to a cliffhanger, meant to leave viewers guessing about whether Victor's character had been exposed. By then it was clear that the undercover cop and the bartender couldn't stay away from each other. Their fourth episode aired during May sweeps. It ended with an on-screen kiss and a 'To Be Continued.' The response from their friends was a barrage of texts ranging from *Fucking finally!!* (Vicky) to *Hot as snot!* (Rory) to *Did your show move to HBO?* (Janis). The media response was explosive.

An online review the next day read 'Finally, a passionate kiss between two adult men on a primetime drama. Finally, not played for laughs. Finally, not teenagers. FINALLY.' The accompanying image was a screen-cap from the episode, showing the moment before the kiss. They were standing at the end of the bar, only a few inches apart. Victor's downstage hand was on Andy's hip. Andy's upstage hand was on Victor's face, his gaze on Victor's mouth. Andy created a frame for the quote and image, and emailed it to Victor with a note: *I feel like this every time I see you*

The reply was: *So do I*

The predictable homophobic flame wars were countered by fan support on a scale neither of them had hoped for, much less expected. For every post or article about how no one should watch this degenerate show, there were hundreds of comments in support of 'Vice' and its entire team.

Aside from the social-media tornado, though, there were solid pieces describing the back half of the season as relevant, topical, and fresh. The writing team and the three leads were acknowledged for having stepped up with vigor and a new warmth to a series previously characterized as no more than a solid procedural. Victor thought, *home run.*

Andy archived much of the legitimate coverage of their prime-time breakthrough, a little proud of having helped set off such an explosion. His second-favorite quote had Victor shaking his head: 'Mr. Martin is not the kind of actor we could see in any role, but he was clearly born to play this one.'

"Why do you like that so much?" Victor said, over the phone since getting together had become, to their mutual frustration, as complex as a royal wedding.

"Because she called me an actor."

"Oh, okay. It's like that review I got that called me an accomplished singer."

"Chorus boys aren't really actors. So I guess I've learned something over the years. Either that or I'm not really acting at all. Because, you know, playing 'falling in love with Victor' is pretty fucking easy."

"I love you too. I hope this shit is going to let up now."

"Well, unless you've heard something, we're done." He spoke too soon. The original outline had sent Victor's character off on a tangent, taking the bartender out of the storyline, possibly forever. But at the end of the week after their kiss aired, they both got word from their agents that the show runners wanted to extend the storyline. Much of the cast was called back to do new scenes for the season's last two episodes, hastily rewritten to get the bartender into protective custody as a witness before the team swooped in to shut down the gang's operation. Bartender and cop shared one more intimate – though not private - moment before being separated by the long arm of the law. The closing shot was the two of them gazing at each other from separate cars, heading in different directions.

They had dinner with Rory and Dana when the re-shoots wrapped. Andy had many annoyed words about how long it took to shoot that last scene on location. Dana said, "Suck it up, you scene-stealing knucklehead." He gave her a middle finger and demanded more wine.

"Turning into quite the diva, aren't you?" Rory said, topping up all the glasses.

"I've always been a diva."

Victor surreptitiously fed a bite of steak to Spike, saying, "I've never had more fun on set. He can steal all the scenes he wants."

"I'm not actually *trying* to," Andy said, checking to see if Victor minded. He didn't think so, but this whole thing had taken on a life of its own. "Eh. It's probably over now. The opening scene of the next season will probably be the car I was in getting shot up or blown up or smashed by a big rig."

"Jesus, I hope not." Victor looked alarmed. None of the cast had any idea what the show runners were thinking at this point. Andy's prediction might give Victor some good scenes, but those weren't the kind of emotions he was hoping to play. "They haven't given us a hint. I'd love to go on with this. Could you tolerate it?" He knew Andy was sincerely irritated about sixty percent of the time.

Andy thought about it, caught Spike's fluffy orange tail a second before it landed in his plate, made eye contact with Dana, then Rory, then Victor, then Spike. He told the cat, "You are a little stinker," set him on the floor, and finally answered Victor's question. "I don't know. It's not the most fun thing in the world to do even with you in all my scenes. It eats up a hell of a lot of time. On the other hand, I'm not sure our work here is done, and it's not like there won't always be weddings to shoot." He shrugged. "Wait and see, I guess."

They didn't have to wait long. Two days after the season finale aired, Raquel forwarded a contract for a recurring role through the next season. Half delighted and half panicked, Andy called Victor. "Hi catnip. God I miss you."

"I miss you too. I love you. I was so tempted to barricade us in the makeup trailer." He was smiling, but he really meant it.

Andy heard the smile. "Jesus I wish you had. I love you. Did you see this blogger? She's all why didn't they get to kiss again, there should have been another kiss, I can't stand the suspense, will they ever see each other again, on and on." He was giggling, but he couldn't help being glad. The outrage camp was still loud, but the 'we want more' camp seemed to be getting louder.

Victor had the same thought. "Yeah, I saw that. There's a lot of that out there. What do you think?"

"Frankly I'm tempted to comment on it and say 'our real life is just as suspenseful, send help.' Of all the moments when we should be together, this is it."

"That's for sure. I need to see you."

"I need to see you too. I have something to show you. And it's not what you might be thinking." He heard Victor laugh. *I need to see that face.* He suggested a rendezvous at Chrome. "Dress to impress. There'll probably be paparazzi by the time we leave."

Victor made a sound that was half a laugh, half a sigh. "Yeah, you're right. See you ASAP." He disconnected. Andy went to get into his new meeting-the-people suit.

June 2015

They met up in the green room, since it wasn't a show night. After they kissed hello a few times, Victor said, "You look really sharp." Andy's suit was a lightweight silk blend in a color somewhere between lavender and gray. The white shirt looked familiar, but the oxblood wingtip shoes were new. "Where'd you get that?"

"Kenji. I like your pinstripes, too, you gangster you." Victor's navy suit looked great over an orchid silk shirt. He had that silver chain on. Andy kissed him again. Then he pulled the contract out of his jacket's inside pocket and handed it over without comment.

Victor read it quickly, then with more attention, and looked up. "I am *so proud* of you. I know you don't even like doing TV. You've been fantastic. Everybody on set loves you."

"I don't give a damn if they do," Andy said bitchily, because all he really wanted was to put Victor on the couch and do things. "What do *you* think? Do you think I should do it?"

"I'd love it if you did," Victor said. "This is the biggest thing I've done on the show. Or basically ever. I loved how you did it, and how I got to be with you." He handed back the contract, watched as Andy stowed it away. "Also I think if I get to work with you some more it might, possibly, make up for the way this has turned into a three-ring circus." He gazed at Andy hungrily. "Jesus I wish there was a lock on that door." Before too long they were on the couch. Andy was flat on his back and fully prepared to not give a damn about the door. Because there wasn't a lock,

Victor sat back, trying not to imagine the body under the clothes. It seemed like an awfully long time since he'd seen it. "I'm hearing from people, everybody's so impressed with you."

Andy had heard things too, many of them in the 'where have you been hiding' category. It was kind of a thrill. All the same, the experience was not wholly fun. "Raquel says this is a generous contract. But I don't know. If we can't live in peace, is it really worth it?"

"Well, I got a raise. We're both pretty well set now. You still want to take that vacation up to Washington?" It wasn't the only question Victor wanted to ask.

"Boy, do I ever."

*Here goes nothing.* "Maybe while we're away from all this nonsense we could talk about getting a place together."

Andy's mind went blank for a moment and he stared up at Victor. Then his brain clicked back on. He blinked. "Did you say 'getting a place together' or was that a mild stroke?"

"I said that." Victor was laughing with relief because Andy's expression said pretty clearly 'what a great idea.' "I know we need to find a place where you can have your studio. But wouldn't this whole thing have been so much more fun if we'd been living together? I feel like I've hardly seen you, compared to last fall."

"That is a thing I had not even considered. I am an idiot. That could make all the difference." Andy hadn't lived with a romantic partner for a long time. Maybe it should have been a scary idea – it was quite a leap from making an extra key – but it sounded like heaven.

They were holding hands. Victor wasn't sure when that happened. He was so happy he almost didn't recognize the feeling. "So? Should we start looking for a house?"

"I don't want to do it myself at this exact second. I want to go on vacation with you." Andy sat up and squeezed Victor's hand. "So how about we find a realtor person to do it for us?"

"All right." Victor smiled. "Let's see if we can sneak out of here for some hanky panky." Andy apparently liked that idea too; there was a lot more kissing. Before that got completely out of hand, Victor put some space between them and called in reinforcements. Within an hour, both their cars had been taken away by friends, to be parked at their respective homes, and they were on their way in a chauffeured car to Oxnard. It was the closest beachy place that was not Los Angeles. They didn't expect anyone to come looking for them there. For most of the drive, they sat quietly holding hands, thinking. When they turned off the 101 highway, Victor said, "I'm having such an is-this-real feeling. I've just had the best year of my life and now it's going to get even better. What the actual fuck."

Andy squeezed his hand. "I was thinking that same exact thing."

Chapter 14

"This is better," Andy sighed. He was stretched out on a king-sized bed, a glass of wine was on the nightstand, his best beloved was right beside him, and they were naked. The room's sliding doors were open and they could hear the ocean. "I'm going to feel so decadent going down to breakfast tomorrow in that suit."

"Who says we have to go anywhere? I vote room service, all day every day." Victor rolled onto his side, reaching across Andy for that glass of wine.

"Hey. Drink your own."

"Already did." Andy laughed. Victor set down the glass and kissed him again. "I'm going to abuse this situation," he said softly, lips against Andy's face. "You remember our second night?"

"I remember." Victor's hand was stroking lightly up and down Andy's body. His breath hitched. "God, don't stop doing that. Let's do it till we can't stand up. Oh wait we already did that." Victor had his mouth on Andy's neck; he was smiling. Andy rolled them over. "I remember our first night, too." *I remember all our nights.* "I can't wait to spend every night with you."

"Neither can I. I hated to leave you that first night. Forgive me?"

"I forgave you the second you told me about your mom." Andy gazed down at him, brushing a knuckle up one of those elegant cheekbones, a fingertip across his mouth. "Jesus, Victor, I can't stop with you. I think we're done, and then you touch me again, and this mouth of yours." The next kiss was as hungry as the first one after the hotel-room door closed behind

218

them. As hungry as the kisses they hadn't shared on the long drive; kissing in the car would have been such a bad idea. "You want me too. Again."

"Always. I want to wreck you. I want to wreck this fucking room. I want the people on each side, and the people downstairs, thinking there was an earthquake. Jesus!" They were moving against each other.

Andy was propped on his elbows, mouth open against Victor's. They were both panting. Andy had enough rationality to reach for the lube. He slid to one side, squeezed some into his hand and warmed it. "On you or in you?"

"On me. Let's make a mess. God, I love you." Andy lunged for his mouth again.

They spent a happy few days doing nothing but being together, and wearing next to nothing aside from – when absolutely necessary - the tee-shirts and shorts sent up from the hotel's gift shop. Midway through the second day, Andy talked through his mixed feelings about joining the cast. He hadn't been an employee for a long time. On the other hand, if the series was willing to commit to the storyline, they had an opportunity to do something for all those unrepresented gay men. All the men who still, this far into a new century, couldn't see themselves on screen. "I've never really been an activist," he admitted. "Doing a Pride parade or donating art to a fundraiser isn't the same as speaking at rallies or whatever."

"Everybody's got their own way," Victor said. "Obviously I never did any good for the rights movement till now. Being able to do this would be major. But there's another thing to consider."

Andy didn't even need to ask. "Security. Well, if we do get a place together, that would be easier too.

*When* we do," he amended, because he didn't want Victor to think he was ambivalent about it. "It's going to be a big adjustment. I'm probably going to bitch about it."

"I'm counting on that." Victor leaned over from his lounger; Andy met him halfway for a kiss, then they settled back. "So what do you think?"

"I'll sign it. Even if it's only for one season, that's so much more than anyone's done before. I'll be notorious forever, and everyone will see how awesome you are, and the show runners will get major props."

"And we'll be together. It won't be like the past few months." They both knew it was going to take a while to find a place. It might not be move-in ready. But simply knowing it was going to happen made them feel closer. "Want to go walk on the beach for a while?"

Andy looked over, smiling. "Might as well get some more use out of those shorts."

Toward the end of the fourth day, Victor said, "Is this what a honeymoon is like?" They were on their hotel room's balcony looking at another sunset, room-service champagne at hand.

Andy stretched lazily. He hadn't felt so relaxed for months. "If it isn't, it should be. When do you want to head up north?"

"I guess we have to go back into town and pack some of our own gear. But I haven't booked a thing, and I don't plan to until we get back, whenever that might be. So anytime works for me."

"Being a lady of leisure like this is agreeing with me, too. I don't have anything firm till the first weekend of August. Promo photos for that tango show. They left that kind of late but I'm glad they did."

"They've already got the marketing going."

"They scrounged some stuff from the Cabaret files. I'll say one thing for this TV gig, having that contract does take a lot of pressure off." Andy had sent his back via FedEx from the hotel. "Summer is usually big for me with weddings and shit. It's going to be a while before I can do those again."

"Yeah. You'd be upstaging the bride and groom." Victor's phone pinged. He picked it up. "It's another house. Ugly as fuck." Andy looked over at the picture and made a sound of agreement. Friends of friends had connected them with a realtor within twenty-four hours of discussing a house, and he was already sending them listings. "It's in Glendale, though. Close to work." He didn't really want to focus his life on the job.

Neither did Andy. "No, thanks. I think we should hold out for west L.A. if we can. Close to most of the places we go, and close to most of our friends. And not too bad to get over the hill to Burbank."

"I think you're right. I'll tell this dude to narrow the search a little bit. And hey," Victor said. "We're not going to have any 'it's gotta be fifty-fifty' issues, are we, if we have to go over the original price point? I've been saving for something like this for years. And now you know what those contracts are like."

They regarded each other for a few seconds. Andy thought, *I have no pride in this situation.* "It's usually the older guy who's the sugar daddy," he said. "And I've got more put away than you might think. But while I may have been too much of an idiot to think of this on my own, I'm not so much of an idiot that I'm going to let ego get in the way of what we both want, so let's spend what we've gotta spend and figure it out later."

"All right, then."


Andy told his parents about the new contract, and that he was about to be incommunicado for a while; rumor had it cell phone reception on their proposed route was sketchy at best. A week back in Los Angeles went to seeing people and getting organized. Then they were headed north in Andy's Subaru, bags packed for every contingency, and with only a select few informed of their itinerary. Neither of them had ever driven to Northern California, much less to points beyond, so they didn't book hotels in advance; they wanted to take it as it came. The first big decision was 101 or I-5.

"If we take the 101 it looks like we run out of road at Arcata," said Andy, studying one of several maps. "If we take I-5 we'll go right through Ashland."

"We could stop there, maybe we could see something. The Shakespeare Festival, right?

"Yeah, good idea. Okay, that's day ... whenever."

They stopped for the first night in Sacramento, and for the second near Mt. Shasta. "It's a good thing I brought that parallel hard drive," said Andy. "I know half of these are crap, but I can't stop taking pictures." They were swapping shifts driving, so each of them had a chance to watch the world go by. Andy was shooting out the window a lot.

"No hurry, no worries. That bridge in Redding was cool, too."

"The coolest. Actually, you're the coolest." Andy set the laptop aside. "Are you super interested in that movie?"

"No," said Victor, and reached for his lover.

At Ashland, they managed to get tickets to three plays, so ended up staying four days. Andy didn't say anything about getting back to his routine. He simply did it. Victor woke up alone on their first morning at the Festival. For a moment he was disoriented; he was already so comfortable sleeping with Andy (and waking up with him) that the absence confused him. Then he blinked, looked around the room, and remembered. In Oxnard they'd both turned to each other immediately. Even if one or the other of them went to the bathroom after waking, they went straight back to bed and into each other's arms. The same was the case their first couple of nights on the road.

Now Victor swung his legs out of bed, amazingly conscious of that absence. The room could have been a suite, or a full apartment, and he still would have known Andy wasn't there. He went to the bathroom, had a drink of water, and made a cup of coffee. There was a note on the desk: GONE OUT TO FIND SPACE FOR MORNING CLASS, BACK SOON. XOX.

Victor pulled on some sweatpants, went to the window, and looked out. There wasn't much to see: a parking lot and some trees. He found the hotel's guide and noted the location of the gym. Andy might have gone there. He might have gone to the pool. Or he might be out in the trees somewhere, preferring not to be found. Victor wanted to find him, but didn't want to bother him. He decided to follow Andy's example and do some stretches. His trainer always told him he needed to work on flexibility.

He was still on the floor when Andy came in. "Well hello. I thought I'd get back before you woke up. Did you find my note?"

"Yes, thanks for that. It was weird waking up alone."

"It was weird leaving you. But if I don't keep up with things they go downhill fast." That was as close as Andy could come to saying anything about his age.

It didn't even occur to Victor to comment, aside from, "Feel better?"

"Yes I do. I could use some floor time though. Is there space for me?"

"Always." Victor moved over. It wasn't a lot of space, even though he'd shoved the coffee table out of the way, but it was enough. Especially since Andy's version of each stretch fit on the outside of every one of Victor's. He told himself to remember that whole dance career. "Goddamn, Andy," he said after a while. He was bent toward a knee – only 'toward' it. Andy had his ribs on his forward thigh, his other leg extended in nearly a full split. "Can you actually do the splits?" Andy didn't answer, only took a breath, shifting as he exhaled. "Holy shit."

Andy laughed silently. He still had his ribs on that forward thigh. After a few breaths he folded his legs and sat up. "I should do that every day. A little tight." He changed legs, doing the open angle stretch and then the split on the other side, aware that Victor was watching. "I've always been bendy."

"You've always been incredible." They stretched for a few more minutes. Victor wanted to ask why Andy still did this if he didn't plan to perform again.

Instead he tried to figure it out. There was a difference between giving something up as a profession, and giving it up altogether. He knew how much Andy loved to dance. Maybe keeping the possibility alive was more about simply feeling capable than about what-ifs. But what if he got offered another gig that called for dancing? He might take it now. And he'd be capable. *Good role model*, Victor thought. He'd said so before, and he'd meant it. Two years ago he didn't even know the half of it.

Andy was very aware of being observed. For once it wasn't the hot stare that presaged some kind of overture. It was a professional, almost clinical interest. He could feel Victor thinking. He hadn't expected questions, but he wouldn't have been surprised. On the other hand, it wasn't surprising that Victor was apparently working things out for himself. That's what he was used to, after all, and what Andy had told him to do two years ago. *Two years*, Andy thought. It seemed like so much longer. And if he counted from when they first met, which maybe he should, it was three. Three years of thinking about each other, wondering about each other. Learning about each other. Now Victor was sitting up, eyes closed, in a half-assed half lotus. Andy didn't give him any shit about it. Instead he moved in behind and wrapped his arms around his lover. Knees up, bracketing Victor's body, with his mouth on that strong tanned neck. One hand on the stag tattoo, though not overtly caressing. Not this time. "You're so gorgeous. You're so great. Thank you for being here." *Here in this room, here in my arms.* Victor put his hands on Andy's and tipped his head back. A few degrees of turn and they could have kissed, but they didn't. This moment was about something else. Neither of them was quite sure what it was, but neither was in a hurry to figure it out. After a moment Andy kissed his cheek and moved away. "Ready for breakfast?"

"God, yes."

Andy didn't intentionally wake Victor up the next day, but he also didn't try not to. Maybe because they were both well-rested after a day of no travel, a single play, and a relatively early bedtime (it would have been early if they hadn't fooled around), Victor was awake before Andy was ready to go out. He reached out a hand. Andy sat on the bed, took Victor's hand, was pulled in for a kiss. "Good morning, sweetness. Want to join me today?"

Victor couldn't hide his surprise. "You wouldn't mind?"

"Not in the least. If I ever really need alone time, I promise I'll say so. You should too. We're both used to having quiet hours." It seemed like they'd had enough of those so far, but Andy thought it was worth saying.

"Yeah, okay." Victor held onto Andy's hand as he stood up, pulling Victor with him. He swung his legs out of bed. "I'll be ready in a minute."

There was another guy in the gym when they got there. He was running on a treadmill, wearing earbuds, watching a TV news show with the closed captioning turned on. Andy and Victor went to the far side of the room, where the wall had a big panel of mirror and there was some open space. Andy said quietly, "Do you want to follow along or do you want me to talk you through it?"

"If you don't mind talking me through this time, I'd like that."

Andy nodded, unsurprised. Their experience with tango lessons had him halfway expecting that. He said, "Put one hand on the bare wall there just outside the mirror. You can face me and do what I'm doing in reverse."

He led Victor through the whole barre routine, switching sides as needed. Victor was sweating by the end of it. "I had no idea," he said, following Andy down to the floor with obvious relief. They settled in for a round of stretches. "You do more than that with Mandy, don't you."

"All the barre, then center. That's when we review the turns and stuff."

"Before we decide on a place we have to make sure there's a room for this," Victor said. "We can put in a wood floor, a barre, mirrors. My trainer's always bitching at me to stretch more." Andy smiled. "You sure you don't mind?"

"Honey, this is never about getting away from you. When we have our own space we can play music," Andy suggested.

"Tango music. And you can teach me how to do that spinny thing."

Andy smiled at him. "You'll get it in no time."

Victor felt the morning session that night. On their way up to their room after the play, he was wincing. "Ow, dammit. My IT bands are like rock."

"We should have brought a foam roller. I could work on you." Andy was – again – not surprised. The morning routine didn't necessarily look like much, but no doubt it had called for effort Victor didn't ordinarily make. "We used to do that on the road. Some shows would have a medic, a massage therapist, even a PT. But most of the time it was like, get back to the hotel and work each other's kinks out with a drink in hand." Victor laughed. "You trust me, right?"

"With my life." Ten minutes later Victor was re-thinking that. Andy's hands on his body were usually soothing or exciting, not painful. "Ow! Damn it."

"Sorry. Got to get the muscle right off the bone for best results."

"Jesus. Where's that drink you were talking about."

Andy kissed the back of Victor's bare leg. "Hang in there a few more minutes and you'll get a different reward."

"Give me a preview." Victor was smiling into the pillow. He felt Andy's mouth on his skin again, on the back of his thigh, in no apparent hurry. "Mmm."

Andy was smiling too. "If I alternate kisses and torture this could take a long time."

"A kiss like that *is* torture." Andy did it again, on the other leg. Victor made another happy sound, shifting his hips, parting his legs a little more. He heard a soft laugh. Then those hands swept up the insides of his thighs and they both forgot about dealing with muscle fatigue for a while.


After their break for Shakespeare, it was on to Coos Bay for a night at the coast. They found an available vacation cottage with a fireplace, bought food and firewood at a local market, and went for a long walk on the beach. After dinner they watched the sunset, then sat by the window holding hands and listening to a storm roll in.

"This is wild," Victor said, late in the night. The cottage was rocking in gusts of wind. Thunder roared and lightning flashed. "I haven't been in a storm like this for ages."

"Me neither." Andy had his head on Victor's shoulder. He tipped it up a little so he could see his lover's face in the light of the low-burning fire. "Not since a hurricane back in Miami."

"If it's still raining in the morning, what do you want to do?" They'd thought of driving up the coast to the Columbia River.

"I might put the hood on the camera and go out for a while. Then maybe we go back inland?"

"That works." Victor was lightly stroking the arm Andy had across his chest. "I love this. Love being here with you."

"I love it too." They listened to the wind a while longer. Andy closed his eyes, listening to Victor breathe.

Victor woke up alone. The fire was burning merrily again; the cottage smelled of fresh coffee. He didn't even need to look around to know that Andy wasn't inside. The storm had passed; only a light rain was falling now. He got out of bed and into what passed for pajamas (sweatpants and a long-sleeved tee shirt), fixed himself a cup of coffee, and went to sit by the big ocean-view window. He was still sitting there a half hour later when he spotted Andy, moving south toward the cottage. *Those jeans must be drenched*, Victor thought, smiling. The hooded all-weather jacket only came down to his hips. His legs would be cold. He'd need to get those pants off. Good thing Victor was there to warm him up. He was on the bed, naked, stretching, when Andy came in.

"You know," he said, "I was thinking on the way back down the beach, it's a good thing there's a hot

229

Mexican in that cottage." Victor laughed. Andy set his camera on the kitchen counter and took off his jacket, hanging it on a peg by the door. "Did you see me out there?"

"Why do you think I'm naked?" Victor watched Andy strip, wet shoes, socks, and jeans hitting the floor in the entry. The thermal shirt landed on a chair. "God, look at you. Get over here." He yelped when Andy's cold legs tangled with his. Andy laughed against his skin.

After making love, they scattered the fire to let it die while they showered, got dressed, and had breakfast. Andy texted Dana to tell her they were heading into the Willamette Valley. She wrote *BRING BACK WINE*. They probably would have anyway, but that seemed like a really good excuse. "Good thing we didn't tell Charlene exactly when we might be coming," Andy said as they simmered in the hot tub at a winery-adjacent B&B. "No way should we have driven any further today." At the third tasting room, they'd looked at each other and tacitly agreed to call it a day.

"She said she took it slow when she came up, right? Probably not this slow."

"I never imagined ever taking a trip like this. Where I could, you know, just mosey along. It's great."

"Worth all those years of hard work?"

"Definitely. I also never imagined being with someone like you," said Andy, serious for a moment. "Having something like this. And I don't mean the hotels and the wine and the plays and signing autographs and all that shit. I mean *this*, you and me, this. I love it. I love you."

"I love you, too." Victor leaned over for a kiss. "You're great to travel with. It's so fantastic going to sleep with you, and waking up with you."

"Once we get our new place, we'll always have that." They gazed at each other for moment. Andy wanted to say so many things. He wanted to do a few things, too.

Victor might have read his mind. "Too bad this tub isn't in our room."

"We would never get out of it." Andy put his hand on Victor under the water and kissed him again.

Victor smiled against his mouth. "If you don't stop doing that, we're not going to be able to get out of it for a while." Andy did one more naughty thing, then heaved himself out of the water, stepping out of the tub and reaching for a robe, because he was seriously turned on. Victor stayed in the water a bit longer, staring at him. Andy held out the other robe, eyebrows up like 'I dare you.' Victor stood up.

"Oh honey you'd better face away from the pool." They both cracked up.


They skipped over Portland in favor of Astoria, where they spent a night (and gorged on seafood) before getting back on the road. A night in Olympia, and one more day's drive got them to Sequim. Victor had an interest in adding Olympic National Park to his short list of 'been there,' and Andy was agreeable. Until they actually got into it. "These trees." His tone was ambivalent.

Victor glanced over. It was early, and they weren't very far in, but the sky was overcast. The forest was dark. Victor was driving, and he hadn't really noticed. "It's almost like a tunnel, isn't it? I wonder how far up we have to go to see the sky. It didn't seem like any of the roads actually cross this thing."

"No idea." Andy pulled the park guide out of the map pocket and unfolded it. He wasn't sure what he was looking for, aside from a way out, which he didn't want to admit. It seriously didn't look like any of the access roads even connected. To get out they'd have to turn around. He didn't want to ask Victor to do that. He'd never thought of himself as claustrophobic. *Where is that river*, he thought, looking to see if the road they were on went near the Elwha. It didn't appear to. *Fuck*. But surely there'd be a gap in the trees somewhere. They were climbing, there had to be something like a view at some point. Going into the park first had seemed like a thing they ought to do, so they could check it off. They were meeting Dana's friends Charlene and Juan that night for dinner. The weather was tolerable, and they had plenty of time. He didn't know where the hell they were and couldn't see more than a hundred yards ahead on this curvy road. He abandoned the map and tried to watch for road signs.

"You're not digging this, are you." Victor couldn't have said how he knew. Andy's hands weren't noticeably tense, his breathing hadn't changed. But something about him made Victor feel a little anxious too. "It's not what I expected, either. I've been to Kings Canyon and Sequoia, and Yosemite. They're not quite like this."

Andy almost said 'not as oppressive?' Instead he said, "I've never been any of those places. Since settling in L.A. I haven't really taken a vacation. Weekends here and there to go home and visit the parents."

"No vacation for ten years? Damn, Andy."

"Well, I was working." A smile in his voice now. Victor relaxed too, but he was looking for a place to turn around. One came up after a few more minutes. He pulled off. Andy looked over. "What's up?"

"Let's go back. Let's go around on the coast instead. Who knows how long it'll take before we can see anything this way." It was a good rationale.

"You don't want to push on? I mean it's got to open up somewhere." Andy couldn't keep the relief out of his voice.

"I don't think there's anything here we absolutely need to see, do you?" Victor made eye contact. Andy did a half-shrug thing. "We can always do it by helicopter sometime." Andy made a comment about obnoxious rich people as Victor turned the car to go back the way they'd come. Within a minute they were driving in rain. "Now, see. Just as well."

Ninety minutes later they were hiking up the Elwha in a light drizzle, with sky above and the Strait of Juan de Fuca behind them. Neither of them had to say 'this is better.' Andy put his camera away after a while, and they held hands while they walked.

At dinner that night, they traded road-trip stories with Juan and Charlene. She told them about a murder mystery, set in Olympic National Park, called 'The Dark Place.' Andy ordered it for his e-reader immediately. "It's dark all right. I would have killed someone after about an hour in there," he said. "Victor turned around in the nick of time."

Back at the hotel, they exchanged notes on their new friends while they washed up, discussing some of the suggestions that had been floated for other ways to enjoy the peninsula. Once in bed, Victor moved in, head on Andy's shoulder and arm across his chest. "You know I expected to learn a lot about you on this trip," he said softly. "It's surprising how much I'm learning about myself."

"Same here." Andy was petting Victor's arm. It always happened, whoever was being held. Neither of them could simply hold the other, there was always that extra element of touch. "I had no idea how much it would freak me out not being able to see the sky. I guess I've never been somewhere without a horizon."

"I'm glad we were together." Victor moved his head so he could see Andy's face. "I love you so much."

"I love you too." Andy kissed his forehead. "Thanks for getting us the hell out of there." He rolled them over, kissing Victor's laughing mouth.

Chapter 15

Over the next week they spent time with Charlene and Juan and their baby, visiting some of the San Juan Islands and taking the ferry to Victoria. They hiked out Dungeness Spit, which suited them both: wide-open views of the water. They also took a few riding lessons from Juan, and went to his tattoo artist. Andy made the suggestion, which surprised Victor. "Matching tattoos, that's not too corny, is it?" Andy said when they discussed it. "I mean, we're too old already to regret it later, right? God knows I am." It was the first time he'd made a joke like that on this trip.

Victor gave him a look, but only said, "I'd like that." He'd been thinking of getting another tattoo – he had something definite in mind – but this suggestion was irresistible. They chose a wristband design based on local Klallam art, a single stylized eagle feather.

Andy had second thoughts as they walked in for their appointment. "The show runners might have a fit."

"They might. They can mask 'em if they want to. You've never thought about getting one before?"

"My body is a temple."

Victor gave him a look. "A temple to alcohol and fucking."

Andy snorted. "Also I heard it hurts. I can only do it now 'cause I know you'll be there holding my hand." Andy was going first, at Victor's suggestion. He didn't fully understand why until the procedure got underway. "Mother *fucker*!"

Victor leaned in close and kissed his cheek. "Sorry sweetheart. It'll be over soon."

"Jesus, no wonder you had me go first. If I'd've seen the blood I would have run out of here. Holy fucking shit." By halfway through, it didn't seem to hurt as much. Maybe all his nerve endings had simply given up. When the artist finished, Andy was given a soothing (though sadly non-alcoholic) beverage. He curled up in the spare chair, tried to ignore the dressing on his wrist, and watched the artist work on Victor. *Doesn't even flinch*, he thought, half admiring and half appalled. It didn't seem to take much time at all, when it wasn't him on the receiving end of that vicious little tool. "Was mine that fast?"

"Yes, honey, it was." Victor smiled back at him. "You did good."

They were on their way back to the hotel soon. Victor ordered room service for dinner, with plenty of wine. Then he made a few overtures, trying to distract Andy from the discomfort. Those weren't entirely successful. "I'm thinking back to when you saw Lola. And you went upstairs with me and *forgot* about it." Andy was not even close to forgetting.

"Well, it hurts but it doesn't bother me, I guess. And I wanted you so much." He was holding Andy now, feeling a little guilty for letting him go through with it. "Why in the world did you suggest this?"

Andy looked up at him. "You remember what you told me about this one?" He touched the tattoo of Victor's mother. "You said you wanted her where you could see her."

*Like a wedding ring*, Victor thought suddenly. They'd never so much as circled around that subject. In Oxnard, he'd made that comment about a honeymoon, and he hadn't even made the connection himself. *Is that what this was?* It was a big commitment, now that he thought about it. They already had so much that he'd never dreamed was possible. The thought that there might be more someday was breathtaking. "I love you," he said, as steadily as he could. "I'm glad we'll have these."

"Me too." Andy had his head on Victor's shoulder. The wrist felt kind of numb now. "Do you ever think of getting another rainbow critter?"

"I haven't thought of one. Maybe I feel like I don't need any more. I can be who I am now. And if I ever forget, I've got you to remind me."

Andy shifted enough for another kiss. "I love you."

"I love you too." Victor had his hand in Andy's hair. "I did have a new one in mind. Different kind of thing."

"What kind of thing."

"Some important dates." Andy tipped his head up to make eye contact, questioning. Victor was nervous about saying this, though not as much as he would have been before the wristbands. "The day we met. The day we became lovers. The day we decided to get a place together." Their first night, even though it hadn't ended well. That one kiss, when he agreed to the Year of Maybe. The kiss at the 'My Pet' opening. New Year's Eve. Victor never wanted to forget any of those days.

Andy blinked, swallowed, and tried to make sure his voice was steady. "Where were you thinking of putting those?"

"I couldn't decide. It's kind of like Mama, I'd want them where I could see them. But I'm hoping the list will get longer, so maybe not on my arm." Andy smiled at that. Victor smiled too. "What do you think?"

Andy moved his left hand, stroking it down Victor's chest and hooking his thumb under the sheet. He tugged it down and traced a couple of lines across Victor's thigh. "Rattlesnake on one leg, datebook on the other?"

"Upside down, so I can read them?"

"That works." Andy's mouth followed his hand. A few seconds later he was between Victor's legs with one hand on the gecko and the other – briefly - on the rattlesnake. "Sexy motherfucker," he said indistinctly. Victor felt him say it and said something desperate and profane in return. A few minutes later Andy said, "I forgot all about this damned tattoo."

Victor laughed. "Get up here. I'll make you forget again." He arranged the pillows behind his head. Andy was straddling his thighs now, fully aroused. Victor wrapped his hand around Andy's cock, swept his thumb across the tip, smiled at the muffled curse. Held eye contact while he licked that salty drop off his thumb. "God I love you. Go on. Fuck my mouth. I know you want to."

"Jesus, Victor." It was true. He moved up again, knees spread wide, and felt that perfect mouth take him. He planted his hands on the headboard and forgot about the tattoo. Not too much later, when he'd collapsed on his back, Victor kissed his ankle and asked if his wrist still hurt. Andy said, "Worth it."

They paid Juan and Charlene another visit two days later, said their farewells, and started back. They were most of the way to Oregon when Victor's phone pinged. "Something always pops in when we're near a city. You hungry?"

"I could eat."

"Let's pull off at Portland and take a break."

"Okay." Andy crossed the Columbia River and took the first exit. He found a diner and pulled in. "Let's look at this thing before we go in." Victor opened the email. "Oh my stars it's a *castle*. It's a faux chateau. What the hell?"

"It's Mid City, between Fairfax and La Cienega, south of Olympic. Elliott says there was a fire and all the tenants had to vacate because the roof fell in. Private owner is motivated. Four units plus large studio over separate garage with parking for four. Large lot, mature pepper tree in back. Front landscaping wrecked, assorted vandalism."

"Four units! Actually five, with the studio." Andy was having an unprecedented attack of house lust. "What's the layout?"

"Two two-bedroom, one bath and two one and one in the main building." They both sat and thought about it for a minute. The asking price was less than most of the single-family home listings they'd seen, thanks to the fire damage and zoning restrictions. "We could ... turn it into a big duplex? With the studio for you?"

"We could get a tenant. That would take a big bite out of the mortgage."

"What about Vicky and Sharon? Look at the size of this back yard. And it's already got a wall," Victor said.

"Great for a little kid. It's even good for them, getting to Century City. It would take, what, a year to renovate?" Andy wasn't thrilled with that timeline, but everything else about it was so tempting.

Victor was watching him. The other listings they'd seen had been uninspiring. "Probably."

"Could he guesstimate how long it would take to make at least one unit habitable?"

"We can ask. But let's go eat first. When I'm hungry, my judgement's off." Andy agreed, and they went inside. "We might not hear back for a couple of days anyway," Victor said. "Kind of a complex question."

"But important." Andy was thinking of ways to make it work. Maybe he could move into Victor's place till the duplex was ready. "I don't want to wait a whole year to actually achieve cohabitation."

"Absolutely *not*." After getting some food underway, Victor went back to the car for his laptop so they could look at the listing on a bigger screen. They studied it, discussing possibilities, until their table was cleared again and they were on a second cup of coffee.

Andy leaned back, stretching out his legs. "I guess another question is, could we cope with squeezing into that studio if we put a lot of shit in storage. If we're both working on 'Vice' all year I'm not going to be able to do much with the photography business anyway."

"Oh damn, that's right. What does this say … well hell, the studio unit is eight hundred square feet. That's bigger than your actual living space. Or mine, for that matter."

"Most of my shit is for the business. And you basically don't even have any shit."

240

"We only need one set of kitchen stuff. One bed. Computers and clothes. Everything else could go in storage." They stared at each other again. "Are you feeling like yes? The location's great, the size is great, the potential is great."

Andy produced one of those complicated expressions that always made Victor smile. This one was a combination of panic, doubt, and 'I want.' "I'm feeling like yes."

"Want to make an offer? Obviously, we know, fixing it up is gonna cost a bomb."

"How about putting it in at three hundred under asking. Let's see how motivated they really are."

"Right. Okay," Victor said, and composed an email to the realtor. They read it over, looked at each other, and smiled. "Here we go." Victor pressed 'send.'

They stopped to spend the night in Eugene, too excited to focus on the drive, and wanting to be in a place where they could send documents back and forth easily. Their offer paperwork came in at five; they signed and returned it by six. Then they went to dinner and fidgeted through the meal. "I can't appreciate this food right now," said Victor. "Might as well be McDonald's."

"For real. God I hate waiting."

"Well, there's one thing that always helps the time pass." Victor put his hand on Andy's thigh under the table.

Andy set his hand on Victor's arm and ran his fingertips lightly across the inside of his wrist. "That there is. Let's go back upstairs, hotness."

They had every intention of going up to their room, but decided to do a lap around the block first.

As soon as they stepped outside Victor said, "You are shitting me. How'd we miss that on the way in?" There was a ballroom studio directly across the street.

"Hell if I know. Want to go check it out?" They hadn't been out dancing – even for a lesson – for a long time. Both of them were happy to fill the evening that way. The other way was obviously still an option. Once inside, they checked with the person at the front desk about the evening's program. When they heard the answer they looked at each other with identical 'really?!' faces. "We have some experience with Argentine tango," Andy said. "Do you mind drop-ins?"

The front-desk girl looked as though she thought she should know them, but couldn't place them. "How much experience?"

Victor said, "Couple of years of private lessons, off and on, with Dmitri Vasko in Los Angeles."

"Oh! Do you know Julia Hart?"

They didn't wonder how this person might know Julia. The ballroom world wasn't that big. "Yes we do."

"Oh, how cool! Look, go on in, I'm sure it'll be fine. Do you mind signing in?"

"Not at all." Victor printed their names on the attendance sheet, paid the fee for the night's class and practica, and they went in. "Good thing we were dressed respectably," he said to Andy. "How many minutes till she figures us out."

"Five or less." Andy was confident the girl up front would be Googling them instantly. By the end of the tango class it was a sure thing. A different class had exited another room while they were in the main one. Through its glass wall they could see that none of the other students were leaving. There was considerable commotion, though everyone was quiet. "We're staying for the practica, right?" Andy hardly even needed to ask. They'd moved from partner to partner during the class; now he was dying to dance with Victor, properly dance. He could tell his lover felt the same way.

Victor moved close enough to murmur, "We are going to be mobbed when we leave this room." Andy snickered. The instructor said something, and started the music.

Andy wrapped Victor into the close embrace, taking only a moment to find the thread of the song. It was as if they'd never left the dance floor. That easy, wordless communication, smooth as honey and warm as sunshine. "God I love dancing with you."

"Me too. How perfect is this? The one night we're in Eugene, a hotel across the street, and they're doing tango?" They didn't talk for quite a while. After four dances – each of them led twice – they tacitly agreed to split up and practice with others. Some of the students from outside had joined the practica. It went quite a lot later than they'd expected. When they finally connected again Andy glanced at the clock in the room. It was time to go. As they headed for the door somebody started clapping. Within seconds everyone there was applauding. They glanced at each other, suppressed laughter once again, and took a bow.

Nobody outside pressed them for any contact. There were shy waves, and some not-too-obvious phone pictures. It didn't seem right to leave without a word, so Andy picked up a flyer from a shelf by the door and borrowed a marker from the front-desk girl to write on the back. He and Victor muttered to each other for a minute before deciding on THANKS FOR WELCOMING A COUPLE OF STRAYS FOR A GREAT NIGHT OF TANGO. LOVE AND KISSES, VICTOR GARCIA AND ANDY MARTIN. They both signed it. The front-desk girl squealed a little when they handed it over. Then she asked if she could take a picture for the studio's Facebook page, so they let her do that before making their escape.

"Wow," Victor said, once they were safely in the hotel and headed upstairs. "I was thinking of stopping at the bar, but I'm exhausted." Andy was cracking up. "Did not expect that."

"Get used to it, catnip." Andy suddenly thought of something he'd been meaning to ask. "Do you mind that I call you that?"

Victor was startled. "No, I like it. I've always liked it. When you said I was a hundred and ten percent of your catnip, that's when I knew I had a chance with you." They were at the room now. He opened the door, then went straight to the late-night room-service menu. "What do you think." Andy studied it over his shoulder. "Couple of Manhattans? And a dessert for you?"

"It's so obnoxious, isn't it." Andy's burn rate was always higher than Victor's. "I'll get the sliders instead of something sweet. A Manhattan is sweet enough. Tell them to put an extra cherry in it." Victor picked up the phone. Andy stood behind him while he made the call, arms wrapped loosely around him. Once Victor put the phone down, Andy kissed his cheek and said, "You would have had to do something really egregious. I was so far gone already, that day at the loft. After you came to find me, and told me why, and it made sense. There was no reason for you to be there unless you cared."

"I was so afraid you'd say no. All along the way, there were so many times you could have said no." Victor tipped his head against Andy's. "I don't know what I would have done."

Andy thought, *I don't either.* "You would have found someone. One of those people you dated. I know those weren't all throwaway guys."

"No. Gino in particular, something could have happened. We talked easily. But it wouldn't have been like this." *Nothing could have been like this.* They turned toward each other. They were still kissing when room service knocked. Andy let go of Victor with a look of promise and went to open the door.

Before noon the next day, an email came in from Elliott. "'Hi guys,'" Victor read. "'The seller countered back at two hundred under asking. She says she likes you on 'L.A. Vice' and you seem like sweet boys.'"

Andy hooted. "If she only knew!"

"'If that price is acceptable, then you've got the property.' Well?"

"Fuck yeah, it's acceptable."

"I'll tell him to tell her we'll put her on the list for the 'Milonga' reboot. It would be cool to meet her." Victor sent the reply. "Honey, we just bought a house. Sort of." They were still in the hotel room, still in bed. He leaned over, bearing Andy down against the pillows, stretching out on top of him. "We're going to have our own place." They grinned at each other.

"I cannot fucking *wait* to actually live with you. Thank you for thinking of it." Andy rolled them over and propped himself on his elbows, kissing Victor's face and neck. Then he started moving down. Victor's hands were on Andy's thighs, then his back, then his shoulders, and finally in his hair.

"Jesus, Andy. Give me something to work with here."

Andy replaced his mouth with his hand. "I am going to work *you*. Because I am worked *up*."

"I noticed," Victor said breathlessly. "Oh God." Andy sat back, pulling Victor up to kneel in front of him, and then moved around behind. He ran one hand up Victor's body to his throat, cupping his jaw. His mouth was on Victor's neck and his other hand where it had been a moment ago. Victor tipped his head up, eyes closed, surrendering.

They were back in California a day later, and it was raining. "This is not right," Andy complained. "It is not supposed to rain during summer in California."

"Well, we're still pretty far north." Victor was driving. Andy was watching the scenery go by, camera held loosely in his lap. "What the fuck." Victor slowed a little.

"What?" Andy looked ahead. "Is that a dog?" They both turned their heads to look at the animal in the median as the car approached and then passed. Andy snapped a couple of pictures out of habit. "Definitely a dog. A dog does not belong there. This is not going to end well."

Victor didn't say anything right away. Then, "Somebody had to have dumped it. We're not near anything. I'm going back for it."

"Huh?"

"I'm going to turn around at the next exit. I'll pull over for a minute, can you find our beach towels? I think they're on top of those cartons of wine."

"Okay. Yeah, okay." In a few minutes they reached an exit. Victor went up the ramp, swung over the freeway, then pulled over on the side of the return ramp. Andy scooted out of the car and did a high-speed rummage through the cargo area, pulling out the beach towels and tossing them in the back seat. He got back in the passenger seat, swiping his rain-dampened hair off his face. "I haven't had a pet since I was sixteen."

Victor smiled suddenly. "Me neither." He pulled back onto the ramp, merging with the light traffic. In a minute or two he moved to the passing lane and then slowed, pulling onto the median shoulder with the hazard lights on. "Where is it? Do you see it?"

Andy put his camera up to his eye to use the zoom. "A little farther." They rolled forward slowly. The rain was coming down harder. "You're going to get hella wet."

"It's only water." Victor stopped the car and set the brake, then got out and started walking toward the dog. Andy shot pictures like his life depended on it. The dog was skittish, but when Victor crouched down and stayed still, it crept forward. A minute later, he was able to touch it, pet its head, then pick it up. He carried it toward the car. Andy thought *oh hell the door* and got out of the car to open the driver's-side back door, camera still swinging from its strap around his neck. Victor smiled and Andy took a picture.

The dog was shaking with cold and fear when Victor placed it on the back seat. "I'll get in the back with it and see if I can dry it off a little. We need a lot more towels." Andy was nearly as wet as Victor. He slid onto the back seat and closed the door.

"It's only water," Victor said again, getting into the driver's seat. "She's a good dog."

"She's not hurt, is she?" He didn't see any obvious injuries as he wrapped her in one towel. He reached over with the other to rub the worst of the water from Victor's head, then did his own.

"I don't think she's hurt. But cold. Me too." Victor turned on the heater full blast, signaled, and merged back onto the highway.

"Are you a good girl? Who did that to you?" Andy turned his attention to the dog's wet paws. She bent her head alongside his. "You're a sweetheart, aren't you," he said quietly. One more turnaround and they were headed south once again. Andy kept rubbing the dog's fur with the damp towels.

The nearest town of any size was Redding. They pulled into the first motel that said 'pets allowed.' They checked in, and took turns getting the bare minimum of gear to their room. Then they brought the dog in.

"She doesn't have a collar. How are we going to walk her?" Andy thought for a second. "Hang on." He dug around and found a belt, looping it twice around the dog's neck and attaching the sturdy strap from his camera as a leash. "There we go. Okay, lady? Want to go for a walk?" There was no argument from the dog, so he took her outside. After a while they came in again.

"Anything?"

"She didn't have much to give, but a little something. She should be okay for a while. She is a good dog." The dog looked up and thumped her tail once.

They used half of the towels getting the dog dry, and then took turns in a hot shower. In dry clothes and properly warm, they sat on the bed and looked at the dog, curled up under the desk.

"She's pretty," said Andy. "Like a border collie but blonde." He took another picture. "Why would someone dump such a pretty dog? She's leash-trained. She's potty-trained. She doesn't growl in a situation when I would be biting people's legs off."

Victor made a soft sound. "People can be awful."

"Well, yeah, we both know that."

"What should we call her?"

"Let's sleep on it. But first, let's see if we can order some pizza." It turned out that was possible. The pizzeria even sold meatballs, so they ordered a few for the dog. Andy waited for a break in the rain, then went back out to the car. Victor laughed when he returned with a bottle of wine from their stash. "What? We are, unexpectedly, pet parents; this calls for a little wine with our pizza."

"Come here and kiss me."

"Okay." A few minutes later Andy pulled back. "I think she's watching." Victor made an amused sound and pushed him down. "You don't know how fast this pizza guy is going to be."

"Let's race him."


It was still early after they ate. They both got on their laptops to start catching up with correspondence. "Parker sent me an audition," Victor said. "For a feature, filming next summer. I can go out for it next week."

"What's the part?"

"Action comedy. Second lead, sidekick. That's a really good part for me." His tone may have betrayed his surprise. He'd had movie parts before, but never something so close to the top.

Andy was watching him. Along with the surprise there was relief, and something close to disbelief. "Is it a straight character?"

"Yeah." It didn't specify in the notice. It didn't specify Latino, either. Victor knew that meant the script hadn't been written with him in mind. It also meant the casting director had thought of him in spite of the fact that he was Latino and gay.

*Yes.* There was a time Andy wouldn't have thought about the implications. Now all he could think was 'hallelujah,' because coming out hadn't fucked Victor up, being with Andy hadn't ruined his career, even this wild rainbow tangent that the series had taken wasn't going wrong. He tried to sound casual. "Well, you can't have everything."

Victor responded to the subtext. "It's actually great. There was always the chance, you know, that after going all Ellen on 'Vice' I would be the gay cop forevermore. Parker says they're seeing three people for it, this round. Had one guy in mind but he wasn't available, next choice didn't want to take second lead. So they opened it up."

And one of three people they went to was Victor. More hallelujah. "Who's the lead?"

"Jonathan Morris. Used to be a pro wrestler, got recruited for a bad guy role, and stole every scene. He's been working his way up the past ten years. A couple years older than me."

Andy Googled the guy immediately. "Whoa, looks like a bruiser. Must have a sense of humor, though. Well, cool. By the way I have sent a dog rescue photo essay to Raquel and Parker, figured they should know in case they need some human interest. Raquel hasn't heard from me for weeks, she probably thinks I've been in a blackout celebrating that contract."

"A lot of people would be."

"The only reason I even care is because I get to work with you." Andy turned his laptop so Victor could see the pictures. "You're awfully hot-looking for someone so wet. Did you know that line of trucks was going by? I didn't even see them until I looked at the files."

"Yeah, I knew they were there. It felt like they were *really* close. All I could think was, dog, please don't run."

"For real."

In the middle of the night, Andy woke up to a nudge on his arm. He looked over the side of the bed and saw the dog. She put a paw up suggestively. "Okay. Come on up." He patted the bed. She jumped up, turned around, plopped down by his leg, and thumped her tail once. "Good girl." He went back to sleep.

The next morning, they both had emails from their agents. Andy laughed until he choked when he read Raquel's. "What?" said Victor. Andy turned the laptop around.

> Dear Andy,
>
> Please tell Victor to stop being so adorable. Do you really want to release those pictures? Because if you do, the internet is going to go nuts all over again. Not a bad thing for your careers but I know you were getting a little tired of the shenanigans.

Btw thanks for sending back the contract so fast. Your last check from the first round is in the bank.

Cheers – Raquel

p.s. where the hell have you been??

"Why was that so funny?" Victor asked.

"Because I thought that exact same thing when you bought the print for Rory and Dana. Like, how was I supposed to hold out against this? But you just can't help it, can you?" He sent back a quick email telling Raquel to release the story, that they had a plan to deal with the shenanigans, then set the laptop aside and reached for Victor.

They found a diner for breakfast, bringing the dog back a takeout container full of sausage and scrambled eggs. "Okay," said Victor. "We've really got to name this poor girl. I can't be thinking of 'the dog' all the time."

"Yeah, it's demeaning."

They discussed a few ideas while the dog ate her breakfast, then settled down with a sigh of apparent contentment. The final decision was to call her Molly, after the 'Titanic' survivor. "She wasn't dumped in the North Atlantic, but she was definitely shipwrecked. That work for you, Molly?" Victor addressed the dog. She looked up, thumped her tail once, then settled back down. "I guess that's her name, then."

The next-to-last thing they did before loading the car and getting back on the road was send a text to Vicky and Sharon: *Hey ladies we've got a proposition for you. We're buying a thing that will be a duplex and we'll need tenants. Approx one yr to livability. 3 br 2 ba unit is yours if you want it. We'll call you when we get back to L.A. OXO*

*p.s. we seem to have acquired a dog. Hope you and Simka are well!*

The very last thing they did was send a text to Rory and Dana, with a picture of Molly: *Hey girls we need a foster home for our new dog till Andy can move to the new job site slash studio. Her name is Molly. Do you have capability? OXO*

Andy got a return text almost immediately from Rory: *OMG SHE IS SO PRETTY I WANT HER ok the cat says hell no but Dana says we can keep her for a while. Did you buy wine?*

*What do you think?*

*Bring us some when you bring Molly. Also WTF moving?*

*Bought a house!!*

*SQUEEE*

*LOL*

Chapter 16

They considered pushing through to home in one day, but decided that was too many hours in the car and no way to end a vacation. During a stop at a roadside diner with WiFi (and outdoor tables so they could eat with Molly), they located a pet-friendly hotel in Fresno, and re-routed themselves to Highway 99.

"You are an excellent traveler," Andy told Molly on their post-arrival walk. "A very good girl. Whoever threw you away did us a favor. Right, honey?"

"I didn't even know I wanted a dog until I saw her in the median." Andy snorted. Victor glanced over at him. "Now I'm going to have a dog, a house, and you. I'm the luckiest guy in the world." Andy leaned over to kiss him. Molly, already used to this, sat down to wait.

Back in the room, Andy washed up first. "I keep being surprised when I see this tattoo," he said when he came out of the bathroom. "The first few days when it was still sore, I thought I would never forget it was there. Weird, huh?"

"How do you feel when you see it?" Victor was sitting on the side of the bed. Maybe because of the thoughts he'd had up on the peninsula, he never stopped noticing the wristband. Every time his hand moved, he thought, *this is proof of love*. The only way it could have been better was if they'd done a custom design. He still didn't know if Andy fully recognized the implications of the wristbands. He wasn't going to ask.

"I like it." Andy sat beside him, kissed his cheek, reached across for his hand. "I like the way they look side by side."

"Your hands always kill me."

"They are pretty good hands," Andy agreed. "But yours are talented."

"Someday all this TV craziness will be over. Will you wear jewelry again?" Victor leaned his head against Andy's, eyes on their left hands. Andy's was wrapped over the back of his, fingers pressed between Victor's, thumb caressing the inside of his wrist.

Andy wondered if that was a hint. If Victor had the same thoughts he did. It was hard to believe. Impossible not to hope. "I probably will. Someday." Andy kept hold of Victor's hand with his left, but now his right went to Victor's throat, closing lightly over it, turning his face for a kiss. "God, I love you." Victor's mouth opening, that insatiable hunger, the flood of passionate desire. Victor's right hand on the inside of Andy's naked thigh, moving up. "Jesus, Victor."

"More. Now. Everything."

Quite some time later, when Victor was doing his delayed washing-up, Andy lay on the bed idly stretching, and thinking. He was fairly sure Victor knew the why of the wristbands. There was absolutely no sign that he regretted it. Quite the opposite, in fact. *Someday*, Andy thought, *I will come right out and say it*. He would say, you are the one and only, the one I wanted all my life, the one I will never leave. Someday, when he'd had a little more time to get used to it. When the sight of that perfect Valentino face so close to his didn't reduce him to this dazzled mess.

If it had been only the man's beauty, he wouldn't have fallen so far, so fast, so thoroughly. It was the intelligence, and the talent, and the core of toughness. The generosity, the courage, and the sweetness.

Molly gave an inquiring wuff beside the bed. She never barked. "Your voice is as soft as a summer breeze, Molly. Hop on up." Andy patted the bed. She jumped up, turned around, and flopped down beside him, where he could wrap his arm over her shoulder. She thumped her tail once. "You are a very good girl," he said. She rested her chin on his chest. Brown eyes gazed into brown. Andy heard Victor come back in the room. "She's trying to hypnotize me again."

Almost the first thing they saw driving into Sherman Oaks, aside from a never-ending river of brake lights, was a 'for your consideration' billboard for 'L.A. Vice.' It featured the full regular cast, plus Andy, shown with Victor in the moment before the kiss. "Did you see that?!"

"Watch the road! Jesus, Andy." After a second to make sure they weren't about to crash, Victor said, "They've never gotten an Emmy nom for best drama. How did we not see that campaign online?"

"I don't know about you but I was avoiding the news. Except for, you know, the Google alert which I still have on you. It's not stalking if you're my boyfriend, right?" Victor snorted. Andy went on, "When do the nominations come out, anyway? Oh shit, it's next week. We were gone for a while, huh."

"If we get the nomination, that's going to help when I go to that audition."

"Oh, you know you're going to get it. You always do."

"No I don't," Victor said automatically. "Not always." He thought about it for a second, realizing that he was doing that self-deprecating thing. *Own it, pendejo.* "Just usually."

Andy made an amused sound. "I guess you have a sense for what you're going to get hired for. I never did have any sense about that. I went out for the most ridiculous things."

"You could probably get name parts now, if you wanted. You could play, like, Nathan Detroit. The Wolf. Captain Hook."

One of those was a part Andy had actually played, but he didn't see the need to say so right this second. "Holy shit, that's a *great* idea. We could do our very own summer stock series. You could play Sky Masterson. Rapunzel's Prince. Smee." Victor laughed. "But only if it's here in town. I'm not going out on the road again with anyone but you. You and Molly," he added, glancing over his shoulder at their pet. "Best vacation ever." He took one hand off the wheel and put it on Victor.

"Stop that! You'll kill us all."

"So you see me as the Big Bad Wolf, huh." Maybe someday he'd 'fess up to that.

"Honey, you *are* the Big Bad Wolf. The whole world should know."

They drove over the hill, then to West Hollywood to drop Molly off with Rory and Dana. "Wow, that is one amazingly dirty car," Dana said, stepping out of their cottage. "Where all did you go?"

"Sacramento, Redding, Ashland, then we went over to the coast for a day, got plenty of mud there. Astoria, Olympia, peninsula. And back. I almost filled up my parallel drive," said Andy.

"So what's the story on the dog?"

"Found her on the highway. Where's Spike?"

"He's shut up in the den. He's good with dogs though. He'll probably put on some kind of song and dance but he doesn't really mean it."

"We don't know how Molly is with cats," Victor said. "In general, she's really mellow and quiet." He let her out of the car, wearing a new collar they'd picked up before starting out of Redding.

"She is super pretty. On the highway, seriously? Come on in, Rory made some cookies."

They all went inside. Rory greeted them from the kitchen. Dana went to open the den door. Spike swaggered down the hall, stopping short when he saw the dog. Molly's ears perked up and she wagged. Spike's back went up and his tail puffed out. Molly lay down, alert and interested, with her head low. Spike hopped around for a minute, trying to look big and tough. He feinted at her nose without connecting. She gave him a look of such sorrow that all the humans laughed.

"I think we're good here," said Rory. "Quit dancing around like a fool, Spike, you know you like dogs."

"She is just about the perfect dog, isn't she?" Victor was already completely moony about their rescue.

"Yeah, yeah. I'm jealous. Come and have some cookies and tell us about this house."

"It's a fucking mess," Andy said cheerfully. "Burned out. We have to get ten thousand inspections. But it's a faux chateau. It has *turrets*."

"Okay cool, but wait. What the fuck." Rory took his hand, inspected the tattoo, looked over at Victor. He held up his left hand. Her eyebrows shot up. He did a little 'yeah I think so' thing and she cut her eyes over at Andy. "This is not what I was expecting by way of souvenirs. A very fine dog, and matching tattoos. Andy?"

He looked around at everybody. Everybody seemed to be staring back, even the cat. Victor was wearing that wicked-sweet smile of his. "I know, they're feathers, which is your thing, but you don't have an exclusive." Rory didn't say anything, but she also didn't let go of his hand. Andy sighed. He knew this was going to happen, knew he'd have to verbalize. "Yes, okay, and it was my suggestion. I wanted us *branded*, all right? Labeled. He's mine, I'm his, hands off, fuck off." Rory and Dana made identical 'aww' noises. Victor moved close, leaning against Andy, who put his arm around his lover and kissed his cheek. "Also it hurt like hell, and now every time I see *your* feathers I'm going to be thinking OW." Trying to make a joke out of it, because this was getting kind of sappy.

Rory moved in on him. A second later all four of them were hugging. After a minute she stood back. "You got those from Juan's guy, didn't you."

"Yep. We had a great time with them."

"Can you come in and tell us a few stories?" Dana looked hopeful. "I really want to hear about the dance thing."

"Oh, did that get on the internet?" Andy was grinning. "Talk about being in the right place at the right time."

"I'm still not over that," said Victor. "We had no plans to stop at that particular hotel. We only wanted a place to sit still and do the offer on our castle. And then here's a dance studio across the street, and they're doing tango. It was freaky."

"The second-best kind of freaky," Andy said.

"I'm assuming there was plenty of the other kind." Rory picked up the container of cookies and started moving toward the den. "You don't need to tell us about that. Weren't you supposed to bring wine?"

"Jeez, okay." Andy went back out to the car.

August 2015

Andy and Victor had to scramble over the next few weeks, working with their lawyers and accountants on the house closing. Andy talked to Patrick, who'd been handling his taxes for years. "How did you guys work it? If you don't mind my asking."

"I don't mind." Patrick leaned back in his office chair. He and Dmitri had been observing the whole Andy-and-Victor thing with growing interest, ever since that first tango performance. They'd read the review, followed the links, and been mutually astonished. But it was clear that Andy was not interested in revisiting his years as a dancer, so they minded their own business. "We didn't do it like you guys. I bought the house. Dmitri was making a decent living back in '05, but we weren't living together yet. We registered the partnership after he moved in, and then did our whole estate plan. Doing that twice was a giant pain in the ass. Are you going to register? Or are you going to get married?" Patrick thought he could be forgiven for asking. After all, he had several legitimate reasons for wanting to know the answer.

Andy made an 'eek' face and hesitated. "We haven't talked about it yet. Either of those things."

"Yet."

Andy sighed. "Look, if we were two guys who worked at, you know, Starbucks? If we were the same age? I'd ask him today. To marry me. But we have all this stuff going on, and there is a lot of money in the mix, and I'm ten years older than he is. It's non-trivial shit."

Patrick did a 'that's true, but' thing. "And we had a new house, new cohab, my firm, his high-risk business. Before long we were opening the studio, and that could have gone up in flames in about ten different ways. That's what happens when people come together as grown-ass adults. Imagine what it's like for people who've been married and divorced, or who have kids to consider." He studied Andy for a few seconds. "We talked about it after he moved in. First it was about registering the partnership, because that was going to make a difference for a lot of legal things. The house, healthcare, whatever. But while we were talking about that, it was, if it's ever legal for us to get married, do you want to. Both of us did. There was never any doubt about it. He had an ex back on the East Coast who got married the second it was legal. First in line for a license. There was this huge party where the guy taught."

"You two didn't have a huge party."

"No, because Dmitri was up to his ass in that first title campaign. This is the first year since then that he hasn't been up to his ass in a campaign, and he's been up to his ass in the Cabaret instead." Patrick sounded exasperated. The summer pro show wasn't officially a presentation of the Underground Cabaret, but so many of the same people were involved that everyone tended to forget that. "I'm hoping we can get out of town for a week or so at the end of the year, but I doubt there'll ever be a party. It's old news now."

"Is it ever old news, though?" Andy leaned forward, resting his elbows on Patrick's desk, eyes on that wristband tattoo. "I see this every day, a dozen times a day, and I think wow. Don't you look at your wedding ring and think, holy shit?"

"Oh yeah." Patrick was smiling. "I seriously recommend it. I understand why you don't want to rush it, but … don't wait too long to talk about it. It meant so much to say those things to each other."

"I know." Andy wanted to ask how long was too long, but he needed to wrap things up. Patrick had another appointment, and he had ten thousand things to do himself. *This is the whole problem*, he thought. But someday it would ease up. They'd have that minute to sit down together, maybe in their new house, and say 'do you want to.' Or maybe someday he would simply not be able to wait another second, and he'd ask.


Victor went out to the Valley at the end of their first week back, totally focused on acing his audition. He'd watched as many of Jonathan Morris' previous movies as he'd had time for, and looked up some of his old WWE things online. Parker had sent the full script, something Victor rarely got to see before an audition. He liked it. It was action-packed, funny in both broad and subtle ways, and ended with a bang. Victor's character was an ATF agent, which was something new for him, and meant a little more research. When he went in, he met with the producer, director, and casting director first. Then they had him read a couple of scenes early in the script, before he and Jonathan's NSA officer hooked up. After that, they left him alone for about ten minutes. He didn't know if that was a good sign or not; it was a first. But when they all came back in, Jonathan was with them.

"Hey Victor," the star said. "Thanks for coming out today." He offered a hand.

Victor shook it. "Happy to. I've been watching your movies."

Jonathan winced. "Oh, shit. I've been hearing about some of those ever since the word got out I was cast for this thing."

"Yeah, I'll bet. I've been hearing about some things I was trying to forget ever since my new stuff on 'Vice' dropped."

Jonathan mentioned something truly embarrassing, which astonished Victor; he hadn't expected the star to do any homework on him. There was no sign he had an issue with Victor being gay, or out, or in a relationship with another man. They were given a few more minutes to get acquainted, and then it was on to some scenes. Victor was feeling hopeful about it by the time they cut him loose. He and Jonathan had good chemistry, and they'd had the watching bigwigs laughing more than once. He texted Andy before leaving the production company's office: *Hey good looking, this went well. Jonathan is a kick. I missed you last night so I'm planning to use my key*

A reply came back as Victor was starting his car: *God I missed you too, got really spoiled on vacation. Apologies in advance for mess at loft*

*It's never a mess*

*Oh yes it is I usually clean it up before you get here but doing the book thing*

*OMG okay*

*LOL see you soon XOX*

*XOX*

Andy was serious about the mess. Moving in together was going to take a lot of advance planning. He had several photography jobs to do – things he'd booked in the spring, or that had come up for Cabaret-related reasons - before wrapping up the 'out and about' part of that career for a while. With the expectation of 'for a while' being 'at least a year,' he'd decided to take the book problem to the mat. He wouldn't need the books while he was being an actor. They'd served mostly as props for years. Therefore, it was time to do a serious cull.

When Victor walked in, he saw that all of the books previously shelved above the desk were out on the floor, as was Andy. "In a minute I'm going to see if I can figure out your method," he said. "But can I kiss you now?"

"You absolutely can." Andy stood up and stepped over a stack of books. Quite a few minutes later, he finally leaned back. "God it's good to see you."

"You too. I brought food."

"You are the *best*. Hungry now?" Victor nodded; Andy let go of him. "Shall I open a bottle of Oregon?"

"Yes please." They sat at the desk to eat (and drink) while Victor told Andy about the audition. "Anyway, I sent Parker a note. It felt like a win."

"Here's to that." They clinked glasses. "So I started going through those thousands of photos from the trip. It seems like there's enough time to throw together an exhibit before I move out, and I might as well," he told Victor. "It's something completely different for me, but what the hell." A little something to remind the world what he did, since he hadn't had time for a spring show.

"What are you going to call it?"

"I'm thinking 'Pacific.' For a few reasons."

Victor nodded. The word had several meanings. "What are you going to do with the ones you don't keep?" He was looking at the books again.

264

"Open house. Get the word out around the complex, come and get 'em. By the time everyone's come and gone, there will be no getting out of this. Everybody's going to know I'm moving in with you. Still want to do it?"

Victor wasn't expecting that. He turned his head; Andy was sitting there with both hands on the desk, tightly clasped. His manner so rarely betrayed any anxiety. *You are a better actor than you think.* Victor reached over with his left hand, took Andy's left wrist, and gently pulled that hand away. Locked his with it, palm to palm, wristbands meeting in the middle like infinity. "You see these?"

"Uh-huh."

"I'm yours. You're mine. Right?"

"Right." Andy kept some tension in his arm as Victor pulled, bringing the two task chairs closer. "I really love you," he murmured against Victor's mouth.

"I love you too. Never doubt it." One more kiss. Then, "Do I want any of those books?"

"Let's find out."


The schedule never let up. Victor got a contract for 'Countdown' five days after his audition. There was a celebratory dinner with Rory and Dana. Then more business having to do with the real-estate deal, and the first of many meetings with contractors. There was some press to do about 'L.A. Vice,' some press about the movie deal. None of the interviews were joint, so nobody picked up on the new tattoos. They both had a chance to say some things about each other. Someone asked Victor if he ever regretted settling down so soon after coming out. He said,

265

"Andy Martin is my inspiration as well as my true love. He is incredibly talented. And seriously, is there anyone anywhere of any gender who doesn't think he's gorgeous? Was I going to do *better*?" It made the interviewer laugh, and got Victor a flurry of texts from friends. Including one from Rory: *That would be No and No.*

Andy was interviewed because of the Emmy nomination for 'L.A. Vice.' People wanted to know if he thought the romance arc with Victor contributed to that. He said, "I hope so. It's a major departure for the show. I know it's had a positive effect on their viewership. If the production community thinks that's worthy of notice too, I'm delighted." Then he was asked for his opinion about Victor as an actor. He gave the journalist a look. "You know we're a real couple, right? In all seriousness. I've worked in and around showbiz for a long time. Mr. Garcia is one of the most talented people I've ever met. I don't think he's even begun to scratch the surface of what he can accomplish. I hope he gets a chance to do everything, and I hope I'm around to see it."

They caught up with Janis in August, too. She was in the studio recording her third album, and would be going on an even bigger tour in the fall. Andy dealt with the book situation and wrapped up his other projects so he could focus on 'Pacific.' They found time to get to Shall We Dance, resuscitating their tango routine for the upcoming reboot of 'Milonga,' and then having dinner with Dmitri and Patrick. Anytime either of them was anywhere near West Hollywood, they dropped in to see Molly.

They also got together with Vicky and Sharon to discuss the Faux Chateau, meeting for lunch at a sushi restaurant on La Cienega. "That's, like, three blocks from my parents' house," Sharon said, looking at the Google map they'd printed out.

"Did you leave Simka with them today?" Victor asked.

"No, she's at the studio with Dmitri. They're so cute I can't stand it."

"Miriam is already on board for daycare when Sharon goes back to work next month," Vicky said. "It's too bad we can't move right away."

"So you want to do this?" Andy asked. "I know it was kind of out of nowhere."

"Are we seriously going to turn down living in a castle?" Sharon said. "And that *yard*. The apartment only has that crappy patio."

"It's not crappy," Vicky protested.

"It is compared to a yard, with a tree and everything."

Victor had to agree. "I've never had a yard. I'm not going to know what to do with it. We have to put together a team." They made a list of their friends, family, and connections who might be roped in.

"And I guess I'm the point person," Andy said. "As soon as we close, we're going to spruce up the studio unit so I can move in there. We'll get security for the main building right away, and then get started."

Vicky said, "You're back on the show next season. What else will you have going on?"

"Not a hell of a lot. We're doing 'Mating Game' again, plus Dmitri wants to choreograph 'Moondance' for us, for Halloween. We don't really have time to do it but we both want to do it. Once the show from this trip is down I'm not going to try doing much with photography. I've got a ton of stuff in the archive that I can freshen up for the online store, but doing gigs for hire is definitely out till I'm not a celebrity anymore."

"Will you miss it?" Victor said. "Because what if you're never not a celebrity?"

Andy waved that off. "Yeah, right. But no, that was always only for the money. Maybe I'll do a 'we conquer the castle' series, to keep the camera dusted off."

"Maybe you should do a reality show," said Vicky. She was half kidding, but they all looked at each other speculatively, and nobody laughed. "Huh."

"Let's go see the place," said Victor. "Fair warning, it looks worse in real life." He wasn't kidding. "And we can't go inside."

About ten minutes later they were parked out front. Victor unlocked the front door and pushed it open. "Wow, you guys," said Sharon, looking in. "This looks like it was bombed."

"It's been inspected. Amazingly, not bad enough to be condemned. I had my fingers crossed about the turrets, but they're both good. So first we get the roof rebuilt, then everything else starts." Andy looked around. The center hall had a staircase going up to the second floor, and doorways opening into the two ground-floor units. The doors themselves were long gone. The front rooms were high-ceilinged and would be bright when they had picture windows again, instead of sheets of plywood.

"If we hire your dad to do the engineering, can he pull the original plans?" asked Victor. "And then maybe work with Mateo on new floor plans?"

"Well, sure. I guess it would be, living room and guest rooms and kitchen and laundry and bath on the main floor, gigantor master suite upstairs?" Sharon leaned further in. "I wish we could go in!"

Andy had his arm around her waist. "I wish we could too, but I don't want anything falling on anybody. That would not be a good start for this project."

"Do we get to pick the colors and shit?"

Vicky snickered. "Sharon's been designing kitchens and bathrooms ever since you sent that text."

"Somebody has to," said Andy. "It's basically a gut job, so we're starting from scratch. And you've seen my place."

"Yeah. Honey, we'll stop for graph paper and mechanical pencils on the way home." Sharon laughed. Vicky looked around once more and raised her eyebrows at Victor. "I hope you got a good deal on this place."

"We did." Victor smiled. "Little old lady who thinks we're sweet boys."

Vicky patted him. "You are sweet boys."

"So, are you going to do a reality show?" Sharon asked.

Andy made a face. "Eh. I can't imagine trying to cope with that on top of the actual renovation. So, probably no. It's too bad though, we would have blown Bronson Pinchot out of the water."

Chapter 17

It was strange to look around the loft, his home for more than seven years, and think 'goodbye.' Andy wondered if he would miss it. Miss the community, and the solitude-by-choice. If that's really what it was. The people who were truly friends would stay in touch, he and Victor wouldn't be on top of each other constantly – even on that vacation, they'd found a little pocket of time every day to be separate creatures – and the benefits were legion. From now till the new studio unit was ready, he had to go through all his personal stuff, decide what he needed to keep for the future, decide what he needed to use in the present, and get rid of everything else. *Start with the kitchen*, he thought, because that was easy. He put in a couple of hours, keeping an eye on the clock, then downed tools and settled in for an overdue call to his mother. She'd been making do with occasional texts, but her replies had become more and more openly impatient.

He'd chosen his time well; she picked up on the second ring. "Hi Mom. How are you? How's Pop? Yes, the vacation was completely spectacular. I have a ton of news." Pause for laugh. "No, you go first, seriously, it's going to take a while." He listened, smiling, as Eva gave him the 411 on Miami. "Okay, great. Glad to hear it. Well the first thing is Victor and I are buying a place together." He held the phone away from his ear for half a minute, waiting for the excitement to abate. "Yeah, I know. Believe me, that's exactly how I feel. Well, partly because of the TV show. It's hard work, and the hours are long, and there are security concerns. So there are practical reasons. Mostly we want to be together. It was his idea. I said

270

yes before he finished talking, basically." Another pause for laughter, and another question. "Yes, it's right in the middle of town, close to our friends. It's a mess, there was a fire. We're having to do a giant remodel but we got it for an amazing price. There's a separate unit, a studio over the garage. We'll be able to fix that up fast so I can get in and supervise the main job. Yes, it's big enough for both of us. Or all three of us. We got a dog." He had to wait again. "Found her on the highway. Someone dumped her, I guess. Her name is Molly. I'll send you a picture as soon as we're off the phone. In other news, Victor and I are doing two more dances this fall. One is that same one again, from two years ago. God, I know, I can hardly believe it's been that long. I can't believe we weren't actually together then. It feels like we've always been together." A pause for some commentary, and a question. "I don't know. I haven't gone there yet. No, not even circling around it. I'm so much older than he is. He might not want to tie himself down like that. I did something else though. You know he's the tattoo guy. I suggested we might get matching tattoos. In my head I'm thinking this might be as close as we get to wedding rings. He went for it. Oh my *God* that shit hurt. So, let's see. House, dog, dancing, tattoo. Yeah, I have to get ready to move. Time to go through the harvest of seven years. I already found some ancient stuff in the kitchen. Oh! He's making a movie next summer. Co-star. It's his biggest part yet. He's super excited. Yeah, you know 'Rush Hour?' Kind of like that, from the sound of it. Buddy movie, action comedy. He'll be great. I'll try to get over to see you for a minute around Christmas. Oh, definitely. I'll bring him if I possibly can. Eh, I don't know about Molly. She's good in the car but planes are awful for humans, let alone dogs. I'll keep you posted. Love you too." Andy disconnected, blew out a breath, and lay there on the couch, looking up at the Cabaret posters. He needed to put the word out to the company, see who wanted those. Then he remembered he owed his mother a picture of Molly, and found one to send her.

Victor had been in his apartment for six years, but he'd never accumulated much. He had a collection of bound plays that he wanted to keep. There were books he had already read, that he wouldn't read again; he took those down to the building's lobby for other residents to pick through. He ran into Mrs. Cohen, and told her that he and Andy were moving in together. "We're renovating a burnt-out four-plex. I'm afraid we're not going to get out dancing this fall."

She didn't need her walker anymore. She said, "I'll think of you when I'm out with my boyfriend."

When it was finally time for him to leave here, it would be simple and painless. There was the framed photo of his mother and Tía Susana; the Oaxacan monster; that little metal-framed mirror; and the framed photo of him kissing Andy at Chrome. Obviously he would take his reading chair (he did manage to read in it) and lamp. He'd cleaned out his closet during the Year of Maybe. They would negotiate whose blender or toaster oven or cast-iron skillet made the move. Victor's TV and DVD player could go in storage, with all the DVDs, until they had more space.

His bed was bigger than Andy's, and had a platform for storage. They would do a swap when Andy moved, so the big one could go to the studio unit. The other one could go in storage, for the future guest room, after Victor got moved in. His couch was smaller than Andy's, and they wouldn't need both. He'd get rid of his when he moved. The big one would go in storage until the house was ready. He kept tripping over thoughts like that. *We're going to have a house.*

He'd never lived in his own house, only in apartments. Living with Andy was going to be spectacular enough. To live with him in their house, something they could make their own, a place that was theirs forever … he sucked in a breath, reminding himself that he couldn't look too far ahead. Someday he would have to ask, is this forever for you too. Andy would know what that meant. He would know Victor was saying 'because it's forever for me.'

September 2015

Victor had more screen time this season than ever before. On the one hand, it was great; on the other, it was annoying, because the hours were longer than ever too. There was suddenly so much going on in his personal life, and he felt like he was missing it. Andy moving to Mid City would make it easier for them to get together – they'd be only twenty minutes apart until he could get moved himself – but for now they weren't spending many more nights together than they had in the spring. It seemed like one or the other of them had something that started early or went late, way too often.

The best thing was the dancing. They still found time for a lesson or rehearsal here and there, if not to get out to a milonga. Doing 'Mating Game' again was even better this time, because this time they could kiss at the end. "I always wanted to do that," Andy said.

"I wanted you to." They were hanging out at the bar during the second-night after-party. "I might have been trying to get you to do that."

273

"I'm aware," Andy said, with a sideways glance. "You and those come-and-get-it eyes."

"You and that come-and-get-it mouth." Victor was smiling. "This place was packed tonight."

"The word got out. 'Milonga' always sells out anyway, but Dana said it went about twice as fast this time." Neither of them had actually thought of that. The club management had to add some security in the parking lot for the second night. "Think we should do the next one on the down-low?"

"Probably. Don't put us on the poster, or the online schedule. It's still the Underground Cabaret, not the Victor and Andy show."

"Not yet." They both cracked up. Andy set his empty glass on the bar. "Want to dance, catnip?"

"I always do." Victor had another early call the next day, but he didn't care. They were here, and dancing with Andy was the next best thing to everything else he wanted.


The loft looked wrong. Andy knew why; it was because the shelf over his long desk was nearly empty, and the Cabaret posters that had been on the wall for years were gone. The display walls were arranged in rows, diagonally across the main space. He'd hung some prints on the interior wall, the one that defined the under-loft spaces, for the first time. It was as he'd told Victor: something different, but he might as well. He meant to exploit his celebrity – minor though it was – while he could. So, also for the first time, he laid the exhibit books from previous shows out on the desk, with order forms. A chance for people to see the work he'd done before anyone heard of him; possibly to sell some more books, or even more prints, through his online store.

By the entry door was a table borrowed from a friend in the complex, with a cooler underneath it. An array of wines from northern California, Oregon, and Washington was set ready with disposable glasses. Andy could hear chatter and rustlings in the hall outside. He checked the time, took a deep breath, wished quite intensely that Victor were there, and opened the door.

Three hours later, most of the crowd was gone. Those who lingered were filling out order forms, or were friends. Victor had arrived close to nine o'clock. Rory and Dana were there, Vicky and Sharon, Dmitri and Patrick. The six of them were chatting, browsing through the exhibit as a group. Andy abandoned everyone else and sat on the loft stairs beside Victor. "How are you doing, catnip?"

"Tired." Victor smiled. It had been another on-location day, this time a day of shooting gang trial scenes at a real courtroom shut down by the furlough. "It was everything they shot with you yesterday, only from my side."

"Ugh." That meant testimony. A lot of it, written in consultation with a team of lawyers. The show would compress the trials into short segments, woven into the four episodes leading up to the mid-season break. The cop and bartender were still walled off from each other at this point. "That gangster dude was scaring the hell out of me for real."

Victor smiled, took his hand and squeezed it. "Isn't he great?"

"If by great you mean creepy as fuck, yes." Andy changed the subject to the one foremost in both their minds. "Two weeks to go." Until he moved to Mid City. "Have you been by the work site?"

"I swung by yesterday on the way home. That security floodlight they put up is really obnoxious."

Andy laughed under his breath. "A person could get a suntan. I was in the studio unit day before yesterday. The bathroom and kitchen renos are done, laundry connections are in, new windows. Next week it's the floor and the paint job. The guy was all, seriously, this shade of white? I was having second thoughts."

"We'll be in the main house before long," Victor said, reading his mind. "You'll be using it as a studio again." They were leaning on each other, both aware of the others in the room but in their own bubble of artificial privacy. "I'm freaking out a little."

Andy turned his head, made eye contact, and thought he diagnosed the source of Victor's anxiety. "You've never lived with anyone before, have you? Not even a roommate?"

"Not even. What if I suck at it?"

Andy tipped his head against his lover's and spoke softly. "Remember our trip this summer?"

"Yeah."

"Remember how we never once tried to kill each other?" Victor made an amused sound. Andy nuzzled his hair. "You are easy to live with. I want to live with you. I love you. It'll be different, but it'll be all right."

"I love you too. How do you always know what to say?"

"I don't. I'm making this up as we go along, same as you." They were quiet for a minute. Some art browsers were heading for the door. Andy stood up to meet them, thank them for coming, and usher them out. Finally it was only themselves and their friends.

Patrick came over to the stairs. He and Victor had already greeted each other. "Andy, great show. Really different for you. I saw one of my clients buying something. Gary Fisher?"

"Oh, he's one of yours? Yeah, that beach scene. You never know what people are going to go for. But everybody seemed to be in a gray-skies mood. We sure got a lot of that on this trip." And a lot of the prints were already sold. Every time that happened, Andy was freshly surprised.

"We've never been up that way by car," Patrick said. "Plenty of empty space, isn't there?"

"There sure is. It would have been spooky if I'd been out there alone. Fortunately I had my cop to keep me safe." Andy had his hand on the rail of the loft stairs, right next to Victor's, their little fingers touching. "So can I sell you something tonight, or are you only here for free wine and gossip?"

Patrick said, "Actually you can sell me something. I want that one," he turned and pointed to the print immediately in front of the door, which had a SOLD sticker on it already, "only bigger. For our reception area. There's that tedious abstract thing the decorator gave us."

"Uh-huh." Andy averted his eyes every time he went to Patrick's office. "Ready for some sunshine instead?" The image Patrick wanted was taken on a sunny day, when Andy and Victor were on the ferry from Port Angeles to Victoria. It was a view east, of the early-morning sun breaking through a bank of clouds in a spectacular burst of golden pink, with the San Juan Islands faintly visible through a pink-tinted mist above the dark water in the foreground.

"Well, what I like about it is, it's bright but it's dramatic. And you can't see anything man-made.

Actually all of these are like that. Did you take any pictures with buildings or people?"

"Oh sure. I took hundreds of pictures of Victor." Patrick laughed. Andy was smiling. "And lots of our new friends up there. Dogs, birds, cabins, bridges, falling-down barns. When I was deciding on a theme for this show, though, it came down to water."

"Sometimes in the form of snow. Okay, I get it. Anyway I'm going to have to text you the size, but that's the one I want. I filled out everything else."

"Great, thanks. Give me a second?" Patrick nodded, and went back over to Dmitri and the others. Andy turned to Victor. "Honey, you look exhausted. I'll shovel these people out." He put his hand on Victor's for a second, then went to join their friends. "Hi again. Thanks for coming. What did you think?"

"It couldn't be much different from that very first show of yours," Rory said. "But a good photograph is a good photograph. How long did you have to wait for an absence of humans, on average?"

Andy was grinning. "Well that's one advantage to being outside when it's raining. Mostly nobody else was. And we were traveling at odd hours, I guess."

"Not in a big rush to get out of bed, I'll bet." Vicky looked amused. "Was it a good break, after all that craziness with the series?"

"It was truly, one hundred per cent, great. There's probably another whole show to pull out of that trip. Thousands of photos. Plus we brought home Molly, and Elliott found the house for us. I'm moving over there in two weeks, they'll have the studio unit livable."

"God, I'm so excited," Sharon said. "I've been driving my dad crazy about the floor plans. When it's done, I want to look at these pictures again. I'm going to want one for our side."

"You know where to find me." Andy tugged on her hair. "And I really do appreciate all of you coming out. But the TV star is about to fall asleep on the stairs so I'm going to have to shut this down." It took a few more minutes – everyone wanted to say goodnight to Victor – but he finally closed the door and locked it. Victor went to wash up while Andy took the leftover wine over to the refrigerator. He did some very minimal tidying-up, glad neither of them had to be anywhere till noon the next day, and turned off the lights.

As usual, Andy woke up early. Less as usual, Victor was awake before him. "Well hi there. Sleep well?"

"Slept great. I've already been down to get some coffee started."

Andy could smell it. "If I go down there, should I come back up?"

"Yes please." Victor was smiling. Andy kissed him lightly, rolled out of bed, and went down the stairs. The ranks of prints on the display walls looked moody in the pale light. Andy went to the bathroom, then fixed two mugs of coffee and carried them back up to the sleeping loft. Victor was sitting up, stretching. "I never used to do this," he said. "You set a good example for me."

"Also you don't want to get a cramp."

"Yeah, that too. Thanks." Victor accepted a mug and sat back, watching as Andy arranged himself in bed. "You look sensational."

"I look scruffy," Andy said. "The guys on 'Vice' said to keep my hair a little bit long. Said it gave me the right look, whatever that means." His hair had been cut shorter than usual for the spring episodes.

Victor smiled into his mug. He liked the current look. "I think it means you look like someone in witness protection who hasn't been asked to completely change his look. If this were a legit Mafia story they'd probably have dyed it."

"Gross, no." Andy had managed to make it all those years on stage without ever having to color his hair. For the past few years he'd been getting some gray touched up, a thing he hadn't confessed to Victor but that he knew had been noticed. That whole 'I thought you were my age' thing kept ringing. There were a lot of reasons not to talk about it.

"They'd probably make you grow a beard, and dye that." Victor wouldn't have minded seeing Andy with a beard, or with a mustache. The show would never do that, though; Victor was the only regular cast member with facial hair. He'd come in to audition with the mustache, they'd liked it, and now apparently he was stuck with it. At least he could lose it during the summer breaks. "Thank God I don't have to dye mine."

"Ugh! Stop," Andy said, laughing. "It's bad enough having to wear those phony glasses every time I'm doing a public scene. I keep wanting to snatch them off my face."

"I like them. You have the whole sexy professor thing going." Andy laughed again. Victor sipped coffee, glancing sideways at his lover. "You're sexy whatever you do."

"Speak for yourself." Andy set his mug on the nightstand. Clearly they weren't going back to sleep.

God only knew when they'd get to wake up together again. He didn't say anything else, simply moved down, doing what he needed to do to get the sheet all the way off Victor's legs. He ran his hands up from ankles to hips, heard an intake of breath, and stroked down to Victor's knees. He pushed them apart and put his mouth on the inside of a thigh.

"Jesus, Andy."

"Mmm." Andy heard the mug land on the nightstand.

"I can feel you smiling." Victor's hand was in Andy's hair. "Kiss me." Andy lifted his head, Victor moved, and then Andy was stretched out on top of him.

"God, I love you. How do you want me now." Andy's mouth on Victor's chest, neck, and face. Another deep and hungry kiss. Both as completely aroused as if they'd spent half an hour in foreplay.

"Every way."

Andy nibbled on his neck. "We only have time for one. I hate that fucking show." Victor laughed out loud. "The taste of you. I never get enough."

Neither did Victor. "I love you. Between my legs. Make me come."

Andy levered himself up, reached past Victor to the nightstand drawer, and got the lube. Leaned on one elbow to kiss that perfect mouth again before he slicked himself, then Victor. Heard the hungry sound Victor made. Stroked him again, hand closed, slow. Another kiss, with his leg between Victor's, eyes closed, still stroking. Feeling Victor's hips move, his breath change. "Come for me first." Victor vocalizing, panting into his mouth, so responsive Andy couldn't believe it sometimes. No matter when, no matter how, every time as if he'd never wanted anything more than Andy's kiss, his mouth, his hand, his body. His own erection was hot and hard, throbbing against Victor's hip. "Jesus, you're beautiful. Come on baby. Oh *fuck* yes, there you go, faster. Give it to me. God, yes. Holy mother of God almighty, that *cock* Victor, *now* sweetheart, *Jesus* yes." Victor's body jerked as he climaxed with a guttural sound. Then Andy was on him, erection thrust between Victor's thighs, moving fast, beyond words.

"Fucking hell, Andy, harder, yes, *now*." A low, rough sound from Andy, his mouth open against Victor's neck, and the pulse of his climax. "Holy fucking God." Victor had one arm wrapped tight around Andy's back, the other wrapped around his head. They were both gasping for breath. "My life is going to be so much better when we can start every day like this." A breathless laugh. They both relaxed. Victor kissed the side of Andy's face.

"Exactly like this would be fine." Andy propped himself up a little, taking some of his weight off Victor's chest. "Or the exact opposite would be fine."

"Or your mouth on me, or vice versa."

"So many fun things we can do." Now Andy moved off of Victor, because they were slightly stuck together. Lying side by side, gazing at each other. "Everything with you is fun. I love every picture in this show because you were there when I took them."

"What would Patrick's agent friend think if he knew when that one was taken?" Victor was grinning. Andy was laughing silently, the bed shaking. The rainy-day beach scene had been shot from the open door of the cottage in Coos Bay, Andy standing naked in the kitchen while Victor watched from the bed. "If he knew you were fucking me five minutes before that?"

"Maybe I should have titled it 'Five Past Garcia.' Everyone would know." Victor was giggling. Andy stretched, a happy sound escaping, and pressed his mouth to Victor's chest. "Three years ago all I could imagine was my life getting smaller and smaller. All I could see was my little routine, brushing up against Dana or Dmitri or whoever. People who had a full life. Looking through the window at other people's happiness." He raised his head. Victor was gazing back at him now, serious. "And now I have this vast horizon of joy." Victor's eyes filled. Andy's eyes were wet too. He blinked hard, because he really hated to cry, swallowed and sniffed. "Because of you. I love you."

"I love you." The alarm on Victor's phone went off. "Oh *fuck* you." They both sighed. Victor reached over to silence the alarm.

"Yes. Fuck you, phone. Fuck you, 'L.A. Vice.' What do you want for breakfast, sweetheart." Andy sat up. "Scrambled eggs and chorizo?"

"God, yes. Thank you. Thank you for all of this." Victor got his arms around Andy for a hug. They sat there wrapped around each other for another minute. Then, reluctantly, parted to get ready for the day.


Andy moved into the renovated studio space two months after they closed on the property. Molly came to live with him, though she still spent a lot of time with Spike at the cottage. Andy was called for the TV show at least two days a week, and he didn't like to leave her alone with all the demolition and reconstruction madness happening. He stopped by to get her one day and found Dana alone. "Where's the cherubim?"

"She's over at Dmitri's working on this jazz thing for Halloween." Dana made a move toward the kitchen, pointing at a container of cookies on the counter.

Andy did not say no to Rory's cookies. He took one, saying, "Jazz?!"

"That blond guy Mike, you remember him from the summer pro show. He was nagging her."

Andy laughed, inhaled a cookie crumb, coughed. "You guys got friendly."

"Well, Paula's been around for a while. When she started showing up places with him, it was only a matter of time. Anyway yeah, Miss Kitten Face is doing 'Virtual Insanity' and it is a bona fide trip."

"Can't wait to see it." He accepted a glass of water. "Thanks. So annoying on set today."

"What happened?" Dana and Rory were both hearing a lot about the new season. Andy said 'can I vent to you so I don't bore Victor with my bitching all the time,' and of course they said yes.

"Nothing different. Me in a room with some cops, going over testimony, then me in the room alone freaking out. And no Victor, because he's out on location a-fucking-gain." He growled a little. "We get a reunion scene. It's not going to shoot till after the midseason break."

"But you get a reunion. That's big. I know you were afraid they were going to kill you before that happened."

"Believe me, some days I wish they would. Anyway. What with the shooting schedule, he's not moving in till December, which seems like forever away."

"Everything's still good?"

"God, yes. He's perfect. I have these moments, you know, basically every time we get to spend the night together. I wake up and see him there and it's like, really?" Dana laughed, but sympathetically. Andy glanced down at his wrist. "And I see this and think, I know he knows. I knew he knew, practically from the moment I made the suggestion. Neither of us is saying it."

Dana knew, too. "I keep bugging Rory. Ever since Dmitri and Patrick got married. It's like, see? Now we can, and we should." Being registered domestic partners was one thing, the best thing possible for a long time. Now there was more. "She deflects."

"She loves you." Andy reached down the counter for Dana's hand. "Why doesn't she say yes?"

"She's still got some crazy hangup about money. Unequal partners thing. That's not why you haven't asked, is it?"

"Oh, no. There's just been an awful lot of change in not much time and I'm scared." Scared of letting their momentum propel Victor into a commitment that was all to Andy's advantage. "Maybe once the Faux Chateau is done. After Vicky and Sharon get moved in, and we can sit back and relax for a minute."

"Uh, Andy. Sitting back and relaxing is not your natural state." He snorted. Dana squeezed his hand. "Whatever. If he's not around for dinner, why don't you hang out here and eat with us. I'll ping Rory, tell her you're here."

"Okay. What've you got?" Andy moved past her and looked in the refrigerator. "Hey now. Let me go fire up the grill." All of a sudden there were two interested animals at his feet. "Oh, *now* you wake up. Hi pretty girl. Yes you're a pretty Molly. Spike, do you like your salmon raw or grilled?"

Chapter 18

Trying to fit in the routine for 'Lunatics' was a little tricky. It was a whole new dance, and their schedules didn't get any less crazed. Victor was grateful that Andy and Dmitri both accommodated him, meeting at Shall We Dance at late hours to do the 'Moondance' choreography and for the first rehearsal. After that, Dmitri gave Andy a spare key for the duration. "Patrick suggested," he said, which didn't surprise Andy one bit.

"The fun part about being here this late," he said one night, "is having the place to ourselves. We can sit here eating pizza in Dmitri's office, go out and practice, come back in here and make out for a while, practice some more."

"It'll be even better when we can go home together every time. You need more sleep." Andy's shooting days were fewer, but not necessarily shorter. He was also deeply involved with the renovation.

"So do you." Andy finished a slice of pizza, guzzled some cheap red wine, and studied his gorgeous lover. "You still look incredible."

Victor drained his glass. "So do you. That's the rest of tonight's program, is it? Practice, make out, and practice?"

"Well, unless you'd like to make out first." Andy tried to sound as though he had no preference in the matter.

"I would," said Victor. "But then we might forget to practice. On your feet, diva." They did a pretty good job distributing time equally between practice and making out. But they didn't get to go home together, so there was a little more making out once they locked up the studio and went to their cars. "Tomorrow," Victor said eventually, standing away so they wouldn't completely lose track of where they were. "Supposed to be done early tomorrow."

"If those fuckers ever get done early, they should get a special Emmy award." They were still holding hands. Andy reluctantly let go. "Drive safe."

"You too."

Andy went home alone, took Molly out alone, went to bed alone. "An argument could be made that our fabulous vacation was a bad idea," he told the dog later, when they were cuddled in bed together. "Because I got so very spoiled being with Victor twenty-four-seven. But if we didn't go on vacation I wouldn't have you. Thank you for being a huggable size. I've hated sleeping alone ever since he came back to me, and now I don't have to." Molly licked his nose. "Thank you Molly. You are the best girl."

Twenty minutes away, Victor thought *at least this is the bed he used to sleep in*, and laughed at himself. He was literally counting down the days.


The Halloween show almost always sold out, and the show's theme promised entertaining mayhem, so the added celebrity attraction didn't wreak any havoc at Chrome even on the second night, when word was out. By then Andy and Victor were both so tired that they only stayed at the after-party for half an hour. "Tell me you don't have an early call tomorrow," Andy said, leaning against Victor in the green room after collecting their gear.

"I don't. Can I follow you home?"

"Jesus, catnip, please."

There was a new routine to getting home now, a sweet routine that soon would be every night. First it was locking up the cars. Then going up the stairs, greeting Molly, and taking her outside for some refreshment. Then washing up, taking turns. Going to bed together, kissing goodnight. A murmured 'I love you' from each of them, and then sleep.

They woke up together, Molly curled by Victor's feet, to the sound of hammering. "Ugh," Victor said. "You deserve some kind of award for living through this."

"And that's with all the new insulation." Andy stretched, squirming a little, ending up pressed close to Victor. "Here's my award, right here." A few minutes of kissing later, he said, "If I make some coffee and then come back to bed, are you going to be in it? Or do you have to run for the Valley?"

"You make coffee. I'll take Molly out for a minute. Meet you back here." Victor ended each sentence with a kiss, then pried himself away. They both returned to bed within ten minutes. "Forty days left. I am in here for good on December sixth or there will be hell to pay." The series was supposed to wrap for the year on the fifth. "Have you had any weirdness?"

"Not much." Andy was getting some mail as a result of their storyline. It all went to the production company, then to his agent. She said 'get a business manager for this kind of shit,' but he hadn't done it yet. "Raquel is forwarding anything good and shredding anything bad. I told her I don't want to know." The production company flagged anything that qualified as a threat, but nonthreatening complaint letters still got through. "She was also bitching at me about getting that stuff at all."

"So is Parker. We should find a manager person over the break."

"Yeah, okay. How about you? Anything awful?"

"I hear there have been a couple of things. I got a memo yesterday." What Victor wanted to do was take advantage of this hour to get re-acquainted with his lover's body, but this actually was a conversation they needed to have. "They're going to start providing a car in January."

"Oh shit." Andy pulled away from Victor's arm and sat up. "It's that bad?"

"There are a couple of investigations." Victor sat up too. "They're afraid it's going to get worse after the reunion. And if they decide to go with that other thing, eh." He and Andy had been called into a writers' meeting the week before, to be told the company was considering writing in an actual love scene. The reunion would have kisses; the love scene would have more of those, with partial nudity. They were under orders not to talk about it, and this time they were toeing the line. "If it gets really bad, they'll probably have a car for you too."

"Well, I won't mind being able to sleep on the way over the Hills." Andy studied Victor for a few seconds. He didn't look concerned. It sounded as though the production company was on top of whatever. Andy decided to forget about it and get on top of Victor. A few minutes later, with his mouth on the gecko tattoo, he murmured, "Think they can write a scene we haven't played before?"

"Not a chance," Victor said, a little breathless. "Oh Jesus, do that again."

"Do what? This? Or this?"

"All of that."

Two hours later, Andy was wrapping up a consultation with their general contractor when he got a text from Victor: *Late*

Andy wasn't surprised. He texted *Oops*

Victor's reply made him laugh: *Worth it*


December 2015

Thanks to money and connections, progress was fast. The Faux Chateau still looked like a work site, but no longer like a bomb site. Victor suggested having a Power Is On party, so their friends could get a look at what would be their home. They chose a date in mid-December, and sent invitations. "I can't wait to show it off," Victor confessed. They were all cuddled up in bed in the studio, the dog stretched out alongside Victor's legs. He snickered. "And I can't believe you're playing the Yule log." The faux-fireplace video was running on one of Andy's monitors.

"Well, I considered candles, but there's this fluffy tail situation," Andy said. He leaned his head against Victor's, enjoying having his lover in his arms. "I am counting the days till you're in here for good."

"The hours." Victor was moving in very soon. "Every day I wake up over there I'm like, goddammit." Andy laughed under his breath. "There was kind of a pileup at the end of our shooting schedule."

"I know. Way too many early starts, and I can't even believe how late you were getting back sometimes. I mean, I was getting back late too, but at least it wasn't six days a damn week. I've missed you." He turned his head for a kiss. "I missed you on set, too. The storyline is better than expected but I hate that we're not working together." Their characters were separated at the beginning of the season, with the bartender in protective custody. Thanks to the accelerated timeline of TV, the gang trials were now underway. The bartender was still clinging to faith that the undercover cop had been sincerely in love, because they hadn't been allowed to talk. A certain blogger was covering each episode, breathlessly anticipating their reunion, and speculating about how it would be handled. "Think that blogger will be happy?"

Victor didn't much care about the blogger; *he* was going to be happy. "I never knew how much more like an actual person I would feel with a relationship to play. I'm living for the reunion episode. It's really well-written."

"Yeah, it is." Andy still didn't think much of the show, but at least for now, the writers were putting their hearts into it. "I'm glad they didn't go with a big phony argument about why did you pretend to love me, blah blah." Victor snorted. "These guys are fucking grown-ups. My dude would know better than to think there was the slightest advantage for your dude in starting a relationship."

"The whole thing nearly blew up," Victor agreed. "Because my dude loved your dude." They both snickered. "It's good they gave me that speech. About how I'm so glad you're safe. How the only thing that mattered to me was getting you out safe." He couldn't wait to play it.

Andy squeezed his shoulders. He was fairly certain there wouldn't be a dry eye in any of their friends' houses when that episode aired. "So I was bitching at the contractor about all the sharp shit in the yard. Guess what he's going to do."

"What?"

"He's going to go over the whole thing with a shop vac. I was like *really*? He said hey, I've got a dog too. How about that."

"Thanks Molly," Victor said, petting her head. "If we didn't have you, we'd probably be stepping on nails and broken glass and chunks of stucco for the next fifty years."

Victor hadn't heard from Janis for a good long while, so he sent a text to see where she was: *Hey chica that last album was terrific. Coming back to LA anytime soon?*

He got a reply the next day: *Hey good looking I saw video of you and your hot boyfriend dancing in Oregon. So jelly. My last dates are in the frozen and I do mean frozen north. Going straight home to Mom & Dad, totes exhausted. Will ping you*

*You do that. Can't believe we keep missing each other. Andy is like I thought I met her but does this person actually exist*

*Starting to wonder that myself. Any plans for another concert?*

*We don't have time to plan our way across town. Remodeling a four-plex*

*DUDE NO WAY*

*LOL it's a long story*

*OK well I want to hear it. TTYL*

*Travel safe. Besos a ti.* Victor went to find Andy, to see if they had any commitments beyond the 'Power is On' party. That led to a discussion of a quick trip to Miami

"I used to go in April," Andy said. "For Mom's birthday. Then last year that didn't happen but I took you over there in the summer. And now it looks like next April is fucked because of 'Vice.' So do you mind if we go this month?" He said 'we' for a lot of reasons.

"No, of course not." Victor was delighted, actually. A family Christmas – even if they weren't there on the actual day – was something he'd never had; it was one of those things that went with being in a relationship. And they had so much news to share. They decided on travel dates, Andy talked to his mother, and they booked the trip.

The night Victor moved in, Andy did have candles. Molly was circling the studio, inspecting the things that had arrived with Victor. The men were sitting at the new café set. An open bottle of champagne was on the table with two half-full flutes and a plate recently emptied of fish tacos. The candles were on the nightstands (actually wooden wine crates); they provided all the light in the room. "Well, catnip. This is it."

"This is it. I'm so glad to be here." Victor picked up his glass and clinked it against Andy's. "I'm so glad we got here."

"Me too. I feel like I should make a speech."

Victor struck a pose. "Friends, Romans, countrymen, lend me your … see, here's the problem. I don't need anything else."

"Yeah, that's the problem." Andy drained his glass, stood up, and pulled Victor to his feet. "Only you. That's all I needed. All I ever needed." His hands were on Victor's face. He brushed a thumb over that smiling mouth, then went in for a kiss.

"Take me to bed," Victor said after a while.

"Or lose you forever?"

"You couldn't lose me if you tried. I love you."
Victor started backing toward the bed. Molly, who
recognized this maneuver, got out of the way. Quite
some time later, when the commotion on the bed had
ceased, she hopped up, turned around, flopped down,
and sighed. "Good girl," Victor said drowsily. She
thumped her tail once.

Waking up together the next day felt different.
Andy was staring at the ceiling, telling himself *this is
actually it. This is always. This is forever.* He couldn't
believe it. He turned his head; Victor was still asleep.
Andy got out of bed as quietly as possible, went to the
bathroom, started coffee, took Molly outside. When
they went back up, Victor was standing by one of the
windows in his robe, mug in hand. He turned to look
at Andy. "Three point five years," he said. "That's
how long it took us to get here."

"Another date for the list?"

"You'd better believe it." He was planning to get
the first few dates inked during this break. He watched
Andy brush Molly, then wash his hands and get his
own coffee. They stood by the uncovered window for
a while, watching the day's construction activity
begin. "I have an idea."

"What's that, sweetheart."

"If the crew can do without you for a couple of
days, let's go up to Oxnard. Take Molly to that hotel."
*Have a honeymoon*, he wanted to say, but he knew
they needed some time to settle into this. Someday
they would talk about that.

Andy drifted closer, putting his arm around
Victor's waist. "That's a good idea, catnip."

"I am going to love waking up with you every day." Victor said it softly, face turned toward Andy's, head slightly lowered the way it was when he asked for that one kiss. "I'll love sleeping with you every night. This next year is going to be crazy, but I'll always love being with you. I love you so much."

Andy set his mug down on the café table, took Victor's and set it there too, put his hands on that beloved face and kissed him. "Always. Always, Victor. I love you." He wanted to say 'forever,' but he knew they needed more time to settle into this. Someday they would get there. For now there were more kisses, slow and lingering, with no urgency because they were together for good. At last.

Victor checked in with Janis that afternoon and found out they'd be missing her again. "It'll happen eventually," he told Andy a few days later. They were in bed already; the end of the day was usually a good time to talk. "Now you need to fill me in on the whole family holiday thing."

Andy regarded him for a moment. "Are you thinking there's a whole gift-exchange minefield ahead of you?" Victor made a 'maybe?' face. Andy shook his head. "Not to worry. We agreed a long time ago that the only gift we all really wanted was face time. Let me show you Mom's last text." He reached for his phone and pulled up the message: *So happy you are bringing Victor, can you bring Molly too?? You said she likes the beach!* Victor was smiling. Andy enjoyed the sight of that for a second. "I think she'd be happier with Spike over at Dana's."

"Yeah, I think so too." Victor leaned forward to touch his toes, and coincidentally to pet Molly.

"You're getting stretchier." Andy set the phone down again and put a hand on his lover's back.

296

"I've got a good role model." Victor sat up. Andy's hand stayed on him, sliding up to his neck, lightly tugging him over. "I love how you do that."

"Drag you around by the neck?" Andy was smiling now, with his mouth on that neck.

"Make me feel like you want me."

"I always want you. I wouldn't go to Miami without you. For one thing, I'd never hear the end of it. For another, I don't want to be anywhere you're not, now that we finally have this living situation straightened out." Andy was nibbling his way down Victor's chest. "Someday you're going to get a movie that shoots out of town and I'm going to follow you around like a groupie." Victor was laughing, until Andy pulled him down and it was clear they were done talking.

In a couple more weeks, the place was transformed. "What do you think, Molly?" Andy was walking with her around the yard. "Better, huh?" The building's shell was repaired and the power was turned back on. The debris was gone and they'd had the back yard decorated with a truckload of small trees and flowering plants in containers. Piazza lights were strung across from the studio unit to the main building. "People will be rolling in any minute. Let's go get ready."

Rory and Dana were among the first to arrive. Molly acted like she hadn't seen them for months. Andy took them straight up to the studio, saying, "She misses Spike. Apparently humans alone are insufficient. Good thing Vicky and Sharon will be moving in with Prospero and Miranda. Otherwise we'd have to get a cat."

"Just for Molly?"

"Well, you know. Anyway! Check out the studio! Which is basically a bedroom now. I haven't taken a single picture of anything but Molly and the renovations for weeks. My mother said what a pretty dog and did not comment on the house." He gave a sideways smile at Rory's stifled snort. She knew what the house looked like when they bought it, after all. "Think I should send her some before pictures?"

Rory said, "Probably not."

"It looks good in here," Dana said. "Like your old place but homier." The studio had three new, bigger windows, wood floors, clean white walls, a much-improved kitchenette and a generous bathroom. A laundry closet was at one end of the kitchenette, next to the refrigerator. Victor's reading chair stood by one of the windows. A wardrobe rack stood against the opposite wall. "Really efficient, too."

"It'll do for now. Victor's finally in and that's all I really needed. Anyway, gotta mingle, tell people to feel free to come up here and snoop around. Also, maybe obviously, this is the only functional toilet at the moment." Thus the literal warning sign in the studio bathroom: HANDLE WITH CARE YOUR ONLY OTHER OPTION IS A BUCKET.

"Good to know. We will do that. Hey, Andy," Rory added. "Congratulations. We're really happy for you. This is only the start of what you deserve, but it's a great start."

"Thanks, Rory." He hugged her, then Dana. "I may have had to wait a long time, but he was worth waiting for." Dana kissed his cheek. Rory patted his ass.

Music was playing in the house, a mix assembled by the Cabaret's producer. Andy found Sharon

298

inspecting the new bay window on 'her' side. "This is gonna be *so cool*," said Sharon, spinning around in the big living room that would be hers. "Even after the bedroom's built, there's so much *space*."

"Well, you said you wanted it open, and the kitchen and bathroom had to go anyway. Victor liked the floor plan so much we're doing the same thing on the other side. Want to go upstairs?"

"What do you think?" She followed him up the rebuilt stairs, which now provided private second-story access for each unit. "Andy! Holy shit!" She hadn't seen anything but a picture taken after the roof repair. The interior had since been gutted. "This floor is kind of a disaster."

"The floor is literally toast," he agreed. "But at least we have windows. You already have a good idea what the bathroom will be like, plus we're putting a little sunroom off the back with a door out to the stairs."

"What's the next step?"

"Plumbing, HVAC, and another round with the electricians. Then the interior framing, drywall, floors, and finally the fun stuff can start." If you said it fast, it didn't seem like so much.

"I've got goose bumps." She hugged him. "I can't wait."

They went back downstairs and found Molly mingling with the crowd. Vicky was dancing with Dmitri (who was holding Simka) to 'Papa Loves Mambo.' Andy left Sharon with her wife and went to find Victor, eventually tracking him down on the back patio. That was currently a decrepit expanse of brick, but would soon be transformed. "Hey sweetness. You look exactly like Rudolph Valentino under those lights. Remind me to take your picture out here, like, every night. Everything okay?"

"You look pretty special too. I'm good. I'm just having a moment." Victor smiled, taking a sip of his champagne.

"What kind of moment?" Andy wrapped his arms around Victor, inhibiting consumption of champagne but facilitating some kisses.

"The how did I get so lucky kind of moment." Victor got an arm free and used it to properly hug Andy.

"The how did I end up on an Emmy-nominated primetime show where I get to make out with my real-life lover for money kind of moment? I have those all the time." They stood there for a minute, holding each other, listening to the happy crowd inside. "Come on in. People are starting to dance."

"I love you."

"I love you, too." Andy stole the glass of champagne and drained it just as the music changed. "Oh listen, it's 'Moondance.' Let's see if we can do this without breaking an ankle." He set the glass down on the steps, then scooped Victor into dance hold for a few bars of their number from the Halloween show. "That was a bad idea, catnip." He stood still, holding Victor close, cheek to cheek.

"Great idea, bad patio. Good thing we know someone who can fix that." Victor brushed a hand through Andy's hair and kissed him. Then he stood back so they could settle down. Picked up the glass, held out his other hand, and led the love of his life into the house.

### THE END

*Andy and Victor's story continues in*

**THE GHOST OF CARLOS GARDEL**

*Available now at Amazon.com*

\*\*\*\*\*

About the Author

Alexandra Caluen lives in a small purple house with her husband, a bottle of Laphroaig, a lot of books, and nine pairs of ballroom shoes. She works in patent law and has enough hair for three people.

www.thelastories.com